JON McGREGOR is the author of four novels and a story collection. He is the winner of the IMPAC Dublin Literature Prize, the Betty Trask Prize and the Somerset Maugham Award, and has twice been longlisted for the Man Booker Prize. He is Professor of Creative Writing at the University of Nottingham, where he edits the *Letters Page*, a literary journal in letters. He was born in Bermuda in 1976, grew up in Norfolk and now lives in Nottingham.

Winner of the Betty Trask Award
Winner of the Somerset Maugham Award
Longlisted for the Man Booker Prize

From the reviews of *If Nobody Speaks of Remarkable Things*:

'A dream of a novel … It is not every novelist who has the gift, as Jon McGregor does, of reminding his readers of that heaven in a wild flower, that infinity in a grain of sand'
The Times

'McGregor's publishers must be openly rejoicing … *If Nobody Speaks of Remarkable Things* is the work of a burning new talent'
Daily Mail

'McGregor is an exemplary archivist of the humdrum … written by someone who detects so passionately the remarkable in the everyday'
Spectator

'Extraordinary … McGregor's triumphant prose-poem of ordinariness has a very contemporary kind of spirituality about it'
Sunday Times

'Wonderful … Full of gentle wonder and blinding insight … He has annotated the miracle of life'
Glasgow Herald

ALSO BY JON McGREGOR

So Many Ways to Begin
Even the Dogs
This Isn't the Sort of Thing That Happens to Someone Like You
Reservoir 13

If Nobody Speaks of Remarkable Things

Jon McGregor

4th ESTATE • *London*

HarperCollins
PUBLISHERS
Since 1817

4th Estate
An imprint of HarperCollins*Publishers*
1 London Bridge Street
London SE1 9GF

www.4thEstate.co.uk

First published in Great Britain by Bloomsbury in 2002
This 4th Estate paperback edition published in 2017

1

Copyright © Jon McGregor 2002

The right of Jon McGregor to be identified as the author of
this work has been asserted by him in accordance with
the Copyright, Designs and Patents Act 1988

A catalogue record for this book is
available from the British Library

ISBN 978-0-00-821869-0

Printed and bound in Great Britain by
Clays Ltd, St Ives plc

MIX
Paper from
responsible sources
FSC
www.fsc.org   FSC™ C007454

FSC™ is a non-profit international organisation established to promote
the responsible management of the world's forests. Products carrying the
FSC label are independently certified to assure consumers that they come
from forests that are managed to meet the social, economic and
ecological needs of present or future generations,
and other controlled sources.

Find out more about HarperCollins and the environment at
www.harpercollins.co.uk/green

To Alice

If you listen, you can hear it.

The city, it sings.

If you stand quietly, at the foot of a garden, in the middle of a street, on the roof of a house.

It's clearest at night, when the sound cuts more sharply across the surface of things, when the song reaches out to a place inside you.

It's a wordless song, for the most, but it's a song all the same, and nobody hearing it could doubt what it sings. And the song sings the loudest when you pick out each note.

The low soothing hum of air-conditioners, fanning out the heat and the smells of shops and cafes and offices across the city, winding up and winding down, long breaths layered upon each other, a lullaby hum for tired streets.

The rush of traffic still cutting across flyovers, even in the dark hours a constant crush of sound, tyres rolling across tarmac and engines rumbling, loose drains and manhole covers clack-clacking like cast-iron castanets.

Road-menders mending, choosing the hours of least interruption, rupturing the cold night air with drills and jack-hammers and pneumatic pumps, hard-sweating beneath the fizzing hiss of floodlights, shouting to each other like drummers in rock bands calling out rhythms, pasting new skin on the veins of the city.

Restless machines in workshops and factories with end-less shifts, turning and pumping and steaming and sparking, pressing and rolling and weaving and printing, the hard crash and ring and clatter lifting out of echo-high buildings and sifting into the night, an unaudited product beside the paper and cloth and steel and bread, the packed and the bound and the made.

Lorries reversing, right round the arc of industrial parks, it seems every lorry in town is reversing, backing through gateways, easing up ramps, shrill-calling their presence while forklift trucks gas and prang around them, heaping and stacking and loading.

And all the alarms, calling for help, each district and quarter, each street and estate, each every way you turn has alarms going off, coming on, going off, coming on, a hammered ring like a lightning drum-roll, like a mesmeric bell-toll, the false and the real as loud as each other, crying their needs to the night like an understaffed orphanage, babies waawaa-ing in darkened wards.

Sung sirens, sliding through the streets, streaking blue light from distress to distress, the slow wail weaving urgency through the darkest of the dark hours, a lament lifted high, held above the rooftops and fading away, lifted high, flashing past, fading away.

And all these things sing constant, the machines and the sirens, the cars blurting hey and rumbling all headlong, the hoots and the shouts and the hums and the crackles, all come together and rouse like a choir, sinking and rising with the turn of the wind, the counter and solo, the harmony humming expecting more voices.

So listen.
Listen, and there is more to hear.
The rattle of a dustbin lid knocked to the floor.
The scrawl and scratch of two hackle-raised cats.

The sudden thundercrash of bottles emptied into crates. The slam-slam of car doors, the changing of gears, the hobbled clip-clop of a slow walk home.

The rippled roll of shutters pulled down on late-night cafes, a crackled voice crying street names for taxis, a loud scream that lingers and cracks into laughter, a bang that might just be an old car backfiring, a callbox calling out for an answer, a treeful of birds tricked into morning, a whistle and a shout and a broken glass, a blare of soft music and a blam of hard beats, a barking and yelling and singing and crying and it all swells up all the rumbles and crashes and bangings and slams, all the noise and the rush and the non-stop wonder of the song of the city you can hear if you listen the song

and it stops

in some rare and sacred dead time, sandwiched between the late sleepers and the early risers, there is a miracle of silence.

Everything has stopped.

And silence drops down from out of the night, into this city, the briefest of silences, like a falter between heart-beats, like a darkness between blinks. Secretly, there is always this moment, an unexpected pause, a hesitation as one day is left behind and a new one begins.

A catch of breath as gasometer lungs begin slow exhalations. A ring of tinnitus as thermostats interrupt air-condition-ing fans.

These moments are there, always, but they are rarely noticed and they rarely last longer than a flicker of thought.

We are in that moment now, there is silence and the whole city is still.

The old tall-windowed mills, staggered across the sky-line, they are silent, they are keeping their ghosts and their thoughts to themselves.

The smoked-glass offices, slung low to the ground, they are still, they are blankly reflecting the haze and shine of the night. Soon, they will resume their business, their coy whispers of ones and zeroes across networks of threaded glass, but now, for a moment, they are hushed. The buses in the depot, waiting for a new day, they are quiet, their metalwork easing and shrinking into place, settling and cooling after eighteen hours of heat and noise, eighteen hours of criss-crossing the city like wool on a loom.

And the clubs in the centre, they are empty, the dance-floors sticky and sore from a night's pounding, the lights still turning and blinking, lost shoes and wallets and keys gathered in heaps.

And the night-fishers strung out along the canal, feeling the sing of their lines in the water, although they are within yards of each other they are saying nothing, watching luminous floats hang in the night like bottled fireflies, waiting for the dip and strike which will bring a centre to their time here, waiting for the quietness and calm they have come here to find.

Even the traffic scattered through these streets: the taxis and the cleaners, the shift-workers and the delivery drivers, even they are held still in this moment, trapped by traffic lights which synchronise red as the system cycles from old day to new, hundreds of feet resting on accelerators, hundreds of pairs of eyes hanging on the lights, all waiting for the amber, all waiting for the green.

The whole city has stopped.

And this is a pause worth savouring, because the world will soon be complicated again.

It's the briefest of pauses, with not time enough to even turn full circle and look at all the lights this city throws out to the sky, and it's a pause which is easily broken. A slamming door, a car alarm, a thin drift of music from half a mile away, and already the city is moving on, already tomorrow is here.

The music is coming from a curryhouse near the football ground, careering out of speakers placed outside to attract extra custom. The restaurant is almost empty, a bhindi masala in one corner, a special korma in the other, and the carpark is deserted except for a young couple standing with their arms around each other's waists. They've not been a couple long, a few days perhaps, or a week, and they are both still excited and nervous with desire and possibility. They've come here to dance, drawn sideways from their route home by the music and by bravado, and now they are hesitating, unsure of how to begin, unfamiliar with the steps, embarrassed.

But they do begin, and as the first smudges of light seep into the sky from the east, from the far side of the city and in towards these streets, they hold their heads high and their backs straight and step together in time to the slide and wheel of the music. They dance with a style more suited to the ballroom than to the bollywood movies the music comes from, but they dance all the same, hips swinging, waists touching, eyes fixed on eyes. The waiters have come across to the window, they are laughing, they are calling uncle uncle to the man in the kitchen who is finally beginning to clean up after a long night. They dance, and he steps out of the door to watch, wiping his hands on his apron, licking the weary tips of his fingers, pulling at his long beard. They dance, and he smiles and nods and thinks of his wife sleeping at home, and thinks of when they were young and might still have done something like this.

Elsewhere, across the city, the day is beginning with a rush and a shout, the fast whine of office hoovers, the locked slam of lorry doors, the hurried clocking on of the early shifts.

But here, as the dawn sneaks up on the last day of summer, and as a man with tired hands watches a young couple dance in the carpark of his restaurant, there are only these: sparkling eyes, smudged lipstick, fading star-light, the crunching of feet on gravel, laughter, and a slow walk home.

He was the first to move, the boy from number eighteen.

He was up and across the street before anyone had blinked, before anyone had made a sound.

It was as if he knew what he had to do, as if he'd been waiting for the opportunity.

He moved off the doorstep like a loaded sprinter, and by the time I turned to see who it was he was there.

He was there and then it was over, and it was so sudden that I felt as though a camera flash had exploded in my face.

Everything went white, ghostly, like old news footage, faded and stained.

I couldn't understand what was happening, I couldn't believe what was happening.

I sat there, in the warm afternoon of the last day of summer, and I couldn't work out what I was seeing.

I watched him moving across the street, the boy from number eighteen, and I tried to understand.

I don't remember seeing it, not the moment itself, I remember strange details, peripheral images, small things that happened away from the blinded centre.

I remember the girl next to me dropping her can of beer and swaying backwards, as though from a shockwave.

I can picture the can hitting the ground, the weight of it crushing into the grass, the way it tipped to one side but stayed upright, like a half-fallen telegraph pole in a storm.

I can see a slow-motion image of the beer, frothing from the top of the can, a coil of it rising up like smoke, hanging in the light a moment before spreading flat into the grass and spraying across my lap.

I don't know where that comes from.
I don't know how I could possibly have seen these details.
The fizz of the beer popping into sparkles of air.
Blades of grass straightening themselves as the liquid soaks into the soil, the damp patch on my skirt shrinking and fading and drying in the sun.
The brightness of the light.

There was a woman leaning out of a high window, shaking a blanket.
There were some boys over the road having a barbecue, pushing a knife into the meat to see if it was cooked.
There was a man with a long beard, up a ladder at number twenty-five, painting his windowframes, he'd been there all day and he'd almost finished.
Each frame was gleaming wetly in the sun, a beautiful pale blue like the first faint colour of dawn and it had been nice to watch the slow thoroughness of his work.
There was a boy in the next-door garden, cleaning his trainers with a nailbrush and a bowl of soapy water.
I can see all these moments as though they were cast in stone, small moments captured and enlarged by the context, like figures in a Pompeii exhibition.
The woman with the blanket, interrupted mid-swing, her attention snatched away, the blanket losing momentum and flapping gently against the wall.
Her arms still stretched out, her lips still pursed against the billowing dust.
The blanket hanging down towards the ground, like a semaphore.

Somebody said oh my God.
A boy on a red tricycle rode into a tree.

His feet slipped off the pedals and got caught under the wheels, tugging him from his seat and down towards the ground.

I can see him, falling sideways, his leg about to scrape the concrete, his head about to hit the tree, his tricycle tipping onto two wheels and his attention clamped into the road.

His head kept turning as he fell, and when he hit the ground, he could only lie there, watching, like everyone else.

He can barely have been three years old, I wanted to run to him and cover his eyes but I couldn't move so he kept on looking.

A man who'd been washing his car lifted both his hands to the top of his head, squeezing them into fists.

He was still holding a sponge, water crushing out of it and down his back but he didn't move.

Somebody said oh shit oh shit oh shit.

But mostly there was this moment of absolute silence.

Absolute stillness.

It can't actually have been like that of course, there must still have been music playing, and traffic passing along the main road, but that's the way I remember it, with this single weighted pause, the whole street frozen in a tableau of gaping mouths.

And the boy from number eighteen, moving through the locked moment like a blessing.

It seemed, or at least it seems now, that everything else was motionless.

The beercan caught between the hand and the ground.

The blanket not quite touching the wall.

The boy with the tricycle a flinch away from the tree.

A gasp in my throat, held back, like the air in the pinched neck of a balloon.

9

And it all seemed wrong somehow, unreal, unconnected to the sort of day it had been.

An uneventful day, slow and warm and quiet, people talking on their front steps, children playing, music, a barbecue.

I'd been woken when it first got light by the slamming of taxi doors, people I knew at number seventeen coming back from a long night out and trailing slowly down the street.

I hadn't been able to get back to sleep, I'd stayed in bed and watched the sun brightening into the room, listened to the kids running outside, the familiar rattle of the boy's tricycle.

Later, I'd got up and had breakfast and tried to start packing, I'd sat on the front step and drank tea and read magazines.

I'd gone to the shop and talked briefly to the boy at number eighteen, he was awkward and shy and it didn't make sense that he would be the one to move so instantly across the street.

It rained, towards the end of the afternoon, suddenly and heavily, but that was all, there was nothing else unusual or unexpected about the day.

And somehow it seems wrong that there wasn't a buildup, a feeling in the air, a premonition or a warning or a clue.

I wonder if there was, actually, if there was something I missed because I wasn't paying attention.

The silence didn't last long, people started rushing out into the street, shouting, flinging open windows and doors.

A woman from down the road ran out towards them and stopped halfway, turning back, shaking her hands in front of her face.

The man up the ladder made a call on his mobile before climbing down and leaving the last frame half-painted.

There were people I didn't even recognise coming out of their houses to join the others.

But me and the other girl, Sarah, we just sat there, staring, holding our mouths open.

If we'd been closer, or younger, we might have held hands, tightly, but we didn't.

I think she picked up her beer and drank a little more, and I think I drank as well.

I can't remember, all I can remember is staring at the curtain of legs in the street, trying to see through.

Trying not to see through.

After a few minutes, the noise in the street seemed to quieten again.

The knot of people in the street loosened, turned aside.

People were looking to the main road, looking at their watches, waiting.

I remember noticing that there was still music coming out of half a dozen windows along the street, and then noticing that the songs were being silenced, one by one, like the lights going out at the end of *The Waltons*.

I remember a smell of burning, and seeing that the boys opposite had left their meat on the barbecue.

I could see the smoke starting to twist upwards.

I could see faces at windows.

I could see people glancing up, looking at the one door which was still closed.

Waiting for it to open, hoping that it might not.

I don't understand why it seems so fresh in my mind, even now, three years later and a few hundred miles away.

I think about it, and I can't even remember people's names.

I just remember sitting there, those moments of waiting, murmurous and tense.

People striding to the end of the street, looking up and down the main road, stretching to see round the corner.

Turning back to the others and raising their hands.

The old man from number twenty-five, the brush in his hand, dribbling a trail of pale blue paint, walking towards the closed door.

Rubbing his bearded cheeks with the palm of his hand.

Knocking.

The distant careen of a siren, the man knocking at the door.

A taxi drifts into the end of the street, its engine clicketing loudly as the doors open and half a dozen young people spill brightly out onto the pavement.

There is a pause; payment is made, the doors are slammed shut, and the taxi moves away, out of sight. And they stand there for a moment, blinking and grinning and waiting uncertainly, a tall thin girl with a short short skirt and eyes smudged with glitter, a boy with beige slacks and a ring through his eyebrow, a girl with enormous trainers and army trousers and her hair dyed pink and they are walking down the street, slowly, blissfully, their heads full of music and light, their nervous systems over-stimulated by hormones and chemicals and the exhilaration of the night.

A very short girl wearing nothing but shorts and a bra, her toenails painted the same violets and pinks and greens as her fingernails, she claps her hands, she looks at the sanded bare windowsills of number twenty-five, she says look they look naked, she looks at the tins of pale blue paint, the blue spilling down the side of the tin, she looks at the brushes and the scrapers and she says it's a nice colour it's going to look nice but nobody's listening.

A boy wearing an almost clean white shirt, a tie looped loosely around his neck, he jumps up onto the garden wall of number nineteen, he balances on one leg, he says shush shush can you hear that and when the others stop and say what he says nothing, can you hear nothing it's nice and he topples groundwards hoping the boy with the beige slacks and the pierced eyebrow can catch him.

On the other side of the street, in an upstairs bedroom at number twenty-two, a girl wakes up and hears someone talking about the quietness of the morning. She listens to the loud voice, it sounds familiar, she sits up in bed and puts her glasses on and looks at the people in the street. She knows them, some of them live at number seventeen, she wonders where they've been as she takes off her glasses and gets back into bed.

In the downstairs flat of number twenty, an old man with thinning hair and a carefully trimmed moustache is lying awake, listening to the noises outside. His eyes are open, frowning, focusing on what he can hear. He is listening for tell-tale signs, the crisp sound of a can being crumpled underfoot, the tinkle of a dropped bottle. His eyes sweep from side to side, concentrating, searching. But he doesn't hear anything, and as the voices fade he closes his eyes again, turning face-down into the bed, away from the light, hoping for a little more sleep before the day begins.

Outside, the boy with the white shirt opens the door of number seventeen and the others follow him inside, whirling slowly around, gathering the objects they need to keep them safe, cartons of fruit juice and bottles of coke, bars of chocolate and tubes of crisps, tapes, CDs, cushions, duvets, cigarette papers, cigarettes, candles and burners and matches and drugs. And in the back bedroom they are settling down and they are talking, the tall thin girl with glitter round her eyes says don't be so fucking daft man it'd go all over the floor and down your legs and that, and she giggles and turns to reach for a drink and as her face catches the candle-light her skin sparkles like shattered glass in the sun.

In the front first-floor bedroom of number nineteen a woman wakes suddenly. She looks at the clock, she looks at her sleeping husband, she wonders why she has woken. There is no noise from the street, the children are quiet. She eases softly out of bed, her bladder suddenly straining and full, she stands and she opens the door slowly enough for it not to squeak. On the way to the bathroom, she looks into the children's bedroom and checks on each one of them, she crouches at the lower bunks and stretches up to the top one. She looks with sleepy love at the three of them, she watches their young bodies swelling and shrinking through her barely opened eyes, she holds her hand close to their faces to feel the warm give and suck of their breath. She murmurs a brief prayer for them and closes the door gently, soft-padding to the toilet, sitting and relieving herself and watching the shadows of pigeons flap across the bathroom wall.

The short girl with the painted toenails, next door, she says oh but did you see that guy on the balcony, he was nice, no he was special and she savours the word like a strawberry, you know she says, the one on the balcony, the one who was speeding and kept leaning right over, and they all know exactly who she means, he's in the same place most weeks, pounding out the rhythm like a panelbeater, fists crashing down into the air, sweat splashing from his polished head.

She says once I was there and he got so carried away that he hung from the balcony by his legs, he had his feet hooked under the rail, and she remembers the way his face had stretched into a furious O, going come on let's have some and she remembers his fists still flailing across the void like an astronaut lost in orbit.

A girl sleeps in the back bedroom of number eleven, her hair is pushed out of her eyes by a hairband, her mouth is wide open, the room is warm and beginning to lighten. Bird shadows pass quickly across her face but she does not wake.

A couple in their early thirties sleep in the attic flat of number twenty-one, wrapped loosely in a thin red blanket, he is snoring and she is turned away from him, there is a television on in the corner with the sound turned down, shadows pass through the room but the couple do not wake.

In the back bedroom of number seventeen, the boy with the white shirt and the tie says it was definitely a girl, she didn't have an Adam's apple, I swear, it was a girl definitely, and everyone laughs at him and he looks around the room and joins in the laughter and somebody passes him a long cigarette.

The boy with the wide trousers is quiet, he's looking at the girl next to him, a beautifully unslim girl with dark curls of hair falling down over a red velvet dress, he's looking at the laces and straps and buckles and zips of her complicated footwear and he looks up at her and says so how long does it take you to get those boots off then? She looks at him, this girl, with lips as red as the fire inside a chilli, she looks at the tight spread of him across the bed and she says

I don't know I've never taken them off myself

and she smiles at the sharpness of his intake of breath, she watches his eyes trickle down from her face and roll down the rich geometry of her body.

And everyone else keeps talking, compulsively, talking across each other, talking about the tunes they heard and the people they saw and the next place they want to go. The boy with the white shirt and the tie keeps saying it was definitely a girl, and then he stuffs a pipe full of fresh green herb and the room quietens in anticipation, the conversation dropping, each of them suddenly feeling their minds too frantic, their bodies too tense, and they suck on the sweet smoke in turn, holding the pillow of it in their lungs, closing their eyes, stilling their voices.

And they think about daytime things for a moment, about rolling hills, or beaches, or playing football, or whatever it is they've learnt to think about at these times, and they breathe slowly and move for a moment into a kind of waking sleep. And if someone were to look through the window now, to walk into the backyard and press their face against the glass, cupping their hands around their eyes like a pair of binoculars, that person would see what looked like a roomful of people gathered together in silent prayer, and they would wonder who such a vigil might be for.

Outside, a taxi drives slowly down the street, the driver peering from the window, checking house numbers. He gets as far as number twenty-eight, and then there are no more numbers. He hesitates a moment before driving away, the sound of the car fading behind him like a trail of dust.

And now they are quiet, the girl with the army trousers trying to find a picture on the television, the boy with the pierced eyebrow holding a lighter beneath the plastic lid of a tube of crisps, a look of concentration in his eyes, waiting, watching the plastic soften.

The girl with the boots says I'm going home, I want to go home now.

Do you want to come with me she says to the boy with the wide trousers, walk me home she says, and her voice is thin and tired.

The boy with the shirt and tie is lying down on the floor,

draping one arm across the tall girl who is still chewing gum and staring at the ceiling, dragging a duvet halfway across them both.

The short girl is curled up in a ball in the middle of the bed, waiting for the girl with the army trousers to come and keep her warm.

The boy with the pierced eyebrow lifts the lid to his mouth and blows, and a bubble of hot plastic shoots halfway across the room, flashing into place like a miracle, holding its long airship shape for a fraction of a second and then floating gently down towards the floor.

The girl with the boots offers her hand to the boy with the wide trousers, pulls him to his feet and kisses his forehead. Take me home she says and they drift slowly through the door.

The girl with the army trousers closes her eyes and collapses into the bed, adjusting herself gradually against the outline of the other girl's body, wrapping around her like a nutshell.

In the first-floor flat of number eighteen, a young man sits up in bed, it's early but he feels very awake, he looks around at the mess of his room and he thinks of all the things he wants to do today, needs to do. Sorting, packing, tidying, arranging. He rubs at his dry eyes with the tips of his fingers, he gets out of bed and walks across to the window. He sees two people in the middle of the road, he recognises the girl from number twenty-seven, he doesn't recognise the boy and he wonders who he is. He picks up a camera and takes photographs of the morning, the two people in the street, the sunlight, the closed curtains of the windows opposite, he puts down the camera and makes notes in a small book, he writes the date, he details the things he has just photographed.

18

The young couple in the street, dancing, their arms curled gracefully around one another, the music from the restaurant carpark still in their heads, disappearing into her house, leaving the front door open, the street empty and quiet.

A cat, waiting on a doorstep.

Pigeons, dropping onto chimneytops.

I'd been thinking about it when I called Sarah, the girl
sitting next to me that day, I realised it had been a while
since we'd spoken and it was probably my turn to call.
I said hi I just fancied a chat I wondered what you were up
to and she said oh hi it's been ages hasn't it.
All our conversations seem to start like this now.
Once a month, maybe less, one of us will call the other and
we'll say oh hi it's been ages we should try and meet up,
and a plan will be made, and cancelled, or not quite made
at all.
We're not that far apart, maybe half an hour on the tube,
but it's been months since we've seen each other and
every month it seems to matter less.
And so I sat in my room, that evening, and we talked about
the usual things, about new jobs and plans for new jobs,
about people we both knew and people we were meeting, about dates and possible dates.
I looked out of my open window, across the endless city,
and I imagined her sitting by her window, looking in this
direction, the telephone a shortcut through all those
streets.
I wondered what her room looked like, what she could see
from it.
She said so who have you spoken to lately, have you heard
from Simon, and I said no not for a long time.

I thought about all the time we spent together, the three
of us, the long days of that last summer in the house and
I wondered how it had become so hard to keep in
touch.
I remembered the promises we'd made to each other, me

and Sarah and Simon, and I wondered if I'd been naive to think we could keep them.

I remembered how easily we used to talk, endlessly, making plans, deciding where we'd be in one and two and three years' time, and I don't remember mentioning this.

I had the appointment card on the table, the letter with the confirmation of results, and all I wanted to do was tell her about it, talk it over, like we would have done before.

I wanted to talk about why it was making me so scared, why there was a breathless panic fluttering up into my throat.

Sarah you're not going to believe this, I wanted to say, or Sarah can I tell you something?

I wanted her to say oh calm down why don't you, the way she did when I used to get worked up about deadlines and exams.

To say look no one's dying here, we're not talking about open-heart surgery, it's normal, it's a thing that happens.

I wanted her to give me some perspective, to say things out loud and make them seem a little more ordinary.

But I didn't say anything, I just said oh I had a postcard from Peru, from someone called Rob, I said I couldn't remember who he was.

She said you must do, he was that guy from over the road, he tried skating down that hill in the park, don't you remember?

I smiled and said oh yes, and she said remember how no one went to help him because we were all laughing so much, and I laughed and held my hand to my mouth because it still seemed unfair to find it so funny, the way he went sprawling to the floor, arms flung out for balance, belly-flopping across the tarmac.

I said and remember how he had no skin on his arms for the rest of the summer, just those long grey scabs?

And she said I know I know, laughing, she said I can't believe you'd forgotten, and I could picture the way she screwed her eyes up when she laughed.

We talked about other people, saying do you remember when, and how funny was that, and I wonder what happened to.

We talked about the medicine girl next door, the boy in Rob's house who thought he could play the guitar, the good-looking boy down the road with the sketch-pad.

We talked about the people at number seventeen, Alison who got her tongue pierced, and Chris, and the boy with the ring in his eyebrow but we couldn't remember his name.

I tried to remember what it was like to be near so many people who knew me.

She said what's Rob doing in Peru anyway, and I said I don't know I think he's saving the children or something.

Do you think he's taken his skateboard she said, and I laughed and then remembered the way his hair got in his eyes when he was trying to pull off tricks.

The way his jeans always got scuffed under the heels of his trainers.

I thought about him being all those thousands of miles away, and I wondered how long the postcard had taken to reach me.

I read it again, looking at the long looping letters, trying to imagine the slow slur of his voice.

Things are going massively here it said, I'm having an ace time.

It said I'm not really homesick, but I'm missing decent cups of tea, it said you could write to me sometime.

I looked at the front of the card, at the pictures of Peru,

smiling women in traditional dress, mountains, monkeys in fruit trees.
She said hello are you still there?

I said do you ever think about it, I mean, that last day.
She didn't say anything for a moment, I heard a television in the background and I wondered where she was, if she was with anyone.
She said I try not to, it's weird, you know, I'd rather forget about it.
It seems like a long time ago now she said.
I said I know but I can't get it out of my head.
It keeps coming back I said, just recently, I don't know why.
She was quiet, and I waited for her to say something.
I straightened the flowers in the vase on the table, pulled out the dead leaves.
I watched the traffic lights changing in the street outside.

She said what I always remember is the way everything carried on afterwards.
There were still buses going past on the main road she said, and some of the people on them turned to look for a moment but some of them didn't even notice.
I wanted everything to stop she said, even if it was only for a little while.
There was nothing about it on the news she said, I knew there wouldn't be but it didn't seem right.
It just kind of happened and passed she said, and then we left and there was nothing to prove it had happened at all.
I said, you know, it's the noise I can't forget.
I still have dreams about it sometimes I said.
The way it echoed off the houses, and, oh, it just, I said.

And then we stopped talking and I could hear her breathing.

She said actually can we talk about something else now.
I said yes, sorry, it's just I've been thinking, you know, lately, and she said well it's a long time ago.
She said so anyway are you seeing anyone at the moment, and we talked about recent possibilities and failures, comparing notes.
And she said look my dinner's nearly ready I'd better go.
I said oh sorry I didn't realise, you're eating late aren't you and she said oh I do these days and we both said I'll speak to you soon then bye.
I didn't say who are you eating with are you eating on your own.
I sat there for a long time, after I put the phone down, the letter and the appointment card on the table, unmentioned.
I don't know why I didn't say anything to her about it, I don't understand how I became fearful and closed off like this.
I sat there, watching the flowers quivering each time a lorry went past, feeling the tremble echo along the bones of my spine.

I saw the moon appearing, low and white over the park by the river.
I remembered the time Simon had called me through to his room, saying look out of the window, a dark night and the moon was bright and crisp away to the left, a thin crescent like a clipped fingernail.
And he'd said no no no but check this out, look over there, look over that way.
Pointing away to the right, to a second moon as bright and crisp as the first.

I'd looked at him, and he'd giggled and said how mad is that.

I'd looked at the two moons, each as clean and thin and new as each other, the same size, like twins of each other.

And I'd swung his window closed, and the reflection of the moon on the right swung away into the room with it and he said oh right yeah I thought it would be something like that.

I remembered this, and I wondered what he'd been doing the last few years, I wondered about all the people I haven't seen or spoken to properly since then.

All the emails I get these days start with sorry but I've been so busy, and I don't understand how we can be so busy and then have nothing to say to each other.

I read the letter again, and I sat very still, barely breathing, the streetlight striping the darkening room through the blinds.

I took off my shirt and bra and began touching my skin, very slowly, tracing the contours, pressing against the ridges and lines.

Running my fingers across all the marks and scars and spots, as though I could read my blemishes like braille.

I'm not sure what I was looking for.

I think I wanted to find something new, something visibly changed, something I could point to and say this is what it is, this is where it's beginning.

But I couldn't find anything.

I pressed the palm of my hand against my chest and tried to count my heartbeat.

It felt faster than it should be, and my skin felt hot, shining red, as though the blood was rushing to the surface and gasping for air.

I sat there for a long time, I fell asleep in the chair and when I woke up in the morning I was late for work.

In the backyard of number nineteen, a woman is hanging out her washing, murmuring a song to herself and squinting against the light. She can see people sleeping in the back room of next door, she is glad they are quiet now, it means perhaps her children will sleep more.

She stoops for a handful of pegs and adjusts her head-scarf. She hangs out a row of salwar kameez in different sizes, bright swathes of colour printed on thin fabric, she hangs out shirts, trousers, endless variations of underwear. And when she is done, and the whole yard is heavy with wavering lines of wet bunting, she straightens up and puts her hand to the hollow of her back, curves her face up-wards. She interrupts her murmured song and listens to the muffled rumble of the morning. She breathes slowly and deeply, and for now the air smells clean, infused with the bright wetness of clean laundry.

The young man at number eighteen, with the dry eyes, he's not dressed yet but he's awake and he's busy, he's crouched on the floor, arranging a collection of objects and papers.

A page from a TV guide. An empty cigarette packet. A series of supermarket till receipts, stapled together in chronological sequence. Leaflets advertising bhangra all-dayers and techno all-nighters. Train tickets. Death notices cut from local newspapers. An unopened packet of chew-ing gum.

He lays them all out on the floor, lays them out in size order, rearranges them in date order, blinking quickly. He stands back and looks, and writes out a list of the objects in front of him.

He turns on the television and picks up a polaroid camera. As soon as the screen warms up he takes a photograph of it, scribbling the time and the date on the back of the blank printout, seven a.m., thirty-one, oh eight, ninety-seven.

He lays the polaroid next to the cigarette packet, watching the shapes darken into colour and light. He turns back to the television, blinking, and watches Zoe talking about pop music in a London park, the soft morning light flitting through the trees and lighting up her hair, she says we'll be having it large and he turns the television off.

Next door, in the bedroom of number twenty, an old man is lying awake beside his sleeping wife, he is holding his cupped palms close to his face and looking at the tiny flecks of blood he's just coughed out of his lungs. He is fighting to control his breathing without waking his wife and he is looking at the pictures of their nephews and nieces, their great-nephews and great-nieces, propped up on the dressing table. He feels old, and he feels afraid. He listens to the steadiness of his wife's breathing, and he thinks about the first night they spent together, a smuggled liaison in a seaside hotel nearly sixty years ago. He remembers the pattern on the wallpaper, the luxury of a three-bar electric fire, the view of the hills from the window. He remembers their shyness, standing awkwardly at the foot of the small bed and reaching out very slowly, kissing once, twice, moving uncertainly to hold each other and gradually allowing their curiosity to prevail. He remembers her insisting that the light be kept on until they slept, and that their clothes be folded neatly. And most of all he remembers how wonderfully startled they both were by their eventual intimacy.

He lies still, listening to his wife, waiting for the morning.

In the attic of number twelve, a young man is leaning out of the window, stripped to the waist. He is smoking a cigarette, holding it away to one side and making sure he blows all the smoke out into the air, and he is thinking about the day ahead.

He finishes the cigarette and drops it down into the street, watching it fall, the way it glows brightly as it accelerates towards the ground, the way it bursts into sparks on the pavement below. He turns back into his room, unwrapping a stick of chewing gum from his bedside drawer, taking a wallet from under his pillow and emptying out the cash. He sits crosslegged on the bed, running a flat hand across his forehead and through his thick black hair, looking at the folded notes with a bounce and a jig of excitement. He counts the money, again, smoothing the creases, sorting the fives from the tens, stacking them in ten neat piles of a hundred pounds each. He grins, biting his lip, nodding his head and tucking the notes back into his wallet, the wallet back under his pillow. Today he thinks, today today, and he lies on his back, one hand behind his head, the other hand a fist which he kisses and shakes in the air. He closes his eyes, but he doesn't sleep.

At number eighteen, the boy with the sore dry eyes pulls a shoebox from a high shelf and sorts through the polaroids inside, he picks out a handful and fans them out on the floor like a poker spread. A picture of a lamp-post covered in marker-pen graffiti, Uz 4 Shaf 4 eva 9T7, Izzy is fit signed who, Lee an me wuz busy like bee, Sian equals slag, and so on and so, the soap opera of the street corner marked out in rain-faded initials and abbreviations.

A picture of a fly-posted garage door, poster layered upon poster, streaks torn through the layers of dates and venues and djs and bands, the top corner peeling off under the weight to reveal bare metal.

Empty drums of vegetable oil piled up outside a curryhouse like tins in a nineteen fifties supermarket.

A traffic jam at night, beaded white lights stringing down the road like christmas decorations, rain splashed on the camera lens.

Dark dribbles of blood in a pub carpark.

He picks up the camera again and carries it through to the bathroom, he takes a picture of himself in the mirror. He blinks, tightly and painfully, laying the camera down and holding the palms of his hands to his eyes, screwing his face up, rocking his head.

The colours in the polaroid wake into the light, his selfportrait taking shape while he searches for eyedrops, his blind hand like an addict in a medicine cabinet, knocking over shampoos and deodorants and razors.

In the back room of number seventeen, the girl with the glitter around her eyes is lying awake, chewing gum, looking at her sleeping friends. She knows she'll be awake for some time yet, her brain is piled high with powders and pills and the muscles in her legs are still twitching from the dancefloor. She looks at the girls on the bed, the one curled around the other, protectively, she watches their shoulders and breasts rise and fall, shifting gently into position, she thinks about the piercing in the short girl's tongue and wonders if it's true what they say. The stereo is still playing, very quietly, she watches the small green lights bubbling up and down with the music, she listens to the singer going doowah doowah, I love you so, oohwoah. She feels the good strong weight of the white-shirted boy's arm across her chest, she tilts her head forward to kiss it. The music goes doowah doowah I love you so, and she thinks about the two of them. They haven't spoken about it, they haven't said what will we do when we leave here, do you want to come with me, let's work something out, and she knows that this means they will quickly and easily drift apart, into other people's lives, into other people's arms in rooms like this. She is surprised that this doesn't make her feel sad. She listens to the music, she looks around at the things people dropped when they fell asleep or went out of the room, she kisses the boy's arm again and she feels only a kind of sweet nostalgia. She wonders if you can feel nostalgic for something before it's in the past, she wonders if perhaps her vocabulary is too small or if her chemical intake has corroded it and the music goes doowoah doo-woah.

In the bathroom of number eighteen, a face looks out from the polaroid, wide-eyed, composed. A young man, early twenties, a smooth round face, straight nose, full lips, pale hair losing thickness around the temples, a buckle of skin folded below each eye. It's a good picture, and in a moment he will date it and place it with the other objects he has collected together on his bedroom floor, a magazine article, a half-finished crossword, a twin-bladed razor.

But for now he has his head tipped up to the ceiling, a capful of solution bathing the dryness of his eyes, one hand gripping the sink until the ache subsides.

It's light that makes his eyes hurt, mostly, bright or sudden light, and the dust in the air. It's a rough prickling sensation, like sandpaper pressed up against the skin of his eye, a dryness he can mostly soothe by blinking rapidly, squeezing moisture across the surface.

It's worse in the city, with all the dust and the dirt, and it's worse in the summer, with the long bright days, but usually it's bearable, usually he doesn't notice and he just keeps blinking away that gritted feeling. And if it gets too much, like it has now, he comes to his bathroom and bathes his eyes, and it's a relief like finding a spring welling up in the desert.

He puts the eyedrops back into the cabinet, scratching the back of his hand, he picks up the camera and the self-portrait and returns to his bedroom, he wonders what else he might hide away with this collection. And he thinks about the girl at number twenty-two.

In the street, the front door of number thirteen is swinging gradually open, a young boy who can barely reach the doorhandle is peering around the door, his hair is sticking up and he is still wearing his pyjamas. He climbs onto a bright red tricycle which is waiting for him on the front path, he pushes all his weight onto the pedals and he creaks out of his garden and onto the main pavement. He looks back at the still open front door, he looks ahead of him to the main road, he puts his head down and he pedals, slowly at first, bumping and wobbling over loose paving slabs, picking up speed.

A streetcleaner whirrs past, brushes spinning and skidding across the tarmac, grit and glass and paper skipping up into its innards. The driver stares sleepily ahead, sunglasses curled across his face, lips mouthing the words of the song on the radio, I'll be there for you, when the rain starts to fall. As he passes number nineteen he glances across at a girl sitting on the garden wall, a girl in a red velvet dress wearing very tall boots, she has her face arched up to the sky and a boy in wide trousers is gently kissing the tight curve of her throat. The streetcleaner whirrs away around the corner and the girl takes the boy's hand and bites his little finger. He makes a noise, a soft noise and his eyes are closed and his stomach is like it was left behind over a humpbacked bridge and she says shall we go now and they both stand.

They hear voices then, shouted voices crashing down from the attic flat of number twenty-one, a woman's voice shouting no but listen will you, listen to me, it's not okay is it you shit you weren't thinking about me were you you just went off out and did what you wanted to do it's always about what you want isn't it you selfish fucking wanker and what about me what about me she screams and the woman between the washing in next-door's backyard stands and wonders how these people manage to shout at one another so much and still walk in the street with a hand in a hand. Shut up says the man's voice, just shut up, shut up shut up will you please shut the fucking fuck up please? and his voice rises and rises until it sounds almost like the woman's and it cracks and it breaks.

The girl and the boy outside, they look at each other and they hurry away down the road, and when they turn the corner the street is empty and quiet again.

The street is empty and quiet and still, the light is brightening, shadows hardening, the haze of dawn burning away. The day will soon burn with a particular brightness, hot and lethargic and tense. Later, it will rain, hard, suddenly, and the hot tarmac will steam and shine as water streaks across the surface into the gutters. And windows will be hurriedly closed, and people will stand in doorways, in shocked silences. But now, in this early beginning, it is dry, and the street is beginning to warm, and people sleep, or lie restlessly awake, or make love and sleep again.

The day after speaking to Sarah I tried telling my mother.

I took the phone into my room, I sat on the floor with my knees pulled up into my chest and I started to dial the number.

I looked at a photograph on the wall, taken that summer, taken a few days before it happened.

Half a dozen of us, huddled together in a front garden, ashtrays and cushions spread across the grass, a speaker mounted in the front-room window, a beanbag spilling its beans across the pavement.

It's a photo that makes us look young, it makes all of us look very young.

Our faces taut and shining, grinning awkwardly, squinting into the sunlight, everyone's arms around everyone else.

Waving cans of beer as though they were novelties.

Looking like we thought everything was going to last forever.

I put the phone down before it started ringing, and I looked at the other pictures.

The photo of Simon must have been taken the same day, the day he left.

He's sat in the front passenger seat of his dad's car, window wound down, waving.

His dad's at the back of the car, leaning all his weight on the boot, trying to get it closed against three years' worth of possessions.

Against duvets and pillows, a stereo, a television, books and magazines and folders full of notes.

Against plates, saucepans, cutlery, a shoebox full of half-finished condiments, a food processor with the attachments missing.

A box of CDs, a box of videos, a box full of photographs
and postcards and letters.
And a standard lamp, which he bought in a junk shop to
make his room look civilised, lunging over his shoulder
from the mess behind him.
All of it squeezed into his dad's car, and he sits there and
smiles and holds his open hand up beside his face.
In the background there's a boy on a tricycle, staring.

There's a photo of me and another girl, Alison, and I can't
remember who took it.
I'm standing next to her, pointing, shocked and laughing,
and I'm surprised to see how similar I look, really, the
same short blonde hair, the same small square glasses.
Alison's pulling a wideopen face at the camera, freshly
studded tongue flaring out of her mouth, fingers curled
out like cat-claws.
And I'm pointing at her tongue and looking right into the
lens, looking right out at myself these few years later,
with a telephone in my hand, unable to dial.
I sat there thinking about the day she'd got it done, talked
into it by the boy with the ring through his eyebrow who
lived in her house, how she kept changing her mind all
morning.
Eventually she went to a place round the corner, an upstairs
place with a sign on the door saying no children no
spectators.
It was a week before she could speak properly again, and
then all she talked about was how excited and pleased
she was with it.
She kept sticking her tongue out at men in the pub, just to
see how they'd react.
By the end of the summer she was saying she might have to
take it out to get a job.

36

It was a strange time.

People were slipping out of the city unexpectedly, like children getting lost in a crowd, leaving nothing but temporary addresses and promises to keep in touch.

I didn't know what to do, there was a feeling of time running out and a loss of momentum, of opportunities wasted.

It was a good summer, long and hot, the days cracked open and bare, but it was hard to enjoy when it felt so dead-ended.

We spent our days on the front doorstep, circling job adverts with optimistic red felt-pens, trying to make plans, talking about travelling, or moving to London, or opening a cafe, each plan sounding definite until the next morning.

I don't think any of us had the confidence, not for the sort of plans we were making, not for all those websites and fashion boutiques and doughnut shops.

A time of easy certainty had come to an end, and most of us had lost our nerve.

We used to sit on those front steps long into the evenings, long after the conversations had faltered, dragging our duvets downstairs when the stars finally squeezed out, flicking the ringpulls of empty beercans, blowing tunes into empty winebottles.

Wondering what to do next.

Most of the photos I've got were taken in that last week, rushing around, trying to make up for three unrecorded years.

Pictures of the house, my bedroom, the front door with the number painted on it, the view of the street from my window.

But mostly the pictures are of my friends then, drinking tea in the kitchen, piled up in someone's bed, throwing a frisbee across the street.

And in all the pictures they're looking straight at the camera, always grinning and waving.

I sat in my room that evening, the phone still in my hand, looking at all those photographs, looking closely, as though I'd not seen them before.

Studying the expressions on their faces, looking for hidden details.

It was strange how important the pictures felt, like vital documents that should be kept in a fireproof tin instead of being blu-tacked and pinned to the wall.

Somehow, although we spent the whole summer doing nothing, it felt like the most significant part of my life, until now.

I dialled the number again, and it was engaged.

I don't think I knew what I was going to say.

I don't know why I thought I'd find it any easier to tell her than Sarah.

I think I thought that, once I'd managed to say it, she'd at least be the one who would be able to help.

I think I hoped there would be shock and tearful reaction, that then she'd offer practical help and sensible advice.

That maybe she'd say why don't you come and stay for a few days and we'll talk it through, you and me and your dad.

Like a family, like a proper family.

I don't know why I thought these things, I don't know why I thought anything would be any different suddenly.

Perhaps I thought that exceptional circumstances could change the way of things.

I sat there, listening to the engaged tone, trying to think of the right words.

Telephone conversations with my mother are never very easy.
There always seems to be a weighting inside them, things left unspoken, things not fully spoken.
She says things gently and discreetly, carefully holding back her full implication.
Like holding playing cards against her chest.
When I told her about my latest new job she said that sounds very nice and what other opportunities have you been looking at?
She says things like, I don't think you're making full use of your degree, my love.
She says things like, it doesn't sound as though you're stretching yourself.
She doesn't say what the hell kind of a job is that, or what are you actually doing with your life here?
I wonder if I wish she would.

I got through eventually.
My dad answered, he picked up the phone and sighed and said yes, please?
He's always answered the phone like that, as though he was afraid of who might be trying to speak to him, of what they might be intending to say.
I said hi dad it's me, is mum there, and he said no, no she's not, she's gone out tonight.
I'm not sure whether I was disappointed or relieved.
I could hear him clutching the phone tightly, holding it away from his face as though he didn't think it was entirely safe, the way he always does, and I knew that I wouldn't say anything to him.

I knew it was a secret I would be keeping to myself a little longer.

He asked me about my job, he asked me about people I haven't seen for a long time and I said they were fine.

I said something about football, and then I let him get back to watching the television.

I put the phone down and imagined what I might have said, mum there's something I have to say, or mum I need to talk to you about something.

Mum I'm not sure how to say this but.

I think I was hoping she might realise something was wrong without me having to say so, that I could talk about my new shoes and she would say so what is it you're really telling me?

Like the mum in the old British Telecom adverts.

I looked at another photograph, of Simon and Rob and Jamie dancing naked down the street in the first pale hours of that summer, celebrating the election.

I remembered that momentous night, looping a cable through the window and setting the TV up in the front garden, gathering around it with pizza and weed and the excitement of history.

I remembered coming back from the garage at midnight, armed with fresh snack supplies and seeing my friends' faces lit up by the shrine of the television.

Shining and blue and flickering in the darkness.

Already looking like ghosts.

The woman at number nineteen, she has finished hanging out her washing, and now she steps into her kitchen and begins to think about breakfast. The children will be waking soon, and the whole household will begin then to fumble into the morning, her husband, her husband's father, her husband's mother. She reaches up to the cupboard over the sink and fetches down boxes of cereal, four packets of sugared grains and flakes which she clutches to her chest. As she turns to drop them on the table she sees her young daughter leaning against the doorframe, watching her with her big worried eyes. Before she can say anything, her daughter is hurrying to the cutlery drawer, counting out spoons, turning to the crockery cupboard, struggling with the bowls. She is still wearing her night-clothes. Hey, hey, says her mother, smiling, dress first, washing and clothing okay? And she takes her little arms and hustles her out of the kitchen. The child does not say a word, and the mother listens to her shuffling up the stairs, a shadow of concern skimming briefly across her face.

She finishes preparing the breakfast table, and as she puts the kettle on to boil the twin boys come rattling down the stairs and launch into the food, clutching their spoons like fighting sticks. She tries to talk to them about the day, what are they going to do and would they like to go with Nana and Papa to see Auntie for tea, but their mouths are full of soggy cereal and it is all they can do to breathe between shovelfuls. She relents, and tells them they must not go further than the shop at the end of the street and that they must not go into people's gardens without asking.

She strokes them both on the head, as if to bless their day, and she tells them to be good, and as they leave the room she sees again her daughter standing in the doorway, her head leaning up against the frame and her big eyes looking blankly upwards. She is wearing the floral dress with the gold edge which was made for her by Auntie, she is looking pretty she thinks. She says what would you like, and the young girl says nothing but slides into the chair vacated by her brother and pours herself a bowl of wheatflakes. She eats slowly, gathering the flakes into small spoonfuls, looking out of the window, chewing each portion thoughtfully.

And when she is finished she turns to her mother and says mummy can I watch cartoons now, just like that, no expression, as if she were a child extra in a cheap soap opera and not the centre of a loving family. Her mother nods her assent and watches her drift through to the front room, trailing her hand along the wallpaper.

Perhaps she is nervous about starting school, she thinks to herself, or perhaps she is becoming poorly. She turns to the window and touches her face, she is feeling weary of the day already. The boys stamp down the stairs and out of the front door. It is not yet eight o'clock. She runs the tap to wash the children's dishes. She clenches her fist under the rushing water until it becomes hot, she holds it there.

The man in the attic flat of number twenty-one, he is watching the twin boys from next door running in the street, he is leaning from the window to smoke a cigarette, he is being watched by the woman lying on the bed behind him. They are both naked. They're out already he says, them kids from next door, they're out already, what time is it? You probably woke them up with your snoring the woman says, rolling onto her side and stretching across the floor to pick up her watch. They're cheeky little shits them two the man says, I saw them throwing stones at those girls over the road last week, when they was sitting in their own garden. Probably just looking for attention the woman says, you know what boys are like. It's not even eight she says, I'm going back to sleep she says, but she doesn't and she lies awake looking at the nakedness of the man, at his feet tilted upwards and the tension rising up the muscles of his legs as he stretches to lean out of the window, and the rise and pause and fall of the curve of his shoulders as he savours his cigarette. At the small dragon tattoo on his shoulderblade. At the long pink lines and the small purple scuff marks scattered all over his skin, scratches and bruises she's gifted him in heated moments of fury and passion.

She props herself up on one elbow and catches sight of herself in the mirror, she looks at herself, her skin clean and unmarked except for a single thumb-sized bruise at the top of one arm. She looks at her hair, newly dyed a deep henna red, she turns a length of it in her fingers. She's still pleased with it, even though he hasn't yet said anything. She likes the way it complements her eyes.

They're looking in people's windows now the man says, his irritation furrelling over his shoulder like smoke, what are they playing at? Forget it she says, come back to bed she says, and she rolls to one side to make room for him. Little fuckers he says, they've got water-pistols he says, and he turns away, back into the room, striding across the floor to squash his cigarette end into the ashtray. What did you say he says to the woman, I missed that. She says, I told you to come back to bed and she reaches out her arm towards him and when he kisses her the stubble on his face smells of smoke and sunshine.

In the street outside, the twins from number nineteen are peering into the front window of number twenty, the slightly older one balanced on a pair of bricks to see better, looking through a small gap in the curtains. In the room in front of them, a man with thinning hair and a carefully trimmed moustache is doing stretching exercises, lifting his pale arms high in the air, lowering them towards the floor, placing his hands on his fleshy hips, arching his body from side to side. He is completely naked, and the boys suddenly giggle out loud and cover their mouths, the man with the tidy moustache turning and waving them away, dragging the curtains more fully closed.

They vanish, and he stands by the now safely shielded window, clenching and unclenching his fists, breathing a little heavily. They are not good boys, he is thinking, they are not good boys at all. He has seen them, he knows about them, he has seen them dropping their crisp bags in the street, their sweet wrappings. He stretches his hands towards the floor, his knees almost straight, his bony fingers only half a dozen inches from the carpet. He straightens, slowly and carefully, he puts on a dressing gown and he steps into his small kitchen, reaching for the kettle, glancing into the backyard and his hands yank suddenly up into the air as if he were shaking out a tablecloth and he mutters shameful words, he says to nobody what is it now? where does it come from all of this? and he pulls down the kitchen blind so that he does not have to look at it.

In the flat upstairs, an old man is looking for a box of matches to light the gas under the kettle, he turns to the table and he sees an envelope lying there, his name scratched across it in wavering handwriting. He smiles, he turns and opens the cutlery drawer of the Welsh dresser, he takes out an envelope with his wife's name on it, his own handwriting as newly unreliable as hers.

He places the two cards side by side, he thinks about

44

opening his for a moment and decides not to. He looks for the matches, and he thinks about that day.

It wasn't a spectacular wedding. It happened in a hurry, and they only spent one night together before he went away again, went away properly. They'd been told to tie up their loose ends, and they knew what that meant, so he'd sent her a telegram, just before his leave, saying are you at a loose end stop buy a nice dress stop will buy rings stop, and they'd rushed off to the registry office, dragging in the woman from the cake shop for a witness.

But it was a wedding, and they looked each other in the eyes and said the words, they made their vows and they have kept them all these years.

Her hand in his hand, watching him say to love and to cherish, watching him say until death us do part.

When they kissed, as they were signing the register, the woman from the cake shop turned her face away, as though she was embarrassed.

And they took the wedding certificate back to their new house, propped it up on the chest of drawers at the foot of the bed, and spent the whole evening looking at it, both feeling as though they'd just stepped off a fairground ride, both feeling dizzy and exhilarated, struggling to get their breath back, struggling to absorb everything that had happened.

She said, tell me the story of us, tell me it the way you'll tell our children when they ask.

She said it a lot, in those first few years, when she was feeling sad, or poorly, or she couldn't sleep. She'd lay her head on his chest, her hands tucked up under her chin, and she'd say tell me the story of us, tell me it the way you'd tell our children.

And he'd always say it the same way, starting once upon a time there was a handsome soldier boy with a smart

45

uniform and he went to a dance with his friends and minded his own business, and she'd always lift her head up and pull a shocked face and say you were not minding your own business you were making eyes at me all evening you're a big fat liar.

And he'd always put two fingers to her lips and say so the handsome soldier boy was surprised to see a nice-looking young lady standing in front of him and asking him to dance, and she'd say what happened then, did they dance, did they dance well?

Oh yes, he'd always say, yes indeed, they did dance, and they danced very well, spinning and twirling and looking deeply in one another's eyes so they didn't know everyone else was looking at them so amazed and you know what happened that very moment he'd say, not waiting for her response, what happened without them even knowing was they were in love.

And then? she'd say, what happened then? Did they kiss? and he'd say no no, not so soon, he was a gentleman you see, a gentleman as well as a soldier and so he didn't kiss her until the second time they met he'd say, and she would ask him for more details and he would tell them to her, their first meetings, where they went to, what they did, the first night they spent together in the hotel in Blackpool and she'd say you mustn't tell the children about that bit and he'd laugh and say no.

And that first time he'd told the story, that night, lying side by side on the bed, fully clothed, neither of them said anything when he finished, they just lay there looking at the certificate, looking at the official type, the formal words, looking at their names laid down in sloping black ink.

And she'd whispered it's a good story isn't it?, unbuttoning his shirt, spreading her fingers out across his chest as though smoothing wrinkles from a bedsheet, and he'd said

46

yes, yes it is, it's a good story. And the last thing she'd said to him, just before she went to sleep that night, quietly, almost as though she thought he was asleep, she said you will come back won't you, you will keep safe, please, you will come home?

When I got back from that first appointment it rained for a day and a half.

It woke me up in the middle of the night, a quiet noise at first, burbling across the roof, spattering through the leaves of the trees, and it was good to lie there for a while and listen to it.

But later, when I got up, it was heavier and faster, pouring streaks down the windows, exploding into ricochets on the pavement outside.

I stood by the window watching people in the street struggle with umbrellas.

I phoned work and said I can't come in I'm sick.

I thought about what my mother would say if she saw me skiving like this, I remembered what she said when I was a child and stuck indoors over rainy weekends.

There's no use mooching and moping about it she'd say, it's just the way things are.

Why don't you play a game she'd say, clapping her hands as if to snap me out of it.

And I'd ask her to point out all the one-player games and she'd tut and leave the room.

I wonder if that's what she'll say when I finally tell her, that it's the way things are, that there's no use mooching and moping about it.

It doesn't seem entirely unlikely.

She used to lecture me about it, about taking what you're given and making the most of it.

Look at me with your dad she'd say, gesturing at him, and I could never tell if she was joking or not.

But it's how she was, she would always find a plan B if

things didn't go straight, she would always find a way to keep busy.

If it was raining, and she couldn't hang the washing out, she would kneel over the bath and wring it all through, savagely, until it was dry enough to be folded and put away.

If money was short, which was rare, she would march to the job centre and demand an evening position of quality and standing.

That was what she said, quality and standing, and when they offered her a cleaning job or a shift at the meatpackers she would take it and be grateful.

She always said that, she said you should take it and be grateful.

And so I tried to follow her example that day, hemmed in by the rain, I sat at the table and read all the information they gave me at the clinic.

I tried to take in all the advice in the leaflets, the dietary suggestions, the lifestyle recommendations, the discussions of various options and alternatives.

I read it all very carefully, trying to make sure I understood, making a separate note of the useful telephone numbers.

I even got out a highlighter pen and started marking out sections of particular interest, I thought it was something my mother might approve of.

But it was difficult to absorb much of the information, any of the information, I kept looking through the window and I felt like a sponge left out in the rain, waterlogged, useless.

I was distracted by the pictures, by all these people looking radiant and cheerful, smartly dressed and relaxed.

I knew I didn't look like that, I knew I didn't feel relaxed or cheerful.

I didn't feel able to accept what my body was doing to me, and I still don't.
It felt like a betrayal, and it still does.

And I kept trying to tell myself to calm down.
To tell myself that this is not something out of the ordinary, this is something that happens.
This is not an unbearable disaster, a thing to be bravely soldiered through.
It's something that happens.
But I think I need somebody to say these words for me to believe them, I don't think I can speak clearly or loudly enough when I say them to myself.
One of the leaflets mentioned telling people, who to tell, how long to wait.
I thought about why I haven't told anyone yet, and what this means.
Perhaps not telling people makes it less real, perhaps it's not even definite yet, really.
Perhaps I need time to get used to the idea of it, before people's good intentions start hammering down upon me like rain.

Another of the leaflets had a section on physical effects.
You may find you become tired it said, you may find yourself experiencing dizziness, insomnia, a change in appetite.
There was a list of these things, half a dozen pages of alphabetical discomforts and pains.
I spent a long time thinking about them all, wondering which ones I'd get, wondering how well I would cope.
I thought about backache, nausea, indigestion, faintness and cramps and piles.

51

I thought about waking in the night with a screaming pain, clutching at the covers with clawed hands.

I thought about banging my fists against my head to distract myself from it.

I thought about religious people who train themselves to walk over burning coals and I wondered if I could control my body in the same way.

I didn't think I could, and I got scared and gathered all the leaflets up, stacked them away in a kitchen drawer with the scissors and sellotape and elastic bands.

By the middle of the afternoon it had rained so much that the drains were overflowing, clogged up with leaves and newspapers.

The water built up until it was sliding across the road in great sheets, rippled by the wind and parted like a football crowd by passing cars.

I was shocked by the sheer volume of water that came pouring out of the darkness of the sky.

Watching the weight of it crashing into the ground made me feel like a very young child, unable to understand what was really happening.

Like trying to understand radio waves, or imagining computers communicating along glass cables.

I leant my face against the window as the rain piled upon it, streaming down in waves, blurring my vision, making the shops opposite waver and disappear.

There was a time when I might have found this exhilarating, even miraculous, but not that day.

That day it made me nervous and tense, unable to concentrate on anything while the noise of it clattered against the windows and the roof.

I kept opening the door to look for clear skies, and slamming it shut again.

And then around teatime, from nowhere, I smashed all the
   dirty plates and mugs into the washing-up bowl.
Something swept through me, swept out of and over me,
   something unstoppable, like water surging from a broken
   tap and flooding across the kitchen floor.
I don't quite understand why I felt that way, why I reacted
   like that.
I wanted to be saying it's just something that happens.
But I was there, that day, slamming the kitchen door over
   and over again until the handle came loose.
Smacking my hand against the worktop, kicking the cupboard doors, throwing the plates into the sink.
Going fuckfuckfuck through my clenched teeth.
I wanted someone to see me, I wanted someone to come
   rushing in, to take hold of me and say hey hey what are
   you doing, hey come on, what's wrong.
But there was no one there, and no one came.

I stopped eventually, when I noticed my hands were
   bleeding.
I must have cut them with the smashed pieces of crockery,
   picking pieces out of the sink to throw them back in.
I stood still for a few moments, breathing heavily, watching
   blood drip from my hands onto the broken plates,
   wanting to sit down but unable to move.
I watched the blood pooling across the palms of my hands.
I looked at the broken plates and mugs.
I wondered where such a fierce rage had come from, and I
   was scared by the scale of it, by the lack of control I'd had
   for those few minutes.
I don't remember ever feeling like that before, and it
   worried me to think that I might be changing in ways
   I could do nothing about.
I washed my hands clean, letting the blood and water pour

over the broken crockery, counting about a dozen cuts, each as thin as paper.

The water began to sting, so I wrapped my hands in kitchen towel and held them up into the air, leaning back against the worktop, watching the blood soak through.

Later, when the bleeding had stopped and I'd covered my hands in a patchwork of plasters I found in the bathroom, I tried to get myself some food.

I thought it would make me feel better.

I'd been planning to go out and buy something, but I couldn't face it so I stayed in and ate what I could find.

Peanut butter, sardines, cream crackers, marshmallows.

It gave me a belly-ache, which seemed an appropriate end to a bad day, a wasted and damaged day.

And it kept on raining, rattling endlessly into the ground, piling up in the streets, wedged into the gutters and the drains.

It made the street look squalid and greasy.

People were scurrying along the pavement, their coats tugged tightly around themselves, their heads bowed as though they had something to hide.

And I was locking the door and closing the curtains, and I did have something to hide.

At number eighteen, the boy with the sore eyes is crouching on the floor among his arrangement of things, he is still thinking about the girl at number twenty-two, the girl with the short blonde hair and the little square glasses, the girl with the nicest sweetest smile he thinks.

He's thinking about the time he met her properly, besides seeing her in the street and sometimes saying hello, the time at a party round the corner when she'd stood and talked with him for a long part of the evening, and hadn't seemed to notice his blinking and hand scratching, perhaps because it was dark or perhaps because she didn't make him feel nervous by acting as though he was, the way most people do. They talked a lot, and laughed, and poured each other drinks and he'd felt comfortable and good and real with her, and she'd touched his arm once or twice, and looked him in the eye without saying anything, and although they hadn't kissed he thinks probably they could have done. It was there is what he thinks. And she'd asked him to walk her home because she felt tired and a bit uncomfortable and so he did and she held onto his arm for support, held on quite tightly because she said the pavement was moving like on a boat and she said sorry I'm not normally this drunk honestly and laughed. She laughed a lot, that night. And just before she went inside he said, very quickly, do you want to go out sometime, for a drink or something or? And she'd grinned a big squint-eyed grin and said yes yes, Wednesday night, I'll come round Wednesday night and we'll go somewhere and then she'd gone in and closed the door and he'd gone home and barely slept until dawn.

Next door, in the back bedroom of number sixteen, a young girl is playing by herself. She has a picture book with removable sticky figures, she is removing them and replacing them, standing them on their heads on the tops of houses, making them swim in duckponds, dropping them from a height and seeing where they land. She is waiting for her father to wake, so she can have breakfast and get dressed.

He rubs at his bloodshot eyes, the young man next door, he piles up his collection of things and squeezes them into a coffee jar, writing the date and his name on a sticker on the lid. He thinks about that Wednesday night, waiting in, trying to be relaxed, waiting for the doorbell, checking that it worked, putting music on and off. Sitting outside at midnight and realising she wasn't coming.

He pulls the large floor-rug to one side and lifts up a loose section of floorboard. His brother, when he'd emailed him about it, had said well she was probably just so drunk she forgot, that's all it is, go and talk to her again, she'll still be up for it, but he'd never been so sure, maybe she'd forgotten or maybe really she'd changed her mind. Maybe she'd been too embarrassed to say anything to him about it. He remembers the next time he'd seen her, how she'd looked at him vaguely and said hello and looked away. He remembers how beautiful he sees her, the way she walks, the way she lifts her head when she laughs. How easily they'd talked together that night, the touch of her hand on his arm. It could have been there is what he thinks.

He places the jar between the floor joists, nesting it among the dust and the cables and pipes like an egg, a bundle of memories waiting to hatch into the future. Tomorrow he will pack his bags and move to another house a few streets away, and he is reluctant to vanish without a trace. He replaces the floorboard, lays the rug over the top, returns the bed to its original position.

Today, he thinks. He could go and talk to her today. Say excuse me I hope you don't mind me asking but do you remember that night, that party? Say excuse me but, really, I am actually very much in love with you. He smiles at the impossibility of it, blinks, scratches the back of his hand.

He puts some bread in the toaster, he walks down the stairs and out into the street. There is hardly anyone out yet, except for the art student at number eleven, and the boy on the tricycle, his head down, rattling and racing along the pavement. He looks up at the clear sky, stretching his arms, turning and briefly looking at the closed front door of number twenty-two. He hears the kerchang of the toaster and goes back inside, leaving the door open.

She opens her front door, just a little, just enough, and she hops down her front steps, the young girl from number nineteen, glad to be out of the house and away from the noise of her brothers. The television was boring and strange anyway, it was all people talking and she didn't understand. She taps her feet on the pavement, listening to the sound her shiny black shoes make against the stone, and then she strides along the pavement with her fingers linked behind her back the way she's seen her father walk when he's walking with the other old men. She watches her feet as they spring between the paving slabs, enjoying the bounce and the hop of it, counting each step, stopping when she gets to twenty because that's as far as she knows.

She looks up, balancing on one foot, and spins around and around and she can see a spiral blur of sandy-coloured houses and blue sky and streaks of red and blue and yellow from people's curtains and all the colours spin round and when she stops suddenly it all carries on spinning for a moment and she feels dizzy. She sees a man sitting on his garden wall, a young man, and he is looking at her and smiling. She looks away quickly, and counts twenty steps back towards her house, bounce bounce, not stepping on the cracks.

The man sitting on his wall, outside number eleven, he is drawing a picture of the street. He has pens and pencils and rulers and erasers and a compass and a protractor, and he is drawing a very detailed picture of the row of houses opposite, trying to get the correct perspectives and elevations, trying to capture all of the architectural details.

That is what he wants to get onto the page, all the architectural details. For now there are just a few lines, faintly etched and erased and re-etched, between a scattering of dots and noted numbers and angles. He wants to do a good job of this today. He's been told that his drawing is weak and that he must improve it, and he doesn't want to lose his place on the course so he is trying very hard. He begins to measure the widths of the houses, squinting along the length of his arm, looking for the correct proportions. These houses are very different from the houses in his street, of course. The colour, the shape, the way they are all joined into one another, the height of them, it is all different from his village at home. But he likes them, there is a pride to see in these houses, in their age and in their grandeur. He knows that they were built over a hundred years ago, and that they were built for the owners of the textile factories, houses big enough to have servants squeezed into the attics and cellars, houses rich enough to have stained glass over the doors and sculpted figureheads amongst the eaves. He wonders about the people who lived in these houses first, the rich gentlemen and their elegant wives, their cooks and butlers and footmen, what they would say if they could see their houses now, shunted into the poor part of town, broken up into apartments and bedsits, their gardens mostly unkept, their paintwork mostly crumbling.

But still he thinks, even if they are not what they were they are still good houses, in a good street with wide pavements and plenty of trees for shade and life. He measures the distances between the ridges and the eaves, calculating the angles, and as he looks towards the far end of the street he notices that the hop-skipping girl is standing right behind him and is looking at his skeletal drawing.

He looks at her. She looks at the paper, at him, and back at the paper.

It is the street he says, and he waves a hand at the row of houses opposite, I am drawing your marvellous street, and she giggles because his accent makes marvellous rhyme with jealous. Where are the windows she says, in a very still and quiet voice, and she rubs her finger on the page.

Not yet he says, smiling at her, first I draw the walls and roofs and then I will draw the windows and doors and all the things. She looks at him, and at the page, and across the street. Where is the dog she says in the same voice, and she moves her finger across the page to where she thinks the dog should be.

Okay he says, I will put the dog in for you. But only after the windows he says, and he smiles at her. She looks at him, she turns around and skips across the road.

He watches her for a moment, he takes a pencil and sketches in the lines of the rooftop, the ground, the eaves, carefully, hesitantly, joining the marks of the measurements he has made. He looks from the page to the building, he sighs and he pulls at the loose skin around the corners of his forehead, it is very difficult he is thinking.

Upstairs at number twenty, the old man stands by the window, waiting for the kettle to boil, watching the twin brothers creeping into the garden of number seventeen, raised up on the fronts of their feet like a couple of Inspector Clouseaus.

The old man pushes his fingers into the thick white strands of his hair, he watches.

The boys are carrying elaborate waterguns, bright coloured plastic, blue cylinders and pink pressure pumps, green barrels and triggers, and they move to stand either side of the open front-room window, pressing flat against the wall like miniature sentries in a Swiss clocktower.

The kettle behind him sighs its way to a boil, and he watches the boys plunge their heads and arms into the billow of the drifting net curtain, their thin high voices echoing up to his window.

They re-emerge, they turn and they run from the garden, waving their guns like cowboys and indians, their faces hysterical with laughter and excitement and fear. A young man with wet hair appears at the window, shouting, wiping his face with the palm of his hand.

The old man laughs quietly. He likes the twins, they're funny, they remind him of his great-nephew, the same energy, the same cheek. He laughs again, and the breath whistles in the top of his lungs, the pain is suddenly there again, like cotton thread being yanked through his airways, the whistling getting louder, the hot red streaks beginning to splinter across his vision and he leans against the worktop, gulping for oxygen, jaw flapping, a fish drowning in air.

The kettle shrieks to a boil. The lid rattles with the pressure of the steam.

Downstairs, the man with the carefully trimmed moustache is getting dressed. He is standing in front of a mirror, fastening the top button of a crisp white shirt. He combs his thin black hair, straight down at the back, straight down at the sides, either side of a straight central parting on the top. He puts the comb back in its plastic wallet and takes a bowtie from the open leather suitcase on his table, where he keeps all his clothes. He loops it around his collar, lifting his head to tie the knot, adjusting it, tweaking at the corners until he gets it straight.

Upstairs, the old man clutches at his throat, head tipped back, mouth gaping, silent, staring at the ceiling like a tourist in the Sistine Chapel.

It took me a long time to get to sleep that night.

The rain was still spattering against the window, and there was a loud fall of water from a broken gutter onto the concrete below.

I blocked my ears with the bedcovers, I breathed slowly and deeply, I counted to a hundred, I counted to five hundred.

I gave up eventually, and put the light on, and sat up in bed to read.

But I couldn't concentrate, I kept thinking about that day, that moment, the afternoon.

About what happened and why there are so many names I can't remember.

About whether I knew the names in the first place.

Whenever I tried to read my book the images kept returning, small moments from that day and I don't understand why I can't leave it alone.

It's a strange feeling, almost like a guilty feeling, almost like I feel responsible.

I thought about going back up to my room that morning, after a shower and a mouthful of breakfast.

Swinging the window open, and the flood of fresh summer air that had come sweeping in, the sweetness of a rolling wind that was still clean from the countryside.

Seeing the guy from over the road poking his head through an attic skylight and tipping a bucket of water over some kids in their front garden.

I tried to remember his name, and all I could remember was the ring through his cycbrow, the way he used to smack the palm of one hand with the back of the other.

63

I remembered how hard it was to pack, how I spent the morning rearranging boxes and bags and rewriting lists.

I hadn't known what I was going to need, what I should throw away or leave behind, what I should give to someone for safekeeping.

I still hadn't known where I was going.

I remembered phoning the landlord and asking for another week, and panicking when he said people were due to move in the next evening.

I remembered looking at my overflowing room, and the empty boxes, and not knowing where to begin.

I thought about how I'd gone and stood in Simon's room for a while, looking at the sunlight brightening and fading on the ceiling.

Thinking about him leaving the week before, and how bare his room was now.

The unfaded squares on the wall where his posters had been.

The naked mattress on the floor, a curve in the middle where the springs had begun to fail.

And the things he'd left behind, unable to fit them into the boxes he'd squeezed into his dad's car.

Coathangers in the wardrobe that rattled like skeletons when I stood on the loose floorboards.

A muted noticeboard on the desk, pimpled with drawing pins.

A paper lightshade he'd taken down but left behind, folded on the floor like a deflated accordion.

The room had a hardness in it without his things there, an emptiness that made me want to close the door, leave a do not disturb sign outside, let the dust settle.

I remembered going to the shops to buy binbags, and saying hello to the boy at number eighteen.

He was on his doorstep, reading, and I caught his eye and he
smiled so I said hello.

I think it was the only time I ever spoke to him.

He said how are you doing, how's the packing going, he said
it with a little laugh, as though it was a joke.

Oh I said, fine I said, and I wondered how he knew that's
what I was doing.

There was a silence, and we looked at each other, and I
noticed he was blinking a lot and I thought he looked
nervous.

He said, last day of summer, everyone's packing aren't they,
and he did the little laugh again, and I said well you
know, all good things come to an end and he said yes.

I said well I'd better get to the shop, I'll see you around, yes
he said, yes, okay, well, see you then.

And he held up his hand, a wave like half a surrender, and
by the time I walked back he had gone.

I remembered going back to my room and trying to imagine
it being like Simon's.

I took a poster off the wall to see how much the sunlight
had faded the paint in the time I'd been there.

I took all my clothes out of the wardrobe and made the
coathangers rattle.

I couldn't picture the room being as changed and empty as
Simon's already was.

I wanted to leave a note for the next tenant, leave a trace of
myself behind, I wanted to be able to go back years later and
find a plaque with my name on it screwed to the wall.

I thought about all this, lying in bed listening to the rain,
looking at the room I sleep in now, another room in
another city.

I looked at the objects that make it my room, the calendar
on the wall, the colour of the curtains, the photographs.

I thought about all the other people who've slept in this room before me, about what traces they've left behind.
It took me a long time to get to sleep.

And when I woke up in the morning the room felt different, haunted, and I had to get out of bed quickly.
It had stopped raining, finally, but the street outside was still wet, swathes of dirty water across the road, sodden pages of newsprint glued to the pavement like transfers.
Perhaps the words will soak into the stone I thought, yesterday's stories imprinted like cave paintings, like a tattoo.
I left early for work, I didn't want to stay in my flat after the previous day.
I couldn't face cleaning up the broken plates or reading those leaflets again.
I got dressed and slipped out of the door without any breakfast, down the steps and past the back door of the shop downstairs.
There was a cold wind, but it was a dry wind and it felt good on my skin and I sucked big mouthfuls of it into my lungs.
There was a girl with a striped overall standing by the back door of the shop, smoking, I've seen her there before.
She smiled and said hello and I was surprised so I think I only nodded.

I walked along the main road, the wind blowing across my face, the traffic steaming slowly past me in fits and starts and stops.
I felt better than the day before, much better, I could feel the blood in my cheeks and the light in my eyes.
I felt like a spring was uncoiling inside me.
I could feel the creak and sing of my muscles loosening, like

a child bouncing on an old leather sofa, and the faster I
walked the better I felt.
I began striding, my arms swinging, my bag banging against
my back, my shoes click-clacking on the pavement like a
runaway metronome.
It had been weeks since I felt like that, since I felt such a
simple exuberance at being alive and outside, and I felt
cleansed by it, by the noise and the light and the wind all
rushing in upon me.
I wanted to sing.
I wanted to run.
But I managed to contain myself, and keep a blank face, and
anyone seeing me would only have thought I was late for
work.

I walked myself out of breath in the end.
I stopped at a cornershop by the ring road and went in to
buy something for breakfast.
The man said good morning and I smiled and nodded.
I bought a bread roll and some fruit, and I sat on an
upturned milk crate outside to eat them.
The man came outside and began arranging his boxes of
vegetables, straightening the price labels, wiping off the dirt.
It's better day is it? he said to me, yes I said, much better.
Yes he said, and he stood back and looked up at the sky like
a soothsayer, too much rain, is bad for the heart, you
know, do you know what I mean?
I smiled and said yes and stood up, holding my banana skin,
not knowing what to do with it.
He looked at it and said ah, bin is over there, pointing to the
other side of the road.

And at work I spent the whole day trying to decide how I
could tell someone, who I could tell.

I even wrote lists, names, opening lines, all by the way and actually there is something and can I tell you.

I wondered if a conversation could turn that way, if I'd get the chance to say oh well it's funny you should mention that because.

I wondered if I'd take the chance, even if it were to be offered.

I still had the plasters on my hands, I had to keep them hidden, I kept my fists closed, hid my hands under the desk to peel them off.

They left sticky trails around the edges, like chalk outlines on crime scene pavements, and when I rubbed at them they curled into dark strings and twisted across my skin.

I looked at the wounds for a long time, turning my hands under the desklight, a dozen pink unstitchings already beginning to fade and heal.

The marks are still there now, and I'm worried they might scar, I'm worried what people might think.

If they saw, if they looked at my hands and they noticed.

He knows. He sits in his kitchen, breathing clearly again, the old man upstairs at number twenty, he listens to the sound of his blood crashing through his ears. He sits, and he looks at the cooling kettle, and he knows. The doctor told him, told him as much as she could, over the course of a few appointments, in between various tests.

I don't like the sound of those lungs of yours she said, first.

They sound rather unhappy to me she'd said, with the ice-cold searchlight of a stethoscope pressed against his chest, with a concentrated look in her eyes like she was trying to imagine herself inside him.

I'd like to find out some more about that she'd said, do a few tests, make sure it's nothing untoward. That was what she'd said, untoward, and he remembers thinking it was a strangely old-fashioned word for a young woman like her to be using.

He remembers noticing that she kept the stethoscope in a long black case with polished brass fastenings and an engraved plaque. It had looked like a present from some-body, and he'd thought it was a strange thing to give as a gift, and he'd wondered how long she'd had it, how many unhappy sounds she'd heard through its earpieces.

That was where it started, with unhappy-sounding lungs. I'd like to find out some more about that she'd said. He hadn't liked the way she'd talked to him, not at first, it had seemed patronising, distant. But now, now that things are how they are, he is glad of her manner. It helps him to hear all that she says, the details, the projections. And he knows.

69

But his wife, she doesn't know. She doesn't know a thing.

That first time, when he'd returned from the clinic with a thumb-sized plaster over the puncture in his arm, he'd said everything was fine there was nothing to worry about, he was fit as a fiddle. And he'd gone on to prove it, in a way which surprised them both and made her feel much younger than she was. He'd only lied to stop her worrying, he'd only lied because he didn't think there was anything to worry about. He'd thought the doctor would call him back in, tell him some things about the blood test that he didn't understand, and then say he should exercise a little more. Cut down on fried foods. Drink less. And his wife does take to worrying easily and he didn't want her fretting over something so insignificant.

Next door, the young man with the bloodshot eyes begins his packing by taking down his work from the walls. He is ready to leave this house now, he has left his mark here and he is ready to pack his things and leave, so he takes down the papers and photographs and objects that are blu-tacked and pinned to the walls.

Most of the papers are to do with his work, notes and plans and quotations to help him structure his dissertation, sketches of burning Viking longboats, of prehistoric burial mounds, of Indian funeral pyres, photographs of mahogany coffins with brass handles, of crematorium chimneys. He takes all these pictures down, rubbing away the blu-tac left on the wallpaper, and he puts them into a large red folder with funeral rites from pre-history to post-history written on it in thick black pen. He takes down photocopied sheets of poetry, of religious text, of lecture notes from his archaeology course.

And from a small shelf in the middle of all these papers he takes down an unglazed clay figure, a replica of a

70

Japanese ceremonial idol, and he wraps it in thin tissue and an old newspaper. He puts it in a box and turns away, he looks out of the window and sees the boy with the tricycle following the twins into number seventeen's front garden, he looks up and sees someone leaning out of the attic window with a bucket of water.

In his kitchen, the old man refills the kettle with fresh water, and sets it to boil again. He thinks about his wife, and he thinks about what she doesn't know. He hears shrieking from outside, laughter, children running.

He hadn't even told her about the second visit to the doctor's, or the third or the fourth. He'd invented stories, walks around town, bowls matches, shopping trips, surprise meetings with old friends. And once he'd started it had seemed so difficult to stop. There was a time when he could have spoken, after another test they'd done which had taken all day, a complicated thing where they'd smeared him with gel and scanned him like luggage in an airport, and he'd felt that perhaps the time had come when he should say something, make hints, leave clues.

A bloodied handkerchief in the washbasket, an appointment card on the noticeboard.

But he didn't want to have to admit to having lied to her at all, and he couldn't bear to think of her worrying and upsetting over him, especially not now that it seems there is nothing really to be done about it. So he knows, and she doesn't know, and this makes it easier, and this makes it harder.

He knows about the look the doctor had on her face when she'd spoken to him about that first testing of blood, the look she'd tried to hide behind a shuffle of papers and a smile. Well now she'd said, things aren't exactly one hundred percent the way we'd like them to be, we'd like

71

to do a little more investigating. I can't pretend there's nothing to worry about she'd said, but the sooner we know what's wrong the sooner we can do something about it, yes? Which had seemed a sensible enough thing to say at the time, except that with each further test they did the likelihood of there being something they could do about it seemed to decrease. And unlike the doctor, he can very much pretend there is nothing to worry about, to his wife at least. All he can do now, it seems, is to protect her from the truth. This is what he thinks.

The kettle begins a low whistle which will soon become a shriek, and as he stands to move towards it he notices that the twins have disappeared. He moves the kettle off the heat and rolls a splash of water around in the pot.

She doesn't know, as he knows, that after that scan with the gel they'd had him in for what they'd called a lumbar puncture, he hasn't told her that the needle in his spine felt like a fist sunk into his bone, much as he's often imagined a bullet might feel. He wore a vest to bed for a month to hide the bruising, bruising which spread across his back like purple flowers opening out their petals, and he could only say he was feeling the cold when she asked him about it. Say he was getting older. Make a joke about it.

In the attic bedroom of number seventeen, the room usually occupied by the tall girl with the glitter round her eyes, the boy with the pierced eyebrow puts down an empty bucket and laughs silently, crouched over, exclaiming a trio of yeses and slapping the palm of one skinny hand with the back of the other. He can hear the children in the street, he thinks maybe he can hear one of them crying a little, he runs his fingers through his short damp hair and laughs again. He looks at the time, it's early but he's wide awake now, he looks around the room and thinks a moment. He looks at the girl's bed, neatly made, unslept in, he looks at her makeup crammed across the mantelpiece, the framed photos on the wall, the textbooks stuffed under the bed. He puts the bucket back where it came from, carefully lined up under the leaky stain on the ceiling, and he leaves the room, running down the two flights of stairs, into the kitchen, and out the back door, crashing it shut behind him, striding out through the backyard and down the alley, a man on a mission, a smile still wrapped around his face and water still dribbling down the back of his neck.

In his room, upstairs at number eighteen, the young man blinks painfully, turning away from the window and holding the palms of his hands over his eyes for a moment. He takes the clay figure out of the box again, unwraps it, looks at it, runs his fingers over its smooth lines and rough texture.

The small figure is the reason he started working on the dissertation subject he did, the reason he argued with his tutors about the boundaries between archaeology and anthropology, and it's the reason he wants to travel to Japan as soon as he has finished his course, to see the real things, to see what he has imagined so many times.

The figure comes from a place somewhere south of Tokyo, a place where mothers go when they have lost young children. Very young, as in not even or only just born; the miscarried, the stillborn, the aborted. The mothers go to this place, a Buddhist temple on a wooded hillside, and they take tiny pieces of clothing for their ghost children, and gifts, and prayers. He has seen photographs of the temple grounds, and he has spoken to a lecturer who has been there, the lecturer who gave him this replica figure, and it's a place and a rite that has stuck in his mind.

He imagines them, the mothers, walking up the steps, between soaring bamboo stems and carefully ordered miniature waterfalls, beside pools with carp drifting slowly among the lilies. He imagines them walking slowly, leaving gentle impressions in the gravelled pathways, moving to the place set aside for them, pressing their flat hands together and holding them against their faces, their limbs a triangle pointing skywards, the small space between their fingers filled with a hot breathlessness.

He opens the red folder again and pulls out a postcard of the place, holds it behind the figure, looks at it for the hundredth time. He looks at the figures in the picture, row after row after row, dozens, hundreds of them, identical little six-inch Buddhas, the smooth domes of their heads like pebbles on a beach, numerous, indistinguishable. Some of the figures, towards the back of the picture, look a little weathered, but mostly they are new and clean. None of them were more than a year old when the picture was taken, and when he goes to see for himself-there will be a new set of figures not more than a year old.

He turns over the postcard, to remind himself of what he always thinks when he looks at this picture, he reads the words he wrote when he first saw it, the words in thick black ink, they are all named it says, each one of them has a name.

He turns it back again, looks closer. Some of the figures are dressed up, in traditional woollen caps and shawls, or in baseball jerseys, or with tiny coloured parasols to protect them from the sun. There is one with an unused Bugs Bunny bib strung enormously around its neck. At their feet are offerings, comforts. Packets of sweets. Money. A yo-yo.

He puts the postcard back in the folder, he takes down a photograph of Graceland, he takes down scraps of paper with marker-pen diagrams and spidercharts, he tries to rub more blu-tac from the wall.

In his kitchen, the old man measures out the tea-leaves, drops them into the pot, fills it with boiling water. He sets out a tray, two cups, two saucers, a small jug of milk, a small pot of sugar, two teaspoons. He breathes heavily as his hands struggle up to the high cupboards, fluttering like the wings of a caged bird.

His wife doesn't know, as he has known for weeks now, that any treatment they will be able to offer him will be, as the doctor had said, with a steady gaze and a hand to his arm, only in the form of palliative care. You do understand what that means don't you she'd said, not even blinking, you do understand? And he'd looked straight back at her, holding her professional eye contact, and said yes, thank-you doctor, I do understand, yes. And he'd coughed, hard, repeatedly, spraying blooded phlegm into his handkerchief as if to prove how much he understood.

Yes, thankyou doctor, I understand.

Things are not exactly one hundred percent the way we would like them to be.

He slips a tea-cosy over the pot and stands by the window a moment.

He sees a young man sitting on the front garden wall of number seven, one of the foreign students it looks like, holding a pad of large paper, staring at the houses opposite.

He sees a dog trotting along the middle of the road, a bald patch across one shoulder, an unevenness in its stride.

He sees a construction crane rising up above the houses away to the right, a few streets away, stretching its neck over the rooftops like an anglepoise lamp.

He picks up the tray and carries it through to his wife.

And so today I'm back on the telephone.

I'm listening to my mother talking, and I'm waiting for the right moment to interrupt.

I know that I have to tell her, I know that I will be able to tell her if I use the right words at the right moment.

I know what the right words are, I've been sitting here for hours, choosing and unchoosing.

And I know that I need help now, that in spite of everything my mother is the person to ask.

I'm scared, I have always been scared at times like this, waiting to say something, waiting to be told off.

Falling off the garden wall, and she says what the hell were you doing up there anyhow while she cleans the graze and presses a bandage around it.

Dropping my dinner on the floor, and she shouts at me and sends me to bed, and when she brings me a sandwich later I throw it out of the window.

My dad, saying nothing at these times, averting his eyes, folding his hands.

I remember my dad taking me to school, when I was very young, when my mother was ill.

The feel of his huge hand wrapped around mine, rough and hard and warm.

The length of his strides, and having to run to keep up.

The very cold days when he'd wrap his scarf around my face until it almost covered my eyes, and when I breathed in I could smell him in my mouth, damp cigarettes and bootwax and the same smell as his hair when he said goodnight.

I remember that once he had to take me early so that he

could get to the shops before work, and I went and hid in the corner of the playground, behind the bins, with the scarf wrapped completely around my head like a mask.

I remember how safe I felt, wrapped up like that, blinded.

He didn't say anything during those walks to school, but I used to look forward to them, I used to be secretly and ashamedly pleased if my mother didn't appear for breakfast, impatient to leave the house.

I wonder if he'll say anything now.

I wonder if he'll turn away from the television, come to the phone, say something.

I listen to her talking, and I remember those times she was ill, those strange blotches on her otherwise busy life.

I remember the way it would go almost unmentioned, as though nothing out of the ordinary had happened.

As though there was nothing to be concerned about.

I remember having to creep into her room to say goodnight, her puffed red face turning to me from amongst the pillows and the blankets, the curtains closed and a desklamp pointing up at her from the bedside table like a stagelight.

I remember trying to hold my breath while she asked me how my day had been, if I had been good, if I had done the washing up.

And her voice sounding strange, thick and slow, as though she was talking from behind a closed door, through a thick wall.

I'm not sure if I held my breath because of the smell or because I was scared of catching her germs, but I always came out of that room dizzy, sucking down lungfuls of air.

And it never worried me, because she always seemed to be better the next day, saying oh it must have just been a bug, one of those things, you know, and she'd be back to normal.

Bustling around the house, cleaning, tidying, baking scones, rearranging the furniture.

She's still talking, and I'm still saying yes and no and I'm sure, and I'm having trouble working out what she's talking about and I want her to stop.

I hear a mobile going off, an electronic *Für Elise*, and I assume it's on the television.

She says oh that's my phone, do you mind if I, and without me saying anything she's pressing buttons on her new phone and saying yes, hello, yes fine, hold on a moment.

She says it's your Auntie Susan, was there anything else?

I say yes, yes there is something else, can you call me back, and she says oh, oh okay, and I hear her talking to Auntie Sue before she's even hung up on me.

I didn't know my mother had a mobile phone.

I make a cup of tea, and I listen to my answerphone, to a message from Sarah.

She says hi again how you doing, I've got something to tell you, I met somebody, I need to tell you about it, call me soon bye.

The phone rings, and I'm talking to my mother again.

She says and have you been eating properly.

I say mum I'm a grown-up now you shouldn't be asking me that sort of thing.

She says well yes of course but.

There's a moment's pause, I can hear the television in the background.

I say and how's dad, oh you know she says.

Same as always she says.

She asks me about friends I haven't seen for months and I say I don't know I haven't seen them.

79

I live in a different city now I say, it's difficult to see people
    so often.
She says he could do with a haircut though.

This needs to be an important conversation, and it's not.
I say who needs a haircut, your dad she says, it's sticking out
    round his ears.
You know the way it does she says.
I loop the telephone wire around my finger, the spirals
    hugging tight between my knuckles.
I say well have you told him, watching the skin beneath my
    fingernail turn red as the wire tightens.
Oh no she says, you know he doesn't like me saying things
    like that.
I think about him there now, watching television, his feet
    up on the table, the dark patches on the soles of his white
    socks.
I uncoil the telephone wire from my finger.
There are red stripes, white stripes.

She's talking about dad's sister coming to visit.
Your Auntie Susan she says, and then she's talking about
    spare rooms, and bedding, and extra pints of milk.
She says you know she's got an insatiable appetite for tea,
    and she does like it with a lot of milk.
I need to stop her talking now.
I need to say mother I have something to say.
Mum, please, I need to tell you something.
It's important mum, and I'm scared and I need your help.
I need to say these things.
My throat feels tight, squashed.

I open the window to get some air into the room, and a
    burst of noise rushes in.

Traffic, and shouting, and music.

And birdsong, from somewhere up on the roof, a thin twitter that creeps and tangles in with all the other sounds.

I breathe deeply, trying not to sigh.

I wrap the telephone cord around another finger.

Mum, I say.

I see the girl from the shop downstairs crossing the road.

She glances up and sees me, she waves and smiles.

I lift my hand to wave back, but it's held down by the telephone cord and she disappears.

Mum, I say, again, can I just, but she doesn't hear me, or she won't let me speak.

And how about you she says, when are you next coming down, it's been a good long while hasn't it?

I don't know I say.

She says your Auntie Susan's slept in that spare room more times than you I should think.

I say mum that used to be my room, I slept in it all my life, she says yes well I mean since I decorated it.

Since it became the spare room she says.

I say mum, there was something I needed to say, can I just, and she says sorry love what was it?

I hesitate, I squeeze a coil of telephone wire into my fist.

I say mum, I'm pregnant.

She's balancing on one foot again, the sister of the twins, and now she is leaning forwards, bringing her face towards the ground, her other leg cocked out behind her and her arms thrust out like glider wings. A young man with very short hair walks past, slowly, his feet are shuffling along the pavement and once or twice he stumbles. She doesn't notice him, and he disappears into a passageway next to number sixteen.

In the back bedroom of number twenty, the wife of the old man with the weary lungs is drinking a cup of tea, standing by the window, looking out across the yards, along the backs of the houses in the next street, down the alleyway. She sees a white cat roll onto its back on the roof of an outhouse. She sees a woman hanging out washing, pegs lined up across the shoulders of her blouse like a queue of trapeze artists. She sees a young man with very short hair emerge from the passageway a couple of doors down and shuffle up the alleyway, towards their backyard. She watches him, she notices his face all screwed up against the sun, his hand held to the walls for support, and she tut-tuts to herself, she sucks in her breath.

She says well will you look at this one.

What a state she says, he can hardly walk.

Been out all night I should think she says, and she watches him stumble into the backyard two doors down, coughing, pulling out a key on a long chain from a pocket halfway down his trousers.

We never stayed out all night in my day she says,

83

watching the door close behind him, it wouldn't have been on would it now?

No love, it wouldn't, her husband mumbles from the bed, deadpan, not at all love he says.

She says and the state of that yard down there is getting a joke.

She turns away from the window and walks across to the wardrobe, looks like a nice day she says, and she rattles through the clothes on the hangers. Her husband looks at her from the bed, good lord he is thinking, but she is still a woman. All these years he thinks, smiling, and no less a woman than she ever was. He looks at her nakedness, savouring it, the sags and the wrinkles, the way her shoulderblades jostle against each other as she reaches up to the shoeboxes on top of the wardrobe, the thumbsized ridges of her spine, the fleshy weight of her backside, the curve of her belly as she turns into the light with a dress in each hand.

He remembers the first time he felt the weight of that backside, the shape of the weight pressed against his knees and his thighs, and not knowing where to put his hands as she sat talking to her friend, giggling and smoking his cigarettes. Knowing she was being improper, both of them, but knowing that somehow there were rules which didn't apply. Of course, later, she'd always denied that that was how they'd met, later she'd told a different story, a more refined and sensible story; but he remembers it well enough, oh indeed, the way she'd wriggled to get comfortable, the way she was making his uniform scratch and pull against himself.

She stands there now, looking at him, weighing up the two dresses, one in either hand like a pair of scales, now then she's saying, look here, which do you prefer?

Downstairs, the man with the carefully trimmed moustache is sitting at his kitchen table with an empty mug of tea, puffing out his cheeks and shaking his head. He stands suddenly, pulling up the blind and reaching for the telephone. It is not office hours, but he will leave them a message, it is easier to talk to them that way, they cannot interrupt or contradict, or pretend they do not understand his voice. Right he says, hello, and he says his name. I have spoken to you before he says, you remember perhaps, about this removal situation in my backyard. He says his address, slowly and precisely, and his lips are quivering with irritation. My backyard is full of rubbish he says, full, and none of this is mine. I feel I am losing control he says. I tell you about this before, five, six, many times, and always you say you coming soon but I don't see you he says. So I will ask you again, and you will come and take them away, please, he says. He begins to list the items in his backyard, individually, the broken chairs and unstuffed mattresses, the milkcrates and binbags and magazines, the pizzaboxes and chipwrappings and small heaps of builders' rubble. He doesn't understand where it comes from. He doesn't understand who goes to the trouble of heaving all this stuff over his wall. He comes to the end of his list, he pauses for breath and says you see there is so much of it now, I don't know but I think when it is here it encourages people, like perhaps they think I am running a scrapyard or something like this? Because this morning he says, and he sighs and he looks outside, this morning this is it, this is the last thing, I look outside and I see three of these shopwindow dummy people there also. Please take this away he says. None of this is my mess he says, and he puts the phone down.

He looks at the mannequins, naked, sprawled across the

rubbish and across each other, their limbs tangled, and he looks away.

In the street, sitting on the low wall outside number eleven, the young man with the sketchpad is pencilling in an outline of the young girl, standing one-legged by the passageway beside number sixteen, peering into it. It is good to put figures in drawings like these, he has learnt this, his tutor said the presence of people lends a sense of perspective, so he sketches her in and later he will include also adults. And the dog he promised her.

In the back bedroom of number seventeen, the boy with the white shirt lies awake, looking at the girl beside him, her eyes, the thin arch of her eyebrows, the dusting of glitter around her eyes. He leans his face towards her to feel the warm push of her breath on his forehead, he leans back to look at her, props himself up on one elbow to look at the whole long length of her. He remembers the way people looked at her last night, in the club, the way people always looked at her when they were out, the way he's looking at her now; appraisingly, admiringly, a breathless yearning which is not really or not entirely sexual but something else, something noble or aesthetic perhaps. He hears himself whispering Jesus I'm so lucky, and he looks up quickly to check no one's awake. But it's true he thinks, he is, and he lies back down, closing his eyes in sweet anticipation of the weeks and months and maybe years to come. They haven't made their plans yet, they're not sure what they'll be doing or where they'll be, but he knows they'll be spending their nights enclosed together like this, he knows he can take that much for granted. The fact that they haven't even needed to discuss it makes it all the sweeter, like it's a given, like it's as natural as a cup of tea in the morning, or a shared cigarette. He kisses the corner of her lips, with his eyes still closed, and he drifts back into sleep.

In the empty back bedroom of number twenty-two, the girl with the short blonde hair and the small square glasses is standing by the window, finishing a piece of toast. She's resting the back of her head against the cool glass and looking into the room, thinking about the boy who moved out a week ago, looking at the bare sagging mattress, the empty noticeboard, the lightshade concertinaed on the floor. The squares of wallpaper where posters had been, the pattern bright and clear and sharp. She thinks about her own room, overcrowded with clothes and books and tapes and all the dozens of bits and pieces that don't seem to belong anywhere but can't quite be thrown away, she wonders where to start.

She goes into her room and takes the posters off the wall, she opens the wardrobe and piles the clothes on the bed. She takes everything off the windowsill and puts it into a shoebox, and then she stops and looks at it all.

She goes downstairs to make a cup of tea.

In the bathroom of number eighteen, the young man with the dry eyes packs his toiletries into a bag and wipes old soap and hairs from around the edge of the sink. He opens the mirrored cabinet, taking down the toppled tubs and cans and packets he knocked over earlier, shaving cream and shaving foam, deodorants, eye lotion, hairgel, shampoo, antiseptic cream, plasters, aspirins, peppermint foot scrub.

He looks at the foot scrub, he takes the lid off the almost full tub and smells it, it's a good smell, a tingling smell, a nose-clearing steam of a smell and he turns his head away from it and puts the lid back on, puts the tub in the bag. He

87

remembers buying it the day before that Wednesday night, the night he'd opened and closed the front door a dozen times, checking. He remembers thinking it would be a nice thing, a thing they could do later, weeks or months after this first night became a reference point, she could say she was tired after a long day at work or whatever and he could offer her this, as a gesture, as a symbol, like it's nothing really it's just a thing I would do for you.

He remembers thinking he was getting ahead of the situation by buying something like that so early, but he'd seen it by chance and he'd thought why not, he'd thought it would be good to have it around so he could make less of an issue of it, like here I've got some of this would you like some.

And he remembers that awestruck Tuesday night, trying on different clothes and making his room tidy but not too tidy, and he'd decided he should maybe try it out, see what it was like, make sure he knew how to use it, and he'd got a bowl of water and a towel and sat on the edge of his bed with his trousers rolled up. Paddling in hot tapwater, dabbling with the possible way of things.

The way he'd scooped out a handful of the cold grainy cream and rubbed it into the skin of his feet, circling across the arches and squeezing between the toes, enjoying the cold lick and tickle of it, pulling at the skin, working his thumbs along the lines of muscle between the bones, the way he'd varied the pressures, a fist twisted roughly into the hard skin of the heel, a finger running like a whisper along the tendons between ankle and toe. He remembers that evening, the excitement and fear and disbelief, sitting on the edge of his bed with his foot in his hands, thinking maybe soon it would be someone else's foot, thinking maybe soon there would be someone else sitting on the edge of his bed, sitting beside him.

Lying beside him, sleeping beside him.

He remembers rinsing his feet in the hot water, padding damp footprints through to the bathroom, pouring the slow swirl of murky water down the sink.

He squeezes his eyes shut, he runs his knuckles along the open space between his lips.

He thinks about her, at this moment, in her house, a few thin walls away, packing her life into boxes and bags and he wonders what memories she is rediscovering, what thoughts are catching in her mouth like the dust blown from unused textbooks. He wonders if she has buried any traces of herself under her floorboards. He wonders what those traces would be if she had. And he wonders again why he thinks about her so much when he knows so little to think about.

She doesn't say anything, I wait and there's only her breathing.

I can hear the television in the background, laughter, applause.

I'm not sure if she's heard me, so I try to say it again.

I'm.

The words falter in my throat, all of the last few weeks trapped in the bottleneck of this moment.

I remember all the times I've thought about saying this.

I remember all the reactions I've imagined.

I say, mum, I'm pregnant.

There's a pause, and I can hear the colour draining from her face.

It wasn't going to be like this.

It hardly seems worth saying, but I'd planned it differently, I really had.

I was going to be ready, financially stable, emotionally prepared.

I was going to be living in a house by the sea.

I was going to be in a secure and loving relationship with a man who was creatively self-employed, a potter or a woodworker, somebody good with his hands.

I used to imagine the hands, strong, large hands criss-crossed with the scars and scratches of hard work, hands that would smell of fresh air and earth and wood.

I used to imagine long walks along wind-harried beaches, hand in hand, wrapped up warm, feeling the cold suck of salty air in my lungs and the bloom of a baby inside me.

I was going to be older than this.

That was mostly what I'd planned, being older than this.

She says congratulations you must be very pleased, and she
   sounds as though she almost means it.
I expected her to be shocked.
She says so when's it due then, do you know, have you had
   a scan, are you eating plenty of green vegetables.
I expected her to be angry, or disappointed.
She says oh you know your dad's always wanted a grandson.
I wasn't expecting this, the things she's saying now, the
   politeness, the indifference.
I'd prepared myself to be defensive, argumentative
   even, to have to listen to criticism and not be
   crushed by it.
She says and of course you'll be okay for money won't you.
I say I don't know mum.

She says and what about names, have you thought of a
   name?
I say no mum, not yet, it seemed a bit early for that, there
   was, there's other things.
She says oh it's never too early to think of a name, and then
   she gives me a list of names, none of which I would have
   thought of, and none of which I like.
Instead of the shock and dismay and disgust I was preparing
   myself for, I'm finding out what I might have been called,
   if things had been different.
I don't ask her what she means by if things had been
   different.
I wonder if my dad can hear her end of the conversation, if
   he's listening, if he can tell what's going on.
I wonder what he'll say when she tells him.
She runs out of names, and without pausing for breath she
   says and will you be using terries or disposables?
I feel like when I was fifteen, when I got a tattoo and I
   couldn't understand why I hadn't been grounded.

I thought she was going to ask the questions, the ones that
start do you and have you and stumble into silence.
Do you know who the?
Have you thought about having a?
But she doesn't, she says actually I really should call your
Aunt Susan back, she was finding out about train times
she says, and she's waiting for me to say okay then but I
don't want to.
I say will you tell dad then?
Oh I will she says, he'll be very pleased she says.
And I say mum, will you call me, tomorrow?
If I get the chance she says, and I can tell she's looking at the
clock.
I say well okay then I'd best be going give my love to dad,
and I put the phone down and I lay a hand on my belly.

I imagine her putting the phone down and picking it up
again to dial Sue's number.
I wonder if she's hesitating, if there's a thickness in her
throat she won't be able to speak through, if she is
blinking back a slight wetness in her eyes, having to
slowly sit down and bite the knuckle of her thumb to
stop herself from crying.
She does that, sometimes, biting and biting, leaving a pair of
small pale bruises like ink on folded blotting paper.
She did it once when we were at the cinema, and when I
asked her about it she said she'd trapped her thumb in
the seat.
I wonder if she's sitting there now, waiting for my dad to
look up, to notice.
I imagine him turning off the television and moving towards her.
Saying, love, what is it, what's wrong love, reaching out a
hand.

And I sit here and I know that none of this is happening.
I know that he is still watching the television with his feet on the table, I know that she is already talking on the telephone, that she will not mention what I have just said.

I listen to the answerphone message from Sarah, and I think about calling her back.
I realise how pleased I am that she's called me for a reason, not just because it's been a long time and she thinks she should.
I wonder what she means by met somebody, who it is, why she wants to tell me.
Perhaps I can tell her my news in return, now that I've spoken the words aloud, now that it's a reality outside myself, perhaps now it can just get easier and easier.
I could just drop it into the conversation, like exciting news, like by the way guess what I'm pregnant I'm having a baby.
We could talk about baby clothes and cute names, meet up and go browsing round Mothercare, pretend that there was nothing strange or frightening happening at all.
She could wind me up about childbirth, make jokes about gas and epidurals and yelling give me some fucking morphine.
Except that she couldn't because she doesn't know anything about it, not really, not anything more than she's seen on television, not anything more than I do.
But I thought my mother would know what to say, and she didn't, she didn't say anything.

She's never said anything to me, not really, not when it mattered.
Our conversations always seemed to be functional, brief

discussions about how something was to be arranged, a passing enquiry about a state of health.

She never told me things about her life, what was happening at work, who she saw at the shops, stories about her growing up and meeting my dad and moving down south.

It surprises me now that I took it for granted, knowing so little about her, knowing so little about her family and where she came from.

And she didn't ask me questions either, she never used to ask where I was going, or who I was going with, or what time I was coming back, and if I mentioned it to my friends they'd say I was lucky but I wasn't so sure.

She never asked me how my schoolwork was going, not even when I was steamed up in the thick of exams, she seemed to take it for granted that I went out in the morning and came back in the afternoon and that was all there was to it.

I asked her once, sarcastic and spiteful, I said how about you mum, how did you get on at school, how did your exams go, did you do enough revision, did your mum help you?

And my dad said that's enough now, leave it now, turning to look at me, reaching a hand out to meet my mother.

That was all he'd needed to say, he only spoke like that occasionally and when he did I knew that I had done something very wrong and it was time to leave the room.

And I think about the question my mother didn't ask.

Do you know who the?

I imagine her asking it just like that, hesitating, unable to say the word, leaving the sentence unfinished.

I don't know what I would have said if she had asked, I don't know if I want her to know who it was.

Or perhaps it's more that I don't want to acknowledge his part in it, to give him a role by giving him a name.

I think about him, and I think about the word father, and it feels like the wrong word to use.

He was there, and what happened turned into what there is now, but there is nothing between us, there is nothing between him and what is inside me.

He was there, and that is all, and I don't feel as though I should give him the place of father for that.

I wonder what he would think, if he knew.

Upstairs at number twenty, in the kitchen, the old man is looking for his hat, he's talking over his shoulder to his wife, he's saying I'm sure I left it on the side have you seen it, he can't hear her reply so he raises his voice, calling through to wherever she is, the bedroom, the bathroom.

She says I've got it right here, and he turns and she's holding his hat out to him.

She says there's no need to shout, and they catch each other's eyes, the day she first said those words to him flashing clear again in both their minds.

The day he'd come back to her, a husband to his wife, the rain had fallen from the sky like it was God's own washday. His kitbag was sodden and heavy, his uniform chafing wetly against his skin. The water streamed off his hair, sending thick dribbles of grease down the back of his neck, and his cigarette hung smokelessly from his lips. All the way home he'd been thinking about comfort and warmth, a pot of tea by the fire, a hot bath, a night's sleep in sheets and blankets, but when he'd turned the last corner into this street he could only stand and look.

He'd looked at the houses, their front-room curtains all drawn and their doors all closed. He'd looked at the gardens, their small hedges all neatly trimmed, their rows of vegetables and herbs all protected from the birds by pegged lines of string. He'd seen a furl of faded bunting tangled in the top branches of the tree opposite his house, a car parked outside number seven, the railings all cut down to stumps. But there'd been no people in the street. There'd not been a crowd of cheering children waiting to meet him, waving Union Jacks and jostling round him while he handed out sweets and stockings and gum. That was not the way it was. People had not been leaning out of windows to welcome him home. There was not even a brass band marching down the middle of the street with a fat man playing a rousing tuba.

There was quiet, closed doors, a grey sky, pouring rain.

He'd stood there, on that day, and he'd called his new wife's name. Dropped his kitbag to the floor, filled his lungs with the cold damp air, and called out her name. He'd wanted to meet her in the street, not knock on the door like a delivery boy, he'd wanted to see her running excitedly towards him. There were faces appearing at windows, but he couldn't see her face and so he flung her name into the rain. Doors had opened, and people had hovered in their hallways, looking at him, but the door of number twenty had stayed closed and so he cupped his hands around his mouth and called and called her name, not caring what people thought, relishing the syllables of it, sending them echoing down the street.

And it had only been when he'd stopped for a long breath that she'd put her shopping bags down and said there's no need to shout I'm right behind you and he'd turned, and they'd held each other, and it was the closest fiercest embrace they have ever had, knocking the breath out of both of them and leaving them unsteady on their feet.

They still say it to each other now, sometimes, making each other laugh, there's no need to shout I'm right behind you they'll say, sneaking around the other's back, slipping a pair of arms around a waist, I'm right behind you they'll say.

They sink back into the bed, the couple in the attic flat of number twenty-one, their breathing ragged and content, each already cleaning themself with a handful of tissues.

The man looks down at his shoulder, inspecting a neat lovebite, freshly planted, beginning to sting a little, so red that it looks as though a glistening bead of blood could pop through the skin at any moment.

He touches it gently, he says I'm sorry about last night I was out of order, saying it quickly and turning away but saying it all the same. He gets out of bed, still holding a clump of tissues, and she looks up at him and says how sorry? He pulls a face at her, wrinkling his nose. A cup of tea sorry? he says, and she tips her head to one side, gazing up at him and pressing a long white finger to her cheek. Outside, down in the street, a dog barks, a door slams, the tricycle clatters along the cracked paving slabs. A cup of tea and two pieces of toast sorry? he says, and she smiles and claps her hands and says oh yes please how nice of you to offer. He smiles sarcastically at her, dropping the tissues in the bin, pulling on a pair of jeans and leaving the room.

She picks the remote control off the floor and flicks on the TV, sitting up in bed and watching someone stirring scrambled eggs and saying now back to you Anthea.

In the darkened front room of number nineteen, Anthea looks out into the sleepy eyes of a short hairless man with a very round belly. He sits forward on the sofa, hands curled around his stomach as though around a warm cup of tea, and he looks at the television and he mutters a song under his breath. He hears his two sons, the twins, they are in the kitchen and they are bothering their mother. Oh and they have so much energy he thinks to himself, and now it is the end of the summer and they have no idea what to be doing with it. It's been a long summer he thinks, it will be good when they are back at school, it will do them good, it will tire them out a little maybe he thinks.

In the kitchen his wife slaps the hand of the older twin as

it reaches up to where she is pressing out pink coconut sweets. No no no! she snaps, and it is her voice which makes him shrink away more than the passing pain of her hand. She turns and throws her frustration at the backs of her retreating sons, keep out of my way now she says, her voice loud and quick, don't you come back in here until I'm ready for you and they disappear squealing into the front room and immediately she feels bad for her sharp words. She rubs her hand where it made contact with her son, as if trying to ease any pain he might have. She makes one of the sweets bigger than the rest, and kisses the sugar-pink taste of it before putting them in the fridge to set.

As soon as the boys bundle into the front room their father starts shaking his head and saying no no not in here, not now, your daddy is watching something okay and they press down on his legs, whining boredom and trying to spark life into him, one on either side like a pair of woodpecking bookends, going daddy daddy we're bored there's nothing to do there's nothing to do.

He sighs heavily, a rumbling gust coming from some-where far down in the roundness of his stomach, and he says boys I said not now, please, go outside and find something to do. It is a big world he says, you can never be bored in this big world he says and he looks each of them in the eye. They stand away from him and sidle out of the door.

Cricket! he calls after them as they disappear, why don't you play cricket? and he settles back in the settee as Jamie welcomes the next guest back to the studio.

His daughter is still balancing on one foot at the other end of the street, and she sees her brothers leaping out of their front door, the older one wielding a cricket bat, the younger one swinging his arms like a dual-action spin bowler. She turns away, keeping her flamingo concentration, and she looks at the ground and she thinks about wings.

In the bathroom of number sixteen, the man with the young daughter looks at his hands, he holds them over the sink and looks at them.

They are better than they were.

The skin does not peel so much, and the colour is gradually returning. But still they are in a bad way. The scarring is hard and shiny and new-looking, swirling across his palms like smoke trapped under glass, damaged skin layered across damaged skin. He turns them over, his ruined hands, holding each side of them under the light as though admiring carved wooden artefacts. But he is not admiring. He looks for the small unharmed areas of skin, on the backs of his hands, towards the wrists, he holds them closer to his eyes, looks at the lines and the pores and the few hairs springing out. He examines the buckles and twists of the damaged skin across his palms, the deep split running diagonally across the left palm. He peers at each of his fingertips in turn, at the marbled smoothness of them, each round tip polished and anonymous.

He stands in his bathroom with the door locked, holding his hands over the sink, looking at his hands. The hot tap is running, the water careering into the basin, steam is billowing up around his face, and he is not crying.

There is a knock at the door, a quiet knocking low on the panelled wood, and his daughter's voice saying daddy I'm hungry now daddy can I have something? Soon okay please the man says, his voice heavy and slow, please ten minutes and I will get food okay? He waits, and he hears that she has not gone away. Please lovey he says, ten minutes okay? and he hears small steps taking her back to her room, and he closes his eyes for a moment but he does not cry. He turns off the tap and watches the water swirl and still, watches the steam skidding across the surface. He hears boys playing in the street, he hears a mother call a child's name. He takes a bottle from the open cabinet above the sink and drips iodine into the water, the drops falling like bombs beneath the surface, the inky stings spreading and staining the water, and then he lowers his cupped hands, holding his breath, pushing them beneath the surface, like the sinking of two upturned boats. And the sharp hurt of it makes him clench his teeth, curl his toes, it makes the breath from his nose hiss like the stutters from a steam-engine pressure valve but he keeps his hands there. He keeps his hands there until the clawing pain settles to a throb and he can breathe again and unclench his teeth again and he can begin to stroke the skin of his left hand with the fingers of his right, the skin of his right hand with the fingers of his left.

Outside, the sound of a tennis ball bouncing in the road, a cricket bat banging against the tarmac, boys shouting, music passing in a car with a heartbeat thump.

He follows the contours of each scar under the water, pressing lightly, pressing as hard as he can bear, trying to soften and ease the skin, trying to massage the flesh back into shape. He watches the colour changing as the heat of the water soaks through, flushing and fading under the pressure of his printless fingers, the blood struggling to follow his touch.

He lifts his hands up into the air, the inky water dripping off them into the sink, and his hands are clean but they are not healed. They are still ruined and useless. He pats them against a towel, careful not to rub the roughness against his skin, waves them through the air until they are dry, reaches up to put the bottle of iodine back into the cabinet. As he closes the cabinet door, a mirror swings into sight and flings him an unwanted glimpse of his face, the sagging mask of it, the familiar wrinkles and twists which mark the face that is not his face. And he looks away, and he opens the bathroom door, and his daughter stands there looking at him.

She says daddy does it hurt?

He says yes my love, it does hurt but it is okay, and he smiles, a small hard crack of a smile, and his voice is thick with it. He touches her on the head, carefully, and he says some food now okay? and she says yay and clatters down the stairs ahead of him.

In the bathroom sink the water sits undrained, cooling, ripples echoing and fading across the surface. A trickle of water weaves its way down the hanging towel, falling away from broken blue handprints, falling softly to the floor.

It was at my grandmother's funeral.

She'd been ill for a long time, and so when she died I wasn't much upset and I wasn't worried about going up for the service.

I took the time off work, I bought a black dress and I booked the train up to Aberdeen.

And on the way up I wasn't thinking about my grandmother, about sadness or loss or any of those things, I was wondering about what would happen, who might be there, what my first funeral would be like.

I was interested to meet all these people my mother had kept us clear of, to perhaps find out more about the whole Scottish side of the family.

I thought I might find out why my mother had chosen to move so far away and stay there.

It was a long long journey, and I spent most of the time staring out of the window, watching the scenery change as we got further north, buildings and roads giving way to empty swathes of heather and sheep.

The rain began to close in the other side of Edinburgh, the wind lifting the water from the sea and flinging it against the side of the train, the landscape shrouded in a grey veil.

By the time we pulled into Aberdeen it was constant, and I was wishing I'd brought an umbrella.

I met my dad at the station, he touched his hands to my shoulders and said hello, and he drove me to the house of one of the many Scottish relatives I'd never met.

My mother wasn't there, and nobody seemed to want to mention the fact, she'd said she felt unable to face the journey and that seemed to be all there was to it.

I didn't even hear anyone asking my father how she was.

It was a small house, and it was soon crammed full of loud-voiced relatives, squeezing into the front room the same way the men were squeezed into their dark suits.

I was disappointed that none of them were wearing kilts.

I perched on the arm of a sofa, sipping the sugary tea someone had poured for me and watching the conversation ebb and flow.

They seemed almost foreign, all bright blue eyes and flushed red cheeks, skin beaten smooth by bitter winds and I couldn't imagine being related to them.

Someone said and what about you hen, what is it you do, and I had to tell them briefly about the office and the work I did there.

There was a pause, and then a silver-haired man piped up with something about football and the room was loud and full again.

In Scotland the men of the family put the body in the ground.

I hadn't known this, I wasn't expecting it, and it touched a place inside me to see it.

Eight of them are chosen, the brothers and cousins and sons, the friends accepted as honorary family, the relations by marriage.

My father was included, and I don't think he was expecting it either.

I saw him wiping his hands on his trousers and loosening his tie.

They are chosen, and given a number corresponding to a position around the coffin, and given this number on a piece of card which they turn over in their pockets throughout the service, checking it occasionally, putting it back, wiping a pair of fingers across a nervous forehead.

They get called by the undertaker, one at a time, and they move away from their women to the graveside.

I spoke to him about it in the evening, the boy, and he said it was like being called to your place in the way of things.

I knew then that I was going to go to bed with him, when he rolled his soft voice around that phrase, in the way of things.

I watched them that day, the eight of them standing around the grave, legs slightly apart, heads slightly bowed, freshly shined shoes pressing into freshly dug earth.

The coffin was hoisted into position by the bearers and held there for a moment.

Suspended over the open grave.

Poised in the outside world.

And then the men lowered it, slowly, each of them gripping their tasselled rope and letting it pass through their hands until the coffin came to rest.

There was a soft muzzle of rain falling, there was a breathless silence in the air, and it was in that moment that I started thinking about it all over again.

About that last day of summer, three years before, the last day in that house.

The child, at the end of the day, and that moment of shocking inevitability.

The ropes were dropped into the grave, and the men returned to their places, and I tried to catch my father's eye but he wouldn't look at me.

It's called taking the cord he said, the boy, when I asked him about it later.

It's a real honour he said, a duty, and but it's a shock as well though.

He said it's a shock because a coffin with a body loaded
  inside, it's a heavy thing you know?
Because even with the eight of you stood around that hole
  in the ground it's a real effort to control the descent like
  it's not just a symbolic thing he said, and I listened and he
  had a lovely voice.
And see this he said, see it takes a long time for the coffin to
  get to the bottom, and you suddenly realise how much of
  a weight of earth is going to press down upon it, upon this
  person you're laying down you know?
He said, and then it really hits you, they're in a box, they're
  being buried and they'll stay gone, like snug in this press
  of thick wet earth, and I nodded and found myself saying
  aye and he laughed and said you going native already?
He said when I put my granda in the ground, it felt like I left
  a part of me there, and brought a part of it away with me.
He said like the smell of the earth, like the burn of the rope
  against my hands, like the minister's voice saying the
  things.
I said do you want to go for a walk?

I met him after the service, at the wake, in the lounge bar of
  a local hotel.
He was working there, serving out the food, and later on I
  got talking to him.
I was sat at a table on my own and he came over to empty
  an ashtray, and he said you alright there then?
I'd already noticed him, he had blond hair and big
  shoulders and a very still way of moving around the
  room.
I'd already smiled at him.
He sat down and said are you a relly then, I said granddaughter and he said oh, sorry, and I said no it's okay.
I said aren't you supposed to be working and he said ah

they'll be alright and he looked me in the eye while I lit
his cigarette.
We talked about each other without really listening, I told
him about my journey up, he told me about what he did
when he wasn't working there.
Quietly, when no one was looking, we left together.

He took me walking through his city.
We walked up past the railway station and the football
ground, up past empty factories and rows of houses built
from grey stone, up to where we could look at the city
lights coming on and sit and talk.
I wanted him.
It was as simple as that, it was shocking and embarrassing
and exciting.
I wonder if I could tell my mother that, if that would be an
explanation for her, to say, mum, he was there, I wanted
him, that's all it was.
I'm not sure if that would be enough for her, if she'd
understand.
We sat on a wet bench and we didn't hold hands, and I
wanted to feel the rough of his face on my skin.
There was nothing very emotional about it, we weren't bond-
ing at a deep level; I was looking at his shirt and imagining the
buttons scattered to the floor like fallen pennies.
He said shouldn't you be getting back and I said I'm sure I'll
think of an excuse.

And we went to his house, and we went to his bed, and we
spent a long time doing the things.
He teased me about my accent, and I stood on his chest and
hit him with a pillow.
He tried to twist my hair into bunches, and I undid the
buttons of his shirt.

He kissed my ankles, and my calves, and he lifted up my
dress and kissed my thighs and I took down his trousers.

And then suddenly a seriousness came over what we were
doing, and I thought about laying my little-known grandmother in the ground, and I thought about that last day
of summer, and almost at once we were making love.

Really, urgently, absolutely making love.

I'd never before felt such a deep need to move that way,
slowly, carefully, inexorably.

It made me feel primitive, rooted, connected to the dirt of
the earth and the light of the stars, a spun thread pulled
across the span of generations.

I was swollen and pregnant with desire, and the need swept
through me in waves, my hands clutching like a newborn
baby, clutching the sheets, his skin, the air, whitening my
knuckles, straining to pull us into closer and tighter and
deeper embrace, and when we were finished the bedsheet was torn and the mattress had slipped to the floor.

And when I left, before midnight, I didn't leave my phone
number and I didn't ask for his.

I don't think my mother would understand that either, if I
told her, if she was ever to ask.

I went back to the relatives' house, and when they asked me
where I'd been I said I'd gone for a walk and got lost, and
they looked at me sweetly and fed me sympathy and
scones.

And the next day I made the long journey home, and I had a
secret dazzle of a thing I could smile quietly about at
work.

Only then it was a secret that was growing, and there was a
becoming place inside me that I hadn't been prepared
for.

Perhaps my mother would say well if you play around like

that you've got no one to blame, if she knew, perhaps she'd say oh my God did I teach you nothing?

Perhaps she'd say you should go and find him, he's got a right to know, and he should be helping to support you, financially.

I wonder if I'd be able to convince her that I didn't want to, that it had been a wonderful one-off and I wanted to leave it like that, unended, a suspended moment.

Maybe I won't tell her any of it, if she asks.

She can hear creaks and sighs coming from upstairs, mur-mured voices, slow footsteps. The flush of the toilet. She looks up at the ceiling, the woman in the kitchen of number nineteen, the mother of the boys playing cricket with milk crates outside, and she wipes her hands clean of roti flour. Darling she says, calling through to her husband, darling, nana and papa are waking up, and she puts the kettle on and begins to lay out another breakfast for her husband's mother and father, bowls of yoghurt sweetened with hon-ey, slices of fruit, juices and tea. Darling please! she says, a little more urgently, and she hears the television going off and she sees her husband appearing in the hallway. Good morning mother he says, looking up as his mother slowly descends, are you well, did you sleep okay? Good morning son she says, her voice heavy with the strain of moving down the stairs, and as she reaches him she pauses for breath, leaning forward to allow him to kiss her on each cheek, yes I slept okay, thankyou, yes I am well she says.

She moves through the kitchen, awkwardly, bulkily, she says good morning child and the mother in the kitchen says good morning would you like some breakfast mother? She pours water from the kettle into the teapot, and they both sit, hands folded on their laps, waiting. The stairs creak and they hear the pained exhaling of a man who does not find walking easy. They hear the son greeting the father and the father greeting the son, and the two men join them and sit at the table. They each murmur a small prayer of thanks, and there is a moment's silence as the first mouthfuls of breakfast are taken. The front door opens and closes, and they all look round but there is no one there. The son calls out the names of the twins, and there is no answer but they hear footsteps and a door closing upstairs. He looks at his wife and she puts her spoon down and goes to see if things are okay, she hears a voice, her daughter's voice, singing very quietly, talking from behind her bedroom door.

She waits outside the room for a moment, wondering if she should ask is everything okay, and then she turns and goes back to her breakfast.

Inside her bedroom, the girl is singing, waving a ribbon around her head in a wide slow circle and balancing on one foot. She is looking at herself in the mirror, pulling faces, tugging her mouth open as wide as it will go, grinning, frowning, tipping her head to one side and cupping a hand around her ear.

Outside, at number twenty-five, a man with a long beard is levering the lid from a tin of pale blue paint, he is plucking the loose bristles from a thin paintbrush, wiping the dust from his downstairs windowframe with a damp cloth, laying the first sticky press of paint across the bare grain of the wood.

The man in the kitchen of number sixteen hears her voice again, saying darling can't you reach me can't you, and the plate in his scarred hand shakes and spills toast crumbs to the floor. He has no way of making silence, so he concentrates instead on the sound of his daughter dancing lightly up the stairs. She is singing a song she has heard on the radio, he listens but he does not recognise it. He puts the plate in the sink, he tidies the other things, the lids on the jam and the honey, the margarine in the fridge, the knives and the cups in the sink. He could not, he tried but he could not reach her.

114

His daughter comes dancing back down again and says daddy can you get my clothes for me, of course he says and he lets her lead the way up the stairs to her room. His steps are heavy and slow, and when she gets to the top she turns around and looks down at him, giggling, saying come on daddy come on.

Her hair, it is the same.

Her hair is long, and dark, and it shines. She is an excitable girl, she talks a lot and she is always busy with something, a song in her head or skipping in the street, but when he sits her down and pulls a brush through her hair she is still. It is the only time, she is still and quiet and learning patience. Or perhaps she understands, even at her age, what happens to her father when he kneels behind a chair and runs a brush through long dark hair until it shines. She is young, she is too young to remember, but sometimes he thinks she understands. She does not often ask questions.

He reaches the top of the stairs and makes a growl like a gorilla, swinging his arms and stamping his feet and chasing her along the landing. She shrieks and runs into her room, and by the time he arrives she has hidden herself in the wardrobe, laughter bursting out of her like air from a punctured tyre. He says where are you? in a big scary gorilla voice, he says I'm coming to get you, he stample-stomps around the room.

He waits a moment, and then he says oh dear she must be somewhere else, in his own voice, he opens and closes the bedroom door.

He waits a moment more, and as the wardrobe door swings open he swoops his arms down around his daughter and hoists her awkwardly into the air, smothering her shrieks against his chest and they both laugh and shout and enjoy the press and tangle of each other until he slumps back onto the bed and says enough now.

Every day it is the same, this hide and seek when it is time to dress her, and every day it exhausts him. He would like to be a better father, to play wrestle games and run in the street and be the gallivanting shoulder-carrying super papa man, but it is too much for him. He is tired so quickly.

He sits and gets his breath back and his daughter watches, she says daddy are you okay and he smiles and nods. Now, what would you like to wear today he says, and they move through the motions of getting her ready for the day, the lifting of arms, the wriggling of cotton vests over reluctant heads, the rolling of socks and the put your feet in here now. The two of them, moving around the small room, circling, from wardrobe to bedside and back again, clothes lifted and held up to the light, clothes dropped to the floor and scooped into a heap. The two of them, a father and a daughter. A man without a wife dressing a four-year-old child.

He crouches at her feet, pushing her shoes on, fastening the velcro straps with a nudge of each wrist. When she learns to tie shoelaces it will not be from him. He says lovey you be good today yes? Every day he says this, and nearly every day she is. She looks him in the eyes and nods, carefully. She is a very solemn child sometimes he thinks, it is strange, and as she leaves the room and walks down the stairs he thinks but I am often a very solemn father. He thinks about what food he will prepare for lunch, how long it will take, he thinks he should begin soon. But first he kneels at the side of his daughter's bed and lets his face press into her bedding, holding his aching hands out into the air.

He looks as though he is praying, but he is not. He holds out his hands, but they are held out to no one.

The young girl from number nineteen, the sister of the twins, she is back in the street outside, holding her balance on one leg. A voice behind her says excuse me now lovely and she looks up to see the old couple from number twenty standing in front of her. She hops out of the way, still with her arms stuck out, and they walk slowly past. As she watches, the old man turns around, lifting his hat from his head like a magician, and winks. She giggles, and the couple continue their procession.

Up in the attic flat of number twenty-one, the woman with the henna-red hair is watching the old couple. She is standing naked at the small high window, a length of hair turned in her fingers, she is looking at the old couple and smiling. She calls through to her boyfriend, in the kitchen, she says have you seen this come and have a look at this, it's those two from number twenty, they're all dressed up for something, it's sweet, and his voice comes back saying yeah yeah in a minute in a minute. But in a minute they will be gone, and so he won't see them, arm in arm along the pavement, heads held high, stepping slowly and precisely. She was wearing a proper dress, not like a granny dress but some kind of elegant fifties thing, and a blue hat with a ribbon, and she had a matching shoulderbag and shoes, this is what she will tell her boyfriend in a moment. And he was wearing a sharp suit, like in a black and white film, he had a white handkerchief in his breast pocket, and a trilby like Sinatra she will say.

And she looks at the two of them, so proud-looking, she wishes she had a camera so she could take a picture, she wonders where they might be going dressed up like that. She watches them until they round the corner into the main road and then she turns away.

You've missed it now she says to her boyfriend.

Outside, the twins have found a couple of milk crates in the tangled front garden of number fifteen and are busy dragging them out to make a wicket with. Their sister is back on two legs, walking carefully behind the old couple, following them around the corner.

The sun is high enough to light up the windows on both sides of the street now, the shade retreating to the cooler paving beneath the trees. The only clouds are pale and thin, hung as high as they can manage, like cobwebs in the high arches of a stairwell, and the sky is a freshly scrubbed blue, as permanent-looking as the first day of the holidays.

The girl sidles around the corner and leans against the wall, peering at the old people in their fancy clothes.

They stand at the bus stop, this couple, this husband and wife of fifty-five years, and they look at each other. Have you got the right change she says, and he pulls a handful of money from his pocket and counts it out in the palm of his hand, nudging the coins aside with a quivering finger. Yes love he says, and he drops it all back into his pocket.

We've not missed it have we she says, and he looks at his watch, unhooking it from his waistcoat and holding it up to his face like a pocket mirror. No love he says, and he looks down the empty road to where the bus will appear.

Do you think the weather will hold out she says, and he doesn't even glance at the gleaming blue sky before he says yes love I'm sure it will love. It's going to be a good day he says, and he turns to her and he puts his hands round her shoulders, just you wait and see he says, and then the burr of the bus creeps up behind him and she points her eyes at the opening door and they step aboard, pay the fares, and take their seats as the bus moves away up the road.

And if either of them were to look over their shoulder now they would see the young girl standing on the corner, watching the bus grind its way up the long hill out of town, lifting an imaginary hat from her head and trying to wink. But neither of them are watching, they're too busy settling themselves in their seats, she straightening her dress, he removing his hat and smoothing his thick white hair, both of them shuffling into a comfortable position.

And behind them, on the corner of her street, the young girl tries again, two winks coming out at once, and she frowns and holds one eye open with a finger and a thumb while she lifts an imaginary hat from her head.

Sarah called me at work yesterday, when I was in the middle of thinking about my mother and what I was going to do next, she said why didn't you call me back?

I said I'd been going to, and it sounded like a lie.

She said she'd been at a party with some people from university and she'd met this guy who'd been asking after me.

I said what party, which people?

She said oh it was nothing really, not really anyone you knew.

But this guy she said, he was asking me how well I knew you, he was asking me where you were living now.

I said who was there that I know?

She said some names, and they were people that I remembered, and I said so how come no one told me?

She said oh it was just a last-minute thing, it was nothing special she said.

But this guy she said, this guy was asking me about you, and he said he wanted to get in touch with you.

She said it was that nervous guy's brother, you know the guy at number eighteen who always blinked a lot, didn't say much to anyone, it was his brother.

I don't know what he was doing there she said, I think Jamie knew him or something but he was dead nice.

She said he wanted to get your number off me, he's heard a lot about you from his brother apparently.

He's really nice she said, I think you should meet him, his name's Michael.

So I said okay, without really thinking about it, and she said she'd phone him up and give him my number.

And he phoned me about half past four, very politely, and
said he hoped I didn't mind him doing this or think he
was strange but he was interested to meet me.
I said no, not at all, no.
He suggested a pub, and a time, and he said you'll know
who I am I look like my brother.

I didn't spend much time getting ready.
I ate something out of the microwave, I put on some clothes
that didn't smell of photocopy ink, I switched the
answerphone on.
I kept wanting to change my mind, but I didn't have his
number and it seemed rude to just not turn up.
So I went, and I met him, and we bought drinks and started
to talk.
And he was very easy to talk to, and we talked a lot.
We said so where do you live, and what do you do, and where
did you live before, and how did you get here tonight.
We talked about people we knew and didn't know, piecing
together our connections like genealogists.
It was tenuous, there was Jamie who used to live with Rob
with the skateboard, and as of a few days ago there was
Sarah.
And there was his brother, although I didn't really know
him at all.

I started to feel relaxed, the way sometimes a new person in
an unfamiliar pub can make you feel, with the loud
music and the smell of beer and cigarette smoke.
I said I thought it was a strange thing to do, to come and
meet him like this, but that I was glad I had.
He said he'd been worried about calling me, but more
worried about not calling me, and did that make any
sense?

I thought about all the people I haven't called or written or spoken to and I said yes it makes a lot of sense.

I said but what made you want to get in touch in the first place, why now?

He said oh no it wasn't deliberate I didn't come looking, it was just a chance thing he said, meeting Sarah at the party and her saying she knew you.

He said my brother told me a lot about you it made me curious, and I said oh nothing bad I hope.

He told me his brother had gone away travelling somewhere, and I said by the way you really do look very much like him.

He said I should think so too we're twins and I said oh I didn't realise.

He said what so he didn't ever tell you about me? and he seemed surprised.

I said well no I didn't really talk to him that much, I didn't know him that well really.

I mean he's quite shy isn't he I said.

He put his drink down when I said this, a little too hard and some of the beer sloshed to the top of the glass and out onto the table.

He said, well, he can be quiet, sometimes, it depends.

I wasn't sure what he meant, I carried on talking, I said I saw him around quite a bit but it's just he wasn't on my course or anything.

It felt as though I was trying to justify myself and I wasn't sure why.

He said, well, that's a shame, I think you would have enjoyed talking to him, he's interesting, he would have had a lot to say.

He said, he wanted to talk to you.

And then he looked at me and said I should tell you
 something, can I tell you something.
He said my brother, he was in love with you.
I said, oh, really?
I said how do you know?
He said he told me, he said I knew it anyway.
He lifted his glass to his face and said and I can see why just
 before the beer reached his mouth.
He moved his eyes around the room, as though he was
 looking for someone.
He wiped the froth from his top lip with the back of his
 hand.
I drew circles in spilt lemonade, I looked at him.

I said but I don't know him, I said I didn't even know his
 name.
He didn't say anything, he looked straight at me and I
 wasn't sure if he'd heard me.
The pub was quite noisy by then, a jukebox and a fruit
 machine and a hundred people gulping down pints and
 raising their voices to each other.
I started to repeat myself, louder, but he shook his head and
 said no hold on you lived in the same street.
He said you lived a few doors away, you saw him nearly
 every day, you knew lots of things about him.
He said you noticed if he got his hair cut, you had opinions
 about his clothes, you knew he couldn't catch a cricket
 ball, you knew he lived on his own, if you saw him in the
 street you knew him enough to say hello.
He said these things loudly, scratching the back of his hand,
 and they were all true, and he drank more beer and held
 up his hands and raised his eyebrows.
He said and you didn't know him?
You didn't even know his name?

He went to the toilet after that, and when he came back it was as if he hadn't said anything, the conversation moved on and he stopped scratching the back of his hand.

We talked about work, about unfulfilling jobs and not knowing what to do about it.

We talked comfortably, way past last orders and I found myself wishing I'd tidied the flat.

Even briefly trying to remember if I was wearing decent underwear.

I could see why Sarah had thought I should meet him, he was interesting and he was funny and he was really quite nice to look at.

He had nice hands, and pretty eyes, and he didn't turn away when I looked at him.

I couldn't understand why, since they were twins, I'd never really noticed his brother that way.

And I couldn't understand how his brother could have claimed to have felt like that about me.

I asked him about it, I said what did your brother tell you about me, but the barstaff were hustling us out and he didn't hear me.

And now, in the slow grey light of the morning, I am looking at him and thinking about it some more, about what he said.

He is so remarkably similar-looking, it feels as though I'm seeing a ghost.

He has the same thinness of hair around the temples, the same curved fold of skin beneath each eye.

I wonder if his brother ever imagined this moment, my pausing over his closed body and examining its lines and tones and folds.

I think about the few times I spoke to his brother, about how little I can remember of those occasions.

I wonder what his brother would say if he knew he was here now.

I remember the edge in his voice last night when he asked how I didn't even know his brother's name.

I put the mug of tea on the floor beside the sofa and turn back towards my room.

I put my hand to my belly and imagine feeling something, a faint shift, a nudge.

The upstairs flat at number twenty is empty for now, the husband and wife gone for their day of quiet celebration, the bed neatly made and the breakfast things stacked in the draining rack. It's a small flat, ordered and tidy, wingbacked armchairs in the living room arranged to suit the television, a welsh dresser in the kitchen parading unused fine china, the bed in the bedroom wrapped in eiderdown. In the kitchen, on the formica-topped wooden table, there are two cards, propped up against the salt and pepper mills like telegraph boys leaning against postboxes. The cards are similar, both cream with gold lettering, both depicting a bouquet of flowers, roses on one, carnations on the other. Happy Anniversary they both say, with all my love. One of them says darling inside, the other says sweetheart. On both of them the handwriting is awkward and scratched, as though written on a moving surface, a table with uneven legs, the dashboard of a cornering car.

There are photographs on the dresser, amongst the decorative teapots and the royal doulton figurines, a life-story waltzing across the varnished wood. A wedding photo, framed in carved oak, he in a soldier's uniform, face shiny and tight and smiling, breast pockets fastened down with rigorously polished buttons, and she tucked into the side of him, the pins in her hair concealed with small white flowers, her dress curving away from her neck and puffing proudly out around her arms.

Another photo, perhaps ten years later, the two of them standing by the sea, somewhere sunny, the sky bright and crisp and he has a handkerchief knotted across his head, the four corners poking up like cloth thumbs, and she has a wide-brimmed straw hat which casts a weave of shadow across her face. There are small boats on the sea behind them, small boats with square red sails and long pointed bows, and there are islands on the horizon, a woman dressed in black in the background, stooping to pick something up off the beach.

There is a larger photo, a wide curve of people standing in a garden, couples with their children, the husband and wife from these other photos standing to one side, smiling as broadly as the rest.

And in smaller pictures, mounted in oval silver frames, the children from that wide photo in the garden grow up, bursting into colour photography, going gap-toothed, long haired, surly, squeezing partners of their own into the pictures, holding scrolls of paper, holding babies.

But mostly there is this husband and wife, in colour photos taken by friends and relatives, or by passers-by on daytrips and holidays. The two of them outside Buckingham Palace. The two of them blowing out candles on a cake. The two of them on a ferry, wind blowing their hair, pointing at the white cliffs of Dover.

On the windowsill, in between the tobyjugs which hide missing buttons and foreign coins, in between the bowls trophies and the decorative egg timers, there is a medal, mounted on a plain white card, propped up against the windowframe. He hadn't wanted her to put it on display, but she had, and he'd turned away from arguing about it. It's a plain-looking medal, like a large thick coin, no ribbon, The Defence Medal written on one side and a young-looking King George on the other. She polishes it sometimes, when she thinks he's not looking. You know it's nothing that, he said to her once, not so long ago, you shouldn't shine it up he said. They only gave them out for making it back home he said, and there's nothing in that worth a medal. She'd looked at him when he'd said that, and he'd left the room. It was the first thing he'd ever said about it.

When he came back to her he knew he would be unable to talk, knew it as soon as he put his hand on the cold metal tailgate of the truck heading home and climbed up into the damp canvas darkness. He could see her face all through that long journey, waiting to hear his stories, wanting to comfort his sadnesses. He could see the expectation she would have in her eyes, not knowing what he would say but knowing that he would surely say something, the same way he'd always told her stories when he'd been away.

But this was different, and perhaps she'd understand. He'd never really been away before, not actually away, he'd only been on training, done exercises, and the stories he'd had to tell were interesting and funny and easy to put into words. Wading through sodden marshland carrying wooden rifles, and his boot had come off and got lost and when he put the rifle down to find it the sergeant had shouted at him for damaging his weapon. Slitting open sandbags with fixed bayonets, the sand spilling onto the ground and the sergeant shouting twist and withdraw, twist and withdraw. Hiding in the forest all night with green makeup on his cheeks, everything silent and black except the red firefly tips of the other men's cigarettes and in the morning the sergeant had said you would all be dead by now. He'd told her these stories over the long weekends they spent together, short snatches of time they were granted between his long spells of duty. What have you been doing this time she'd say, and he'd tell her about the marches, the assault courses, the shooting practice, the running around in deserted villages commandeered by the government. And she'd take off his jacket and circle her fingers around his arm, testing his muscles, telling him what a strong man he was.

He'd thought about that on the journey home, her squeezing the strength of his arm like that, and he'd thought about how much bigger his arms had got while he'd been away, how she wouldn't be able to circle her small hands round his muscle anymore and whether that would make him feel strange to her. There would be nothing else to make him feel strange to her, he'd thought, he had no wounds, no broken bones, no scars or missing limbs. Just very strong arms, and a new quietness.

He'd worried about going back, all the way he'd worried, wondered how she would be, if she would still be there, if things could be as they were before, if they could get on now with making the home they'd been kept from making, and then she'd stood behind him in the rain and said there's no need to shout I'm right behind you and he'd known that things would be okay.

They'd talked a lot about making a home, before he'd gone away, during those weekends, talked about where they might live and what they might do, names they might give to their children, furniture they might buy, or make, or inherit. I'd really like a Welsh dresser she'd say, her fingers tracing absent-minded outlines across the bones of his face, I've always wanted one, with the plates all lined up nicely, and he'd said yes that would be nice and had to ask someone later what a Welsh dresser might be.

In the entranceway of their small flat, their home all these long years, in a small cupboard where the coats and hats and shoes should be, there are gardening tools, a spade, a fork, a hoe, a small trowel, a reel of twine, paper bags full of seed packets and bulbs, an unruly coil of hosepipe. She used to keep all the tools in a small shed on the allotment, but they were stolen so many times that she's taken to wheeling them backwards and forwards in a tartan shopping trolley. She doesn't grow as much as she used to, she gets more tired more quickly, so now she's planted half the allotment with bulbs. It's nice to sit amongst the flowers when she's having a rest, and sometimes in the spring she'll bring a bunch of them home, put them in a vase. It brightens the place up she says and he says yes love it does, thankyou love, and he puts the kettle on and cuts her a slice of cake whenever she comes home from her patch of ground, and she drinks the tea with soil-blackened fingers, eats the cake with a napkin wrapped round it. He never goes to the allotment, he says I don't much like all that gardening, he said I never have done love, when she first got it from the council, he said it's the digging love, I can't be doing with all the digging.

So he lets her go up there on her own, watching her pulling the tartan shopping trolley with the spade sticking out from the top, and when he hears her returning he puts the kettle on and she puts the things away in the small cupboard by the door.

Downstairs, the man with the carefully trimmed moustache is on the telephone again, leaving another message with the waste department of the local council. He says hello, it is me again, I telephoned earlier about the removal situation in my backyard, okay. He says I just want you to note that last time you wrote to me my name was spelt incorrectly, because you used an S and not a Z. This is close, but it is not close enough, he says. These things are important, the way you spell a man's name, it matters, yes? he says, and he puts the phone down. He looks around him, drumming his fingers against his trousers, anxious or agitated or just at a loss as to what to do next. He will be attending a fundraising event at the club later in the day, but before then he has no plans and he doesn't enjoy having no plans.

He takes a brush and dustpan from a cupboard beneath the kitchen sink, and he kneels in his front room, sweeping. He starts from under the bed, and he moves in a methodical line, backwards across the room. When he has finished there will be very little dirt or dust in the dustpan. He keeps his small flat exceptionally tidy, his clothes laundered and folded, his dishes washed and stacked, his rubbish double-bagged and put outside on the correct day. His friends have commented on it, when they've visited, and he is surprised that they consider it unusual. Because you never know do you, he says to them, you don't know when you will be taken and you would not want people to remember you as a person without good housekeeping habits, would you? He is surprised that not everybody thinks like this, he is surprised how casually people will drop things in the street. He asked the lady at the council office about it once, he said do they not care what people think of them, and she didn't seem to know what to say.

He puts the dustpan and brush back under the sink, he takes a duster and runs it around the clean white woodwork of the windowframe. The glass is the worst, he said this to the lady once, these piles of broken glass where people have robbed into the cars, can't you come and at least sweep this away? This is important, he said this to her, please can you understand what broken glass in the street means, to a man of my age, coming from where I come from? He had said this, and she didn't seem to know what to say.

Outside, in the middle of the street, the twins are still playing cricket. The first boy, the older boy by a few painful minutes, he bowls a high loop of a ball which bounces easily, his brother swinging at it with an old split-handled bat and sending the tennis ball pinging towards number fifteen. It bounces off the boarded-up window and buries itself in the overgrown front garden, and the older brother shouts it doesn't count it doesn't count as he kicks around in the brambles looking for it. You're out if it hits the window he shouts, as his younger brother leaps up and down the street counting up his runs.

The young man outside number eleven watches the boy looking for his ball, his sharpened pencil hovering over his sketchpad, his protractors and rulers laid aside. A girl with a hairband flattening her hair steps out of the door behind him, she touches him lightly on the head and says do you want anything from the shop? He says no no thankyou without looking at her, and she says okay and keeps walking, she turns round and says so how's it going anyway, the masterpiece? and he turns and sees her looking at him, she is smiling, he looks at his drawing and looks up, he shrugs and he smiles and he says oh is okay. She says I'll buy you some chocolate, you look like you need some chocolate, and she turns and he watches her walk, he looks again at the boy hunting for his ball, kicking at the tangled overgrowth of number fifteen's garden.

Inside number fifteen, the boy's younger sister is standing very still, looking around in the cool dark silence. The house is almost empty, boarded up and abandoned years ago, and she is excited to be in such a private place. It feels as though she has discovered an underground chamber, a secret garden, an Ali Baba cave. She wonders what would happen if she said open sesame. She's been in here before, once, there's a tiny gap between the boards on the shattered back window, hidden by a huge tangle of weeds, and she thinks only she knows about it, it's scary but it's exciting too. She stands there, waiting for her eyes to get used to the thin splinters of light forcing their way through the cracks and gaps in the boards, and she smells the cold damp air.

Whoever it was who lived here last, whyever it was that they left, they seem to have left quickly, slipping quietly out through the back door perhaps, taking a bag of clothes and a handful of money and leaving everything else behind. There is still furniture in here, just, there are still books on shelves and pictures on walls. There's a clock, stopped. She looks around her, wondering if anyone is here, ready to run. She can hear her own breathing in her ears, like the noise of a television without any pictures. She moves into another room, her imagination and her excitement racing ahead of her, holding her hands out as though for balance, stepping carefully.

She can see, in the near-darkness, a textbook left open on a bed, the pages speckled with mould. She can see a radio with the front hanging off, spilling wires and fuses across a desk, a screwdriver jabbed into its innards. She moves from room to room, looking, occasionally touching. Everything is soft and damp, crumbling wetly beneath her small fingers. She sees a record player with the needle still resting patiently in the groove of a record, she sees a photograph pinned to the wall, curled up and hidden from view, she sees ashtrays balanced on the arms of skeletised armchairs, snuffled clean of ash and still waiting for new cigarettes to be pressed against them.

She treads delicately up the stairs, holding onto the soft banister, swallowing, feeling guilty and delighted and scared. The rooms upstairs are the same, wetter perhaps, a little lighter, she can see more clearly the way that all of it, the carpets and the walls, the beds and the chairs, the record players and the shoes and the clocks and the ashtrays, the way that all of it is hidden, furred over, concealed

134

by a slow slather of wet growth, mould and moss and crusted lichen creeping over it all like a lascivious tongue, muffling the hard edges, crawling across the floor, climbing up the walls, clinging from the ceilings, thickening and flowering and spraying out spores to breed in any untouched corners.

She shivers suddenly, she hears a noise, she turns and treads quickly down the damp stairs, through the back room, squeezing through the secret gap and bursting head-first into the bright clean sunlight of the world, sucking in the sweet air, dazzled.

But if she had stayed, if she had found the courage to poke around in the dank corners, to push open rotting doors, to let her eyes see into the gloom and the shadows, she would have found a lot more.

Mice, making nests from scraps of magazines and bedding, their tiny pink eyes staring back at her. Bats, hanging in wardrobes like tiny folded umbrellas. Pigeons, clustered in the corner of another room, murmuring and scratching and loosening their droppings onto the threadbare carpet. Spiders' webs woven thicker than net curtains, skirting boards honeycombed by woodworm, blue-green algae blooming in the bathroom sink.

And in the attic, if she had managed to find her way up the steep and crumbling steps, she would have found the one room left open to the light, she would have stood, breathless, picking cobwebs from her fingers and her face, staring at a whole meadow of wildflowers and grasses, poppies and oxeyes and flowering coriander, all flourishing in bird droppings and all lunging pointedly towards the one square foot of available sky.

We went out for breakfast this morning.

Michael said he owed me.

We went to a place with plastic gingham tablecloths, and big red and yellow containers of squirtable ketchup and mustard on the counter.

The door jangled when we went in, and a woman in a dirty white apron said in a minute love and went into the kitchen.

The radio was playing a rap song, the singer going my name is my name is, over and over again, as if he'd forgotten.

I said I don't think I've ever been to a cafe for breakfast before, and he said don't worry there's nothing to be scared of it's all quite simple and I said ha ha.

I said, but maybe, I think my mum and dad once took me to a Little Chef, I'm not sure.

We must have been driving somewhere I said, and I tried to remember the journey, where we were going, when it was.

He said what do you want then, and I forgot about it and ordered breakfast.

I said so where's your brother now then?

He said I don't know really.

He said he just went travelling and he didn't really tell us where he was going.

I said oh, but doesn't he send you postcards, hasn't he got an email address?

He said erm no not really well sometimes, and he looked out of the window and said he was in Mexico the last time I heard.

He said hey look at that, and I looked and there was a man in a tracksuit using a bin for a toilet.

He was singing, happy birthday, and he was drinking a can of superstrength lager.

I said I recognise him I think.

He sang happy birthday to me happy birthday dear and then he stopped.

And breakfast came and it tasted good, greasy and squeaky and crisp, solid food to last a long day and we didn't say much while we were eating it.

I tried to remember where I'd been going with my parents when we'd had breakfast at that Little Chef.

I remembered it was a journey started while it was still dark, lying on the back seat under a blanket, watching telegraph wires whipping across a whitening sky.

I remembered my dad rolling his head up and down whenever we stopped the car, squeezing the back of his neck.

My mum saying will you be okay now?

My dad telling me why a haggis has two legs longer on one side and my mum telling him to shush his mouth.

I must have been about seven years old, and I can't think where we were going because we always seemed to go abroad for our holidays, France, Spain, Portugal, always somewhere south.

I wiped the last bit of egg yolk from my plate with a triangle of bread.

He said what's happened to your hands?

I said nothing, nothing's happened to my hands, and I closed my fingers over the cuts and scars on my palms.

He said no let me see, and he reached out to touch my hand and I automatically pulled away.

Oh sorry I'm sorry he said, I didn't mean, and he didn't finish his sentence.

I put my hands in my lap, under the table, and I watched his eyes follow them.

I rubbed them, they felt hot, they felt as though I'd grabbed an electric fence.

He said I'm sorry again, and he was blinking a lot and suddenly he looked exactly like his brother.

I thought about him, that afternoon, sitting on his doorstep looking up at me, the way he spoke, the way he moved through that awful moment.

I said what's his name, your brother?

He looked at me and he looked down and he finished his tea.

He said excuse me, sorry, I need to, and he took a phone out of his pocket and went and stood by the door.

I watched him making a call, I wondered who he was talking to, I wondered why I didn't think it was none of my business.

A man hurried past the window with a huge bunch of red roses, it was twice the size of his head, he didn't look as though he could see where he was going, he was smiling massively and I don't think anyone in the street turned to look.

I thought about his brother, the times I'd said hello, passing him in the street, standing beside him at the shop counter, I wondered why I'd never thought to ask him his name.

I remembered that whenever I saw him somewhere besides our street he'd always wait for me to say hello first, looking at me slightly sideways, as if he didn't quite recognise me, or as if he wasn't sure that I'd recognised him.

Michael came and sat down again, he put the phone on the table and said sorry about that, I just needed to.

The woman came and took our empty plates, and as I passed mine over I saw him looking at my hands again.

I said I'm sorry, I just.

He said I know it's none of my business, but.

I laid them out on the table.

I said oh it's nothing, it's just a bit embarrassing.

He looked at them, and he moved his fingers towards them and this time I didn't flinch or pull away but he didn't touch them.

He said what's embarrassing, what happened?

I said I broke some plates.

I said actually I broke all my plates, I threw them into the sink when I should have been washing them up.

I kept picking up the pieces and throwing them back in and it was only afterwards that I realised I'd cut myself I said.

He looked at me and he didn't ask me why I'd done it.

I said it had been raining a lot that day, I lost my temper.

He looked at me.

He said raining a lot?

I said yes, you know, it just all got a bit, and I couldn't really explain and I laughed a little.

I was embarrassed.

I thought I'd made myself look stupid.

He said and what else, apart from the rain?

I looked at him, I took my hands off the table and closed my fingers over my palms again.

He said I'm sorry, I know, it's none of my business.

I looked at him, and I looked at his hands spread across the tablecloth, and I told him.

I told him that about four weeks ago I'd discovered I was pregnant.

That I was scared and horrified and numb with shock.

That I hadn't been able to tell anyone for a long time and I wasn't sure why it had been so difficult.

And that when I'd told my mum she'd been polite and indifferent and I didn't know what she really felt.

I told him that I'd thought she'd be shocked or cross or upset, but that when she was none of these things I was actually unsurprised.

I told him I hadn't even spoken to my dad yet, that I didn't even know whether he knew.

I said that I wasn't ready to have a baby.

I said that I didn't know what to do.

I said all of this very quietly, and I was amazed to hear the words coming out at all, like butterflies wriggling through net curtains.

He asked me questions, tracing his fingers across the tablecloth as if it was a map.

He asked me for the details, he said stop me if I'm going too far and I didn't stop him.

He asked me the questions my mother didn't ask, the who is the and the have you thought about?

I told him about the Scottish boy, and I said I couldn't do that, I'd never thought about it much before but now that I have I couldn't do it.

And when I started crying a little he unfolded a paper napkin from the rack and passed it to me and looked away.

He said I'm sorry, I said no, it's okay, I'm okay, and I twisted the napkin around my finger like a bandage.

He said, your parents, maybe they, perhaps you could go and see them, perhaps it's just a telephone thing he said.

I said I don't know it's too far, I can't afford it, and he said I'll drive you, please, I'd like to drive you there.

I said, oh, you don't need to do that for me, I couldn't, I mean, and he said I wouldn't be doing it for you.

The daughter of the man with the scarred hands sits in the front doorway of their house, she looks across the street and she sees the boy from the house opposite on his tricycle, he is pedalling along the pavement and his father is walking behind him, carrying a tall glass of water. The boy pedals until he gets to number seventeen, then he scuffles his feet on the paving stones to stop and he looks at his father and points.

His father walks up to the front door and knocks, loudly. He is a tall thin man, with bony hands and a beard cut close to his face. He bangs on the door again, and the twins stop their cricket game to watch.

The door handle moves, and the father straightens his stance, clutches the glass a little tighter. A voice says hold on it's stuck again I'll go to the window, and the father steps into the overgrown front garden. A face appears at the window, the boy with the white shirt and the tie, his shirt very crumpled now, he looks as if he's only just woken up and he squints in the light and he says hello?

The father doesn't say anything for a moment, he looks at him and then he throws the water from his glass into the young man's face.

Bastard! he says, loudly and crisply, and he turns and walks back to his own house. His son drags his tricycle into a U-turn and follows him, and the twins in the middle of the road yell and laugh and point.

The young man watches them, he wipes his face with his hand and he is unable to speak, he closes the window and walks through to the back bedroom, trying to remember something.

He lies down on the floor beside the tall thin girl and squeezes back in under the duvet. She looks at him and raises one of her sleepy eyebrows, still speckled with sparkles. She makes him feel better before she even speaks. She says who was that? A man with a beard he says. He called me a bastard and threw a glass of water in my face he says, and his eyes are weighting themselves closed and he's falling asleep already. She says oh, and she tries to speak some more but she can't remember what they were talking about.

What did you say? asks one of the girls on the bed, but no one answers and she closes her eyes again and she hears shouting from outside somewhere.

In his attic room, the young man with the thick black hair is counting his money again, fanning it out in his hand like a winning set of cards, lining the notes up so all the queens' heads face the same way, holding it up to his face to smell the grubby paper odour of it. The sweet smell of a thousand pounds. He looks out at the street, at his father cleaning his car, he imagines his reaction later this afternoon, the way he'll circle around it, unfolding a white handkerchief from his pocket and dabbing at his face, folding the handkerchief and saying what is this I don't believe it.

He looks up the street, listening for the thump of a car stereo, he imagines his father saying I didn't know, I could have helped you, saying you only had to ask.

He smiles to himself. His father doesn't even know he's passed his test. He tucks the cash back into his wallet, stuffs the wallet back into the pocket of his trousers and checks himself in the mirror. He hears more shouting outside, the shrieks of the twins, he smooths his hair and thinks daddy you going to be proud of me today, believe. He kisses his fist and runs downstairs.

In the street, the twins are still cheering and laughing, running up and down the street as if they've just hit a winning six against England, singing bastard bastard to each other, the older twin swinging the bat around his head like a club.

Hey careful with that one mate says a loud voice, you'll take someone's head out, innit, and the boy turns around and sees the young man from number twelve striding towards him, grinning, reaching out to snatch the bat away, his thick black hair gelled neatly into place. I'll be Imran Khan he says, no I'm Imran Khan says the older twin, no I'm Imran Khan says the youngest. I'll be Imran Khan says the young man again, and you can bowl and you can go wickie he says and he points at each of the twins.

The younger twin takes the balding tennis ball and trots away down the street. I'm Akram he shouts over his shoulder, and he stops and he turns and he throws the ball from hand to hand.

Head down, he begins his run-up.

His brother crouches behind the milk-crate wickets, ready to pounce onto the clipped ball and make a heroic catch.

Wasim Akram leaps and flings his arm over his shoulder, his whole body arching towards the wicket, a shout of exertion crashing out of him.

The ball loops gently through the air and bounces in front of Imran Khan, who steps forward and smashes it back, over the turning head of Akram and towards the main road. Howzaaay! he shouts, six! and the younger of the twins trots away after the ball, running out in front of a bus and sliding under a parked car to retrieve it.

You're out if it goes on the road says the wicketkeeper, reaching for the bat, and you don't get the six, give us the bat, and the young man lifts it out of his reach. No you're not he says, you go and bowl now, and he lifts the bat higher as the boy jumps up for it.

The young man's father is washing his car outside their house, he looks up, and as he dips a sponge into a bucket of warm soapy water he calls eh go easy on the fellow now. The young man looks up at his father and lowers the bat, laughing, saying I'm only joking, taking the ball from the younger twin and saying but I'm still Imran Khan.

His father watches and squeezes soap and water over the already shining roof of his car. He whistles a song from a movie, and as he stretches to reach the far side of the roof his shirt drapes into the suds and soaks up the warm water. He stands back, and the bubbles blister and fizz and pop like glittered skin in a nightclub.

The daughter of the man with the burnt hands, sitting on the doorstep of number sixteen, she watches as the man throws a bucket of clean water over the car. She watches the water skidding across the roof, chasing the dirty soap, swimming down the windows and tipping into the road. She watches the boy with the thick black hair bowling to one of the twins, the twin hitting at the ball and the ball lofting towards number eighteen.

Catchaaaay! shout all three cricketers, Imran and Akram and Younis, and the boy with the bloodshot eyes sitting on his front step looks up, clapping his hands around warm air as the ball lumps past his head. He turns to pick it up, and he knocks it out of reach. He stands to move after it, and he kicks it by mistake, he picks it up and throws it and it doesn't quite reach any of the cricketers. Thanks mate says the oldest of them, and as he turns to the twins he pushes his tongue into his lower lip and crosses his eyes and they giggle and copy him.

146

The boy with the bloodshot eyes sits down again with his paper and pen. He is writing a letter to his brother, he writes last week I saw her loading up a car with stuff as if she was leaving, boxes and bags and even a standard lamp, and I was sick with disappointment but then it turned out it was her mate leaving. He thinks, and he writes I still want to talk to her properly, before I change house, I want to see if well you know, and he draws a row of dots and he writes but I guess if her mate's left then she's probably moving out and today's the last day of the month and so I've missed my chance. He rubs his eyes, blinks painfully, writes I just don't know what to say and I know it's pathetic but I don't, and he looks up and realises the twins are still laughing at him so he picks up the letter and retreats into his house.

A car appears from the other end of the street and hoots at the milk crates, a car with tinted windows and gleaming hubcaps, a car with loud music padooming from inside. The oldest boy raises his hand and throws the ball back to the twins, he walks to the car and clasps the hands of each of the occupants in turn. He calls goodbye to his father, but his father is walking towards him and so his friends climb out and each clasp his father's hand, saying yes my father is well yes my mother is well, thankyou yes, allahu akbar, and then all four of them climb into the car and the father watches them drive towards the main road, he watches a brief flare of flame illuminating his son as a long cigarette is lit behind the darkened glass.

Upstairs at number twenty-four, a girl sits at her desk and watches the car drive past, she thinks she recognises the boy who just got into it, the boy who was playing cricket, she thinks she's spoken to him but she can't think when. She watches the car turn onto the main road, she watches the twins go back to their game, she looks at the old man opposite painting his windowframes, she looks higher and sees a crane lifted high over the rooftops, she wonders what they're building over there now, she screws up her eyes and turns back to the work on her desk. She knows it was a mistake to put the desk under the window, it's good for the light but there is so much to look at outside, there are so many distractions and she doesn't have time for distractions. She opens another textbook, she takes the lids off a trio of felt-tip pens, and she draws another diagram, a delicate weave of veins and nerve endings and cell structures, she annotates and underlines and struggles to understand.

Outside, on the front step of number twenty-two, the two girls are watching a pigeon flying up the street, a leaf in its beak. They've been watching it for a while, arguing about it. They've noticed that whenever it comes back it's not carrying anything, but when it flies up towards the shop it has something crammed in its beak, a leaf, a twig, a piece of string.

The girl with the glasses is saying it must be building a nest, what else would it be doing, and the girl who's still wearing her tartan pyjamas says but surely they're supposed to lay their eggs in the springtime it's about six months late to be building a nest.

Maybe it's confused says the girl with the glasses and the short hair, maybe it's overslept its hibernation, and the other girl says I don't think pigeons hibernate do they? and goes into the house to make a cup of tea and a phonecall.

The girl with the glasses watches the pigeon, she tugs gently at her short hair, pulling it into place, she notices for the first time how graceful the pigeon looks, head stretched forward, feet tucked in under a curved belly, wings carefully angled to catch the breeze.

Across the road, at number twenty-three, a young man with a lot of hair and grazes down both arms is arguing with a young man wearing yellow sunglasses, he's saying we need fire-lighters it'll never get going without fire-lighters. The yellow-sunglasses boy is screwing up pieces of newspaper and dropping them into a rusted metal tray propped up on bricks, he is covering the newspaper with bits of grass and twig, he's saying no it'll be alright, wait up it'll be fine, he nestles a few lumps of black charcoal into the pile of paper and sticks and he lights a corner of the newspaper. Watch this he says, and they peer at the small curl of flame, the paper blackening, smoke twisting off, steam wisping from the ends of the grass.

A twig smokes and crackles, pieces of burnt paper char and break away, the smoke thickens and spirals upwards, wafting up towards the first-floor window, buckling and turning, lifting higher, a catch of it dropping in through the attic window next door, the man with the tattoo smelling a glimpse of it and sitting up in bed to look around, the rest of it drifting further still, breaking and thinning and vanishing somewhere high above the quiet street.

He changes gear.

He says don't you ever wonder about him?

I say who, he says that guy, in Scotland, don't you ever wonder?

I say well no, not really.

I think about it, about him and that night, and an image passes through my mind, all skin and teeth and hands, snagging my stomach like a dress caught in a door, closing my eyes.

I imagine knocking on his door, taking that long walk up the steep side of the city and waiting breathlessly outside his house.

I imagine bemusement on his face, delight, embarrassment.

I imagine him standing with one hand on the door and the other on the frame, his body wedged in between, his uncertainty like a pensioner's doorchain.

I remember the smell of his neck.

I say well no, you know, it was just a thing.

It wasn't anything else I say, it was just a thing that happened.

He pushes a little button, and soapy water squirts onto the windscreen, some of it catches in the wind and flails off to either side.

He says but did you never want to go back and do it again?

He turns the windscreen wipers on, and they squeak back and forth until the soapy water has cleared.

He says didn't you wonder what he was thinking about you?

He says and when you found out did you wonder what he might do if you told him?

I look at him.

I say actually can we talk about something else now.

He says sorry, I just, you know, and he fiddles with the air vents in the middle of the dashboard.

He says are you too warm?

I can change the ventilation he says, and he shuffles the sliding control from left to right, clicks another dial around, holds his palm over the vent to feel the air breathing through.

He says it's just that I've never been in that situation, you know, I just wondered, I didn't mean anything.

I look at him, and his eyes are squeezing and blinking just like his brother's.

I say what did your brother tell you about me?

He says everything he knew, he says which wasn't very much I suppose.

He told me what you looked like he says, and what course you were doing, and what clothes you wore.

He says he told me the way you smiled, what your voice sounded like, who you lived with, what flavour crisps you bought when he saw you in the shop, how different you looked when you took your glasses off, what it felt like when you touched his arm.

I say I don't remember touching his arm.

He says no I didn't think you would.

We overtake a lorry with its sides rolled back and I look at the fields and the sky through its ribbed frame, there are bales of hay rolled up like slices of carpet, there's a sprawling V of birds hanging over the horizon.

I don't know what he means.

He says, my brother, he could, he can be a bit strange sometimes, I say what do you mean.

He says, well, just strange things, like once he sent me a list of all the clothes you'd worn that week, really detailed, colours and fabrics and styles and how they made you look and how you looked as though they made you feel.

He looks at me and says and it wasn't creepy or anything, he wasn't being obsessive, it was just, you know, observations.

He was thinking he wanted to buy you a present he says, and he wanted to get it right.

He winds his window down very slightly, and a thin buffet of air blows in across us both.

He sort of collects things as well he says, things he finds in the street, like till receipts and study notes and pages torn from magazines, and one time he took a whole pile of shattered car-window pieces and made a necklace out of them he says.

He said they were urban diamonds he says.

He made a glass case he says, and he mounted a row of used needles he found in an alleyway.

And if he couldn't take it home he'd take a photo of it he says, he had albums full of stuff.

He says he told me he hated the way everything was ignored and lost and thrown away.

He says he told me he was an archaeologist of the present, and he laughs at this and turns the radio on and I don't know what to say.

There's a boy band on, from years ago, singing when will I will I be famous, and I wonder what Craig and Matt and Luke are doing now.

I say, please, what's your brother's name?

He doesn't say anything, he looks over his shoulder, overtakes someone, changes the radio station.

I say he sounds interesting, it's a shame I didn't get to talk to him more.

He says but you did, at that party, and he looks at me and a car behind us flares its horn as we drift across into the next lane.

He straightens out and keeps his eyes on the road and says sorry.

I say that's okay, what do you mean, what party?

He says there was a party you both went to, he told me about it, you spent the evening talking to each other, he walked you home and then you were so drunk you forgot about it.

No I say, no I don't remember that, and I think and I try and remember, no I say, I really don't remember.

He doesn't say anything, he turns the radio up a little and adjusts his seat, he says do you know the way, do you want to look at the map.

I look at the map, I look out of the window and I recognise the landscape, I recognise the way the fields are tipping up towards the first edges of the town, away to the far left, I look at the map again.

I say but I would like to meet him, when he comes back, do you think he'll want to I say, and he says yes, very quietly, yes I think he would.

We come off the motorway at the next junction, and I start slipping directions into the conversation.

He says do you think it was weird, me saying that about my brother, you know, about him being in love?

I think for a moment, left at this next roundabout I say.

We drive past a retail estate, and I see a line of cars crossing an empty carpark like wagons across a prairie.

I say well yes, I did, it did throw me a bit, it wasn't really what I was expecting.

Straight over at these lights I say.

It's a big word I say, love, it seems a bit, you know, clumsy.

He says I'm sorry, I didn't mean to spin you out, I wanted to tell you, I wanted to see what you thought, I say but I don't really think anything I don't even know him, I'm sorry.

No he says, I suppose not.

Left at this pub I say, and we swing into my old estate, lunging over battered speed-bumps, and I wind down my window and it all comes rushing in, this place, the smell of it, the feel of it, pieces of things that happened when I was younger.

Right at the mini roundabout I say, and I remember falling off my bike and breaking my glasses, my mum stopping my pocket money until the new pair was paid for, left past the shops I say.

Can I ask you something I say, he says yes, he turns the radio off, I say why are you doing this?

He says you said you couldn't afford the train fare, no not that I say.

I say why are you here, now, telling me all these things about your brother, asking me how I feel, what are you trying to achieve?

He stops the car, suddenly, he looks at me and says shit I'm sorry I didn't mean to upset you.

You haven't upset me I say, I just, it's a strange thing to do and I'm interested to know why you're doing it.

I don't know he says, he looks at me, I can't answer that he says.

He says he told me you looked lonely and he couldn't do anything about it.

We drive past my old junior school, left I say, left again, and then round a corner and we're outside my parents' house, my house.

I thank him for the lift, I offer him a cup of tea before he
goes.

He says no, thanks, I should probably leave you to it, and he
gives me the phone number of where he's staying, he says
call me when you want to go back.

He says, if that's okay, I mean, if you don't mind, and I
smile and say of course I don't mind.

He drives away, and I wave, and I stand outside my house
and wait.

I look down at my stomach, and I wonder if it shows
properly.

It feels different to me already, when I lay my hands across
it I can feel the swelling, like a deep breath in a very tight
dress, the stretch of it, and I wonder if anyone else can
see.

I wonder if my dad will be able to see.

I ring the doorbell.

There's a thudding sound from a door across the street, from behind the door maybe, and he looks up to see what it is, the man with the burnt hands, he lifts the cracked shell of his face and tries to see what the noise is.

It's coming from number seventeen, a banging noise of wood against wood, the doorhandle is twitching up and down and the door is pressing outwards with each thud, like the heartbeat of a Bugs Bunny in love, boomba boomba. He thinks to himself, the door must be stuck, it happens, in the heat, in these old houses where the landlords let things slip.

The noise stops. He looks at the door, at the shine of the doorhandle, the metal of the doorhandle warming up in the midday sun.

And then the window next to the door is hauled up suddenly, the sashes squeaking, and a gangly young man clambers out through the opening, the net curtain covering his face briefly like a bridal veil before he emerges into the street and strides away towards the shop. He holds his hand up over his eyes, screws his face up against the glare of the sun, pulls at the collar of his crumpled white shirt. One of the twins stops his bowling run-up and shouts splash sploosh, and the young man ignores him.

The man with the ruined hands sits in a chair in his front garden and looks at the net curtain wafting in and out of the open window.

The veil she wore on their wedding day was white, it was like the curtain. It was smooth, silk maybe, and when she breathed it drifted out from her face like a feather. This was many years gone now, their wedding day, but it is like no time at all.

The look in her face when she lifted the veil, the delight, the pride, the beautiful in her soul, could be yesterday.

Her face, was beautiful.

Her hands, was beautiful.

Her skin, was smooth and clear and unbroken, when she touched him lightly it felt like water trickling across his body. She would move her hand across his face to see if she wanted him to shave before the evening meal, and when she was done his skin would feel clean of the dust of the day.

She was tall, and strong, and she kept her hair coiled tightly around the back of her head and she had intricate paintings on the secret parts of her body. She was a wonderful woman, but this was not enough to help her. He loved her deeply, but this was not enough to help her. Please, darling, she called out to him, through the door, the closed door. Please darling can't you help me she called. He could not reach to her, he was not enough.

The door was stuck, in the heat, it was swollen, the wood of the door in the frame, the frame it was too small, like a wedding ring on a very hot day.

It was so very hot.

She said darling I am very hot I cannot breathe please can't you reach me.

The paint on the door was coming away, it was bubbles, blistering, each time he touched it he felt knives across his skin and into his bones. The metal of the doorhandle, when he touched it, it melted his hand like butter, it sunk into his skin like an axe into a tree and the hot air and the poisonous paint in his lungs, he thought he would die but he did not. He did not die.

She said my God my God what is happening.

He sits in his garden on a folding wooden chair, this man with the burnt hands, and the sun is shining and his daughter is playing with another girl in the street and he is okay but he is not okay.

He watches the young man with the white shirt and the tie loping back along the street with a bag of shopping. The bag is red and white, thin plastic, inside there is a pint of milk, a carton of orange juice, packets of crisps. He watches as the young man clambers back through the open window, he licks a peel of skin on his palm, flattening it, he watches the young man reappear and fiddle with his front-door handle. The young man pushes at the door with his shoulder, he rattles the handle, he kicks the bottom of the frame. He puts his hand through the letterbox and shakes the door.

The man in the chair brings his hand to his lips and thinks of his wife saying my God the door what is happening.

The young man stands back from the door, he looks around. His face is red and he is sweating. He sees the man in the chair, they see each other, the young man makes a face like well what a laugh and the man in the chair replies with a single slow nod.

She said it is too hot I cannot breathe I cannot please my God can't you help me darling please.

The young man turns and lifts his foot high and kicks into the door, his arms raised and his fists clenched, his body all pointed down the line of his leg in a rush and a tangle and the door swings open and his momentum carries him through into the shade of his hallway and there is a sound like he is falling to the floor.

The man in the chair looks, he does not move. He remembers her, she said what is happening, the door, please, can't you reach me, please, the door.

159

His daughter skips past, her shoes are tapping on the pavement, she is singing and she does not look up at him as she passes.

In the kitchen of number seventeen the young man with the creased and sweaty white shirt puts a kettle on to boil. He lines up a row of almost clean mugs and drops a teabag into each one.

The tall girl with the glitter around her eyes comes in and says what was that noise? and her skirt is twisted round almost sideways and there are creases on her cheek from the pillow. He says that was me kicking the door in, oh she says, what for, I couldn't open it he says. The kettle boils and he fills up the mugs, sniffing the milk before he adds it to the tea, he says how are you feeling, she says like shit. He says are the others awake? She says I don't know, she says heal my head and she sits down and takes his hands and pulls them onto her scalp. He rubs his fingers through her hair in circles, squeezing and pressing as if kneading warm dough into life and she says mm that's nice. The short girl with the painted nails comes in and says is that tea for me what was that noise? The boy says the door was jammed, I had to kick it in he says, she says oh, she says where's he gone? He says he must have gone out, he's not in his room, she says oh I hope he's okay he was being a bit weird last night. The tall girl watches the tissue-thin vapours twirling upwards from the mugs of tea, illuminated by the sunlight, she can see each drop of moisture, lighter than air, spiralling together like a flock of birds turning into the sun, like a tiny waterfall reversed, a playful movement, she feels as though if she put her hand in the way it would tickle she says mm oh I feel better now.

The boy says do you want some breakfast then, he sits down again and pushes his fingers through his hair. The tall girl says no I'm not hungry, my stomach feels a bit, and she hesitates and thinks and says beside the point and she smiles a pale smile. The short girl with the painted nails says I want a chocolate doughnut, let's go and buy some chocolate doughnuts, we can sit on the wall outside and eat them, is that tea for me she says.

The door crashes open and the boy with the pierced eyebrow comes in and says those fucking kids I'm going to twat one of them soon. Everyone looks at him. Is this tea for me he says, and he sits down and pulls one of the mugs across the table towards him, and for a moment the tall girl's head is pulled sideways as if by a string as she follows the sight of the spiralling steam. He puts a paper bag down in the middle of the table.

He says I just got hit in the back of the fucking head by their ball, I swear down it was deliberate, little shits, and as he says shits he slaps the palm of one hand with the back of the other. He is talking loudly and quickly, he says they woke me up with water pistols through my window this morning, monkeys, I got them back though, I gave them a soaking, and then he stops and takes a breath and the others look at him and the quietness settles back into the room the way it does once a train has passed.

The boy with the white shirt remembers the bearded man throwing a glass of water in his face, he remembers the crisp and angry way he called him bastard, and he says what did you say what did you do?

The boy with the pierced eyebrow says I got them back, I emptied water over them from upstairs, and as he says it a moment of realisation passes gradually across the other boy's face.

The boy with the pierced eyebrow says oh, I forgot, I bought some chocolate doughnuts.

161

Outside, balancing on the garden wall of number fifteen, the sister of the twins is talking to the daughter of the man with hurting hands, she says do you know what I can see angels, just like that, as if she was saying I had fishfingers for tea, and she takes the yellow ribbon from her hair and winds it around her finger like a yellow bandage. The younger girl looks up at her and says where? but it only comes out as a whisper.

The girl with the ribbon says well it depends, sometimes they come to my room and sit around my bed, they come in through my window if my mum leaves it open. They're really small she says, and she begins to unwind the ribbon from her finger. What do they do asks the younger girl, and her voice is still faint and breathy, they shine says the older girl, like bright bright lights with faces she says, and sometimes they sing, like imams only with girls' voices and the younger girl giggles, claps her small clean hand to her mouth and ducks her head and giggles.

And sometimes says the older girl, they fly around and around like this, and she whirls her ribbon through the air like a majorette, the tail of it spinning and twirling and drawing circle shapes around her head and the young girl giggles but the older girl is not smiling. Ssh she says, and she holds a finger to her lips, can you hear them now she says and the young girl looks up and around and her mouth falls open. Where? she says, where are they? and she looks all around her. They're really hard to see says the older girl, they're really small and anyway it's probably too sunny they're harder to see in the daytime.

She whisks her head round as if watching a passing car, she says there did you see, there was one, it was really fast, did you see, and the younger girl shakes her head.

The older girl keeps talking, she says I think it's gone now, sometimes they stay still but they have to be careful

162

because they can't hardly touch the ground because if they do they die but they can only talk to you if they are touching the ground so what they do is they do this.

She holds out her arms, the ribbon trailing from one hand like a kite-tail, and she lifts up her left leg, leaning forward slightly and holding it out behind her, trying to rise up onto her toes, each wobble sending ripples down the yellow ribbon.

She says and then they're safe because they're not really touching the ground but they are enough to talk to you, and then she wobbles too far and falls back to earth. The younger girl is pulling a frowning face and she says what do they say?

Just things says the girl, winding her ribbon around her finger again, they tell me things about people, things they can see. They tell me what it's like to be an angel she says, it sounds really nice she says I think I might be one one day.

She says and when they talk they only whisper in your ear to make sure no one can hear them and their mouths feel wet on your ears like warm icecream. She says they told me you mustn't stand on the cracks or you'll fall down and be stuck inside the ground forever.

She says do you know what if someone dies all the angels go to their house at night and shine over the roof, loads of them, and they get so bright that the birds start singing because they think it's the daytime but they only stay for a little while, right in the middle of the night so that no one can see them they don't like to be seen, they said I was lucky to see them.

The younger girl doesn't say anything, she keeps looking around her, looking up and down the street, looking for lights hurtling up and down the concrete and touching the ground with only the tips of their toes.

She can see trees, and sky, and houses, and boys playing cricket.

My mother is Scottish, my dad is not, and I've always assumed that this makes me half Scottish, but I don't feel it.

I've got no trace of an accent, I've never eaten porridge, I've never trampled glumly through wet heather whilst my mother told me about her childhood.

My grandmother's funeral was the only time I've ever been to Scotland, the only time I've caught sight of the wilder landscape and the broader sky.

I don't remember my mother talking about these things, or suggesting that we go to these places, and I don't remember her ever having an accent.

Occasionally, when she was very angry, I would hear echoes of it, a naughty that rhymed with dotty, a rolling of the R in girl, a growl over the K in put away your books, but mostly her voice was plain and carefully flavourless.

Her Scottishness, and the portion of it handed to me, was a secret, something to be concealed and denied, and I have never understood why this was.

I asked her once, and she pretended not to understand me.

She changed the subject, asked me if I had a boyfriend yet, and we had an argument and I forgot what I'd asked her.

She was clever, in that way.

And so I wonder if the mathematics of genealogy will make my child three-quarters Scottish, and I can't see how that would make sense.

I put my hand to my belly, imagining the knitting together of cells going on inside me, picturing the swelling of flesh and the stretching of skin, the shaping of limbs and fingers.

I imagine my body suddenly hollow again, a crying baby crushed hushingly against my face.

I imagine my baby's first words, and they're not spoken with a Scottish accent.

I wonder if perhaps I'll become guilty about this, if I'll feel obliged to teach my child about its heritage, if we'll go to Scotland on holidays.

Perhaps we could live there, up amongst the long nights and hard rain and beautiful land, and I could raise a child with clean air in its lungs, and a broad accent, and a strong sense of place.

Maybe one day we could go to Aberdeen, and track down the waiter-boy, and I could say here, darling, this is where half the cells in your body have come from.

I find myself thinking happy families again, and I'm flooded for a moment with the taste of him, the feel of him, the delicious perfection of our passing moment.

And I scrub the image from my mind, like lipstick from a shirt, like graffiti from a wall.

I'm thinking about all this, sitting in my old living room, watching my dad watch the television, listening to my mother crash things about in the kitchen.

She offered to make a cup of tea, but I think really she just wanted to leave the room because I haven't heard the kettle boiling for half an hour now.

I told her about him, about the boy in Aberdeen, and her politeness turned inside out like an umbrella in a storm.

Her face flushed hot and red and shiny, and I'm sure I heard the words you dirty wee something come gasping out before she clamped her hand to her mouth, and the words had a sharp accent running through them and she turned her face away.

She said, not looking at me, and have you spoken to him at all since then, has he been in touch?

I told her that he didn't have my phone number, that I didn't have his.

She said so that's all it was then, a fling in the dark, a one-night stand and no precautions? and she made the last word rhyme with oceans.

I said mum, please, I'm not ashamed and I don't want to apologise to you.

I said, but mum, I do need your help.

She looked at me then, when I said that, and her face softened and I thought I'd got through to her.

Oh but I thought you were an independent woman now she said.

I looked at her, and I realised that my jacket was folded across my lap, like a disguise.

Or like a shield.

I thought you were quite happily making it on your own she said, and her face hardened again as suddenly as a slamming door.

I didn't know what to say.

I looked at my dad, but he was staring fixedly at the soundless television, his fingers scratching the arm of his chair.

She said how much do you need?

I said mum I'm not talking about money.

Nobody said anything for a while.

I looked at the ceiling and I blinked a lot, I swallowed hard, my eyes felt wet and I didn't want them to.

I didn't want my voice to wobble the next time I spoke.

My dad started to turn the volume back up on the television, but he muted it again when my mother gave him a look.

She said and what was he like, this young man, would we like him if we met him?

She said I'm assuming he was a young man was he?

Yes mum I said, he was, he was a bit younger than me I should think.

And then I saw the tight purse of her lips and the puff of her chest and I felt a flush of spite so I said but no I don't think you'd like him, he wasn't so very interesting.

He wasn't so bright I said, he just had a nice voice, and nice eyes, and a great body, and, you know, and I left the end of my sentence hanging in the air like a cloud of cigarette smoke wafting into her face.

She went to make the tea after that, her self-control unwavering, her poise as steady as a gymnast, and my dad waited until he could hear her banging cupboard doors in the kitchen before he turned the sound up on the television.

He'd been watching one of his boxing videos again, I didn't remember seeing it before but then they all look the same to me, two men in a square of ropes, grainy black and white picture, fists slamming into faces.

My dad, overweight and unexercised, is a great boxing fan, knowledgeable and opinionated and passionate.

He used to spend hours talking to me about it when I was a kid, the stories going straight over my head while I dreamed about being a fashion designer.

I look at him now, his eyes dancing across the screen like a fighter's footwork, the light from the television making his face shine.

He says look at this, do you know this one, it's Ali versus Terrell, Terrell's been calling him Cassius Clay, he said I don't know no Ali, but you see to Ali the Clay name is a slave name, like a white man's name, he doesn't want it he says.

When he talks about boxing his face comes alive, his voice comes from a different part of him.

He says look, here, Ali could have knocked him out ages ago, but he wants Terrell to say his name, look he keeps asking him, hitting him again, asking him, look.

I watch, and I hear Muhammad Ali's voice ringing out of the television like a song, saying what's my name? what's my name?, the fury of the question channelled into petrol-bomb punches, holding his fists up like hammers over rocks, singing what's my name? what's my name?

I say dad, do you think I'm a bad person as well?

Your mum doesn't think you're a bad person he says, she just, she needs a while.

It's not what she was expecting he says.

It's not what I was expecting I say.

I look at him, I want to ask him this, I think he'll be honest with me, I say but what do you think dad?

He breathes heavily, he squeezes his forehead with his thumb and fingers, he says I don't know love.

He says I think you've been very unlucky.

He says I think you need to make some difficult decisions.

He says but I'll get used to it.

And mum I say, do you think she'll ever get used to it?

He picks up the remote control and presses the red button and the screen goes blank and I realise I've never seen him do that before.

You have to give your mother some leeway he says, she doesn't always mean to be the way she is.

You're a clever girl he says, but there are some things you don't understand.

He's looking straight at me now, leaning forward, talking
quietly.

He says when your grandmother died your mother cried
solidly for a week, solidly.

She was crying with relief he says, it was like as if a door had
been unlocked and she'd been let outside, she said to me
I'm safe now.

He waits, and he says this kid, when it's born, you mustn't
ever let it think it's anything other than a gift and a
blessing, do you hear me?

I nod, and he sits back in his chair looking tired and old.

He watches the video again, and I watch him, the way the
light shines blue and white across his worn-out face.

Ali is looming up above the camera, a man on top of the
world, saying I wrestled with the alligators.

I look at the lines on my father's face, my daddy's face, each
one carved out by the long passing of a year, and I think
about how little I've known all this time.

I want to run my thumbs across his face and smooth those
creases away.

Muhammad Ali dances on the tips of his toes, saying I'm so
quick I make medicine sick, the two dozen cameras and
microphones around him laughing and drinking him in,
calling his name.

My father, the strongman, holding my mother up all those
years.

I want to go to him and hold him like a baby.

I sit on the sofa and listen to my mother moving around in
the kitchen.

I hear her going up the stairs, slowly.

He opens the front door, the man with the carefully trimmed moustache who lives downstairs at number twenty, he touches a hand to his bow-tie and he steps out into the middle of the day. He glances up and down the street, he sees a ladder propped up against the wall of number twenty-five, he sees a young girl with a ribbon balancing on the wall opposite, he sees the twins arguing about whose turn it is to bat. He looks higher, he sees a construction crane hanging over rooftops a few streets away, his heart bangs a little harder but he smiles and sets off in that direction.

He remembers what they'd said, at the club, when he'd first put his name down for this, are you sure they'd said, at your age they'd said. He'd smiled then, pointed at the heading on the sheet, what does that say he'd asked the young lady trying to dissuade him, and she'd read it out for him, as though his eyesight was poor, it says Veterans and Widows Benevolent Fund she said. Well then he said to her, I am not a veteran, I was too young to be a veteran, so do not be saying this a man of my age, I am too young for you to be saying this to me he told her. These people, he said, his finger jabbing at the word veterans, these people did everything for me, and for you, don't forget this. She had been quiet by this stage, embarrassed, and he'd felt bad for her. This, he said, this is the least I can do, this I can do with my eyes closed. And he'd paused, looked around, picked up his drink, and said I bloody will have my eyes closed for certain, and everyone in the club laughed and the young lady had looked at him and smiled.

He chuckles now, remembering it, pleased with himself, and he walks down the street, past two girls drinking tea and reading magazines, past a boy scrubbing his shoes, past a house with all the curtains closed still, turning right at the end of the street and then he is gone and nobody notices him leaving.

Outside number seventeen, they are sitting on the wall and eating chocolate doughnuts, they are talking with their mouths full, the boy with the pierced eyebrow is saying and I don't think anyone really believed in this thing, that was the problem, no one believed in it. He says I know I didn't, or any of the other sellers, or the managers or the printers or even the pilots who go around taking the pictures.

A girl with a yellow ribbon trails past them and pushes open the door of number nineteen. She stops in her hallway for a moment to outline a pattern on the wallpaper with her fingers, and then she drifts into the front room. Her parents and grandparents are all sitting there, watching the television, John says there is a small band of low pressure sweeping northwards this afternoon and nobody in the room is speaking. The girl's mother looks up, she speaks quietly so as not to disturb the others, she says love why don't you go and play with your brothers? and the girl says they're playing cricket they won't let me play they say girls can't play and as she talks she is backing out of the room. Her mother says tell them they are wrong, tell them I say you can play, and the girl drifts out of the room, her ribbon trailing behind her like the wake of a boat.

Outside, she looks at her brothers playing cricket, she looks away and she walks straight past them. The tall girl on the wall next door sees her and says hello but the young girl pretends not to hear.

The tall girl is looking at her eyes in a silver pocket mirror. They are watery, greasy-looking, and the skin around them, without the glitter now, is swollen and grey. She dabs cream onto the skin with her little finger and rubs it in, wincing. She puts the mirror down on the wall beside her. It's engraved with the name of a women's magazine. She picks up a pipette of eyedrops and leans her head back into the sun.

The boy with the pierced eyebrow says and the worst bit was each evening we had to boast about how many people we'd sold to that day, they did this thing where we all stood in a room and played a different musical instrument depending on our numbers. The other boy reappears in the doorway behind them, doing up the buttons on a freshly ironed shirt.

What's he talking about he says to the girl, his job she says without turning around or sounding very interested.

Outside number twenty-three, the boy with the big hair is saying you've got to use something else, the charcoal's not getting a chance to catch, try some lighter fluid or something, and he presses down on the lighter tab, he sprays a thin drizzle of fluid over the coals and the singed newspaper. The boy with the yellow sunglasses says that'll do that's enough try that, and he lights it and flinches back as a halo of soft blue flame wraps suddenly and briefly around the cold coals.

In the doorway of number seventeen, the boy with the white shirt unrolls a navy-blue tie and slings it around his neck. The tall girl says yeah well at least you got to work outside, I've been stuck inside all summer, and the eyebrow boy looks at her and says what were you doing anyway?

She tips her head back and drops another splash into her eye, and she says I've been ripping free gifts off magazines. He looks at her.

She blinks rapidly and lowers her head, I've been sat in a room without windows she says, ripping the free gifts off magazines so they can be recycled. The boy with the pierced eyebrow looks at her and doesn't say anything.

The boy in the white shirt does up his tie and says have you seen my black shoes to the girl.

No she says, and she turns and she says your tie's not straight.

The eyebrow boy turns round and says where are you going dressed up like that and the smart boy says new job, telephone helpline at a mortgage company.

The boy with the pierced eyebrow slaps the palm of one hand with the back of the other and makes a loud noise in the back of his throat. He says, for fucksake, didn't our parents used to make stuff for a living?

On the front step of number twenty-two, the girl with the short blonde hair and the small square glasses is watching the boy from number twenty-four cleaning his trainers. He is sitting on his front step, his hands wrestling in a bowl of hot soapy water, thrashing around as though the shoe were trying to escape, she wonders why he's so keen to get them clean, she watches the soap bubbles sparkling in the air like a flung handful of crushed glass.

Across the road, outside number twenty-three, the boy with the big hair and the grazes is watching the other boy put together another careful pyramid of paper and sticks and charcoal, shielding it with his hands as he lights it. He says what's with the yellow glasses anyway, where'd you get them from? and the other boy takes them off and looks at them, help the aged or something he says, try them on. He puts them on, the boy with the big hair and the grazes, and the other boy says the woman in the shop said they used to give them to mental patients, like to cheer them up or something. The boy with the big hair looks around at the street, grinning, everything gone a strange saturated yellow. He takes them off and hands them back, he says well mad and he rubs his eyes as if to get rid of any leftover tint. They both turn back to the barbecue just as the pyramid of paper and sticks stops smouldering again, and the boy with the big hair and the grazes says fuck this I'm going down the shop to get some fire-lighters or something. The other boy says no hold on hold on, but when he turns round the big-haired boy has already picked up his skateboard and stepped it onto the pavement. He watches as he kicks up some speed, bending his knees as the wheels knock over the uneven slabs, holding his hands out slightly and, as he passes number seventeen, leaning the board towards the road, shifting his weight suddenly, pushing down with his back foot.

And they all watch, the people outside number seventeen, the two girls at number twenty-two, the man with the burnt hands, the twins in the road, the boy in the yellow sunglasses, they watch as he lifts off the pavement and the board swings up beneath him, his body crouching suddenly and his hand grabbing at the illustrated underside of the board before the wheels hit ground again and the momentum carries him forward towards the shop.

The boy on the tricycle stops pedalling, he drifts to a halt as he turns and watches the skateboard pass, his mouth is open and he doesn't understand what he has just seen, when he tries to tell his mother later he won't know what words to use, and she won't understand what he is trying to say, so she will stroke his hair and fetch him a drink of juice.

The boy with the skateboard jumps off and disappears into the shop, and the boy outside number twenty-four goes back to cleaning his trainers and the girl next door looks at him again.

She says excuse me sorry and he looks up, his hands stop moving, she says sorry but what are you doing, it's way too nice a day to bother with that isn't it, and he holds up a dripping shoe with his hand inside, like a glove puppet coming out of a bath, he points to a dark brown stain curled like a foetus across the white toe. He says I'm trying to get rid of that, these trainers are new and I'm not having that staying on there.

The girl says what is it, curry sauce or something, and he smiles and says no, he says no I was out last night and the bloke I was with got into an argument with someone. He puts the wet shoe down and turns to face her, he leans towards her slightly so she can hear him better. He says I knew it was trouble but I couldn't split because he'd given me his drink to hold and I couldn't see anywhere to put it down.

He wipes sweat and soap from his forehead with the bottom of his t-shirt, he says next thing I knew was he was biting a chunk out of this bloke's nose, I couldn't believe it, there was like blood and shit all over the place he says, and now I can't get my trainers clean he says.

The girl with the glasses says what's that noise? and they turn and they listen and they look at each other.

They listen, and there's a rumbling from somewhere, becoming a rattle, a rattle like the window-frames of a drum and bass club, they can't tell what it is but it sounds like it's coming from further up the main road, they stand and they look, it sounds like a car without tyres rolling down the hill, the twins stop playing cricket and run to the end of the street, even the man with the burnt hands stands and looks and the noise is now so loud that none of them can speak, the rumble rattle hudderjudder, and they hear shrieks and whoops and yes alrights and

And a dozen chairs roll past the end of the street, office

chairs with swivel bases and ergonomically adjusted back-rests, racing down the steep main road, eleven riders cling-ing onto them, trying to steer by stabbing their feet onto the tarmac, hollering encouragement to each other, bracing themselves for the inevitable fall, an empty chair following behind them like a riderless horse at the Grand National, and then they are gone, the noise fading quickly, and the people in the street turn to look at one another, blinking, saying what the and then carrying on with what they were doing, talking, drinking tea, eating doughnuts, getting ready to go to work, playing cricket.

A bus stops at the end of the street, the doors open and the old couple from number twenty step awkwardly down. The old man says thankyou driver, turning to touch his hat as the doors flop closed. As the bus pulls away, a young boy squeezes his face through a window on the top deck, spitting out a spray of phlegm which falls towards them accompanied by the high-pitched wail of children's laugh-ter.

She looks at him, she feels his body stiffen like a stretched rope, she squeezes his arm and they turn and walk away.

She doesn't say anything as they walk down the street, she doesn't need to and she knows he doesn't want her to.

He takes a handkerchief from his breast pocket, wiping at the thick string of spit on his sleeve, carefully folding the red silk and holding it out to one side.

The boy with the tricycle rattles towards them, head down, and they step neatly around him.

He walks calmly, his back as straight as ever, his breath-ing a little loud but his face still impassive.

They cross the street to their front door, he says which one of you two is Ian Botham then, but he says it quietly and the twins don't know who he's talking about.

And it's only when they have closed the front door behind them that he says what did I do? I didn't even look at them. I know love she says, I know, and she takes him by the arm and they walk up the stairs.

And as he stands by the coat-hooks and takes off his hat, he sees a spade and a fork through the open cupboard door, he thinks of the things he's never talked to her about, he thinks of the medal propped on the windowsill, he thinks about her walking back from the allotments on her own.

He turns and watches her moving through to the kitchen, he remembers those first few months and years after he'd come back, when she'd asked him, pleaded gently with him to tell her something, to not hide it all but to share it with her.

He takes the handkerchief through to the bathroom and rinses it under the hot tap, squeezing and soaking it until the steam rises.

He didn't tell her anything, because there was nothing to tell. There was no answer to the question of what did you do in the war, because he had done nothing. After years of training and preparation, after days of tension and a terrified journey across the channel, after all that he had done nothing and he had nothing to tell. He had travelled halfway across Europe, and when it was over he had travelled back, but somehow the war had passed him by, as if he'd been asleep when the others had started and he'd spent the whole time trying to catch up.

At the beaches of Normandy he had leapt into the cold sea and waded onto the desecrated sand with no more need for caution than on a daytrip to Blackpool. Across northern France and Belgium he had marched in time along cratered tarmac roads, past flattened woodlands where single bare trees stuck uselessly out of the desolate soil like dead men's stiffened arms jabbed accusingly at the sky. He had passed through towns captured for the fourth time, crossed rivers bridged by floating pontoons and planks, seen farmhouses broken open and smoking from battles which had only just moved on, eaten meals with bandaged men heading in the other direction.

He wrings the hot water from the handkerchief and hangs it from the line strung over the bath. He looks at his hands, wide flat hands with uncalloused skin and neat fingernails, and he scrubs them clean with a nailbrush.

He'd dug graves. Right the way across the new map of Allied Europe he'd dug graves, following in the costly trail of liberation, his shovel cutting into the bloody soil and carving holes just deep enough for the uniformed bodies of young men. They had a chaplain assigned to their unit, an older man who would run short of breath as he scurried from hole to hole to offer blessing and sanctification to each fresh mound of soil. Between them all, himself and the rest of the men in his unit, they could dig hundreds of graves in a day, spread out across a field like farmworkers, their shovels rising and falling in unison, the chaplain standing beside each one in turn, naming each body if he could, commending each blank face to the company of saints as the soil shushed and fell back into the ground.

And they did this all the way to Berlin, the crack and thump of battle always off to the east, a fresh supply of bodies rolling back to them on flatbed trucks driven by men with faces as undisturbed as their own, handing over half-phrases of information with the bodies and the marker-sticks. Pushing through steady they'd say, or bit of a tight one, or got the bridge last night. And a few days later they'd be there, where it had been steady, or tight, or at the bridge. Sinking shovels into soil, beckoning over the redfaced

179

chaplain, painting a name and rank onto a marker-stick ready for the stonemasons. Or, if there wasn't a name, writing Unknown beneath the date.

Sometimes, when he was sure nobody was looking, he would make up a name, look at a man's young face and decide a name on the spot, like a fresh baptism, trying to disguise the brutal anonymity of what they were doing.

Those were the memories he carried with him when he travelled back home to his wife, picking mud from his fingernails and thinking of all the things he would be unable to tell her.

And they are the memories he's been shuffling around with all these years, unspoken because there is nothing to say, burying them deep down and finding them risen up again, the faces of the men, the smell of soil and flesh, the stumbling words of the chaplain drowned out by the distant noises of war.

And she doesn't understand why he doesn't want to put out his medal like a trophy.

And he can't tell her that he liberated Europe with a spade.

Next door, at number eighteen, the young man with the blinking eyes leans out of his window and takes some final photographs of the street, his packing almost completed. He squints through the viewfinder and snatches the images in quick succession.

The boy with the yellow sunglasses poking at the barbecue.

The man with the burnt hands sitting on an old wooden chair.

The twins playing cricket, arguing.

A crane, looming brightly over the rooftops.

And on the way home I hardly say a word to Michael.

He concentrates on driving, making small adjustments to the heating, the stereo, the angle of his seat, the speed of the windscreen wipers.

I look out of the window, or close my eyes, and I think about the way of things now.

I think about my mother crying for a week, and I try to imagine her hard dry face changed in that way.

I picture precious water falling on desert ground and rolling across the surface like beads.

I picture a tap left on in a deserted house, reconnected at source and suddenly gushing forth with bright clean water.

And I picture my mother, actually, her face bloated and streaked, her eyes bloodshot and waterlogged, a handkerchief squashed into her hand like a sponge.

I wonder if she stayed in bed that week, buried in a mound of bedclothes, or if she stalked the house like an exorcist, or if she just fell to the floor beside the telephone and refused to move.

I wonder how my father felt when he heard her say the words, I'm safe now, if his heart leapt up inside him, I wonder if he was holding her at the time.

I remember that breakfast in the Little Chef again, a tiny brick building tucked into a valley of stone and pine and heather, I remember looking out of the window as though I was just waking up, saying where are we, looking up at the endless reach of the mountain into the sky.

And the whole thing creeps back to me, and I wonder how

such important memories become veiled from us, like front rooms hidden behind net curtains.

My dad saying we're in Scotland now, look at it love, this is Scotland, and me not understanding what he meant.

My mother slamming down her knife and fork so hard I thought she'd broken the plate, saying we're not going, I can't do it, we're not going.

My dad talking quietly to her, trying to touch her hand and she kept moving it away.

Like two magnets face to face.

And he was talking so quietly that I couldn't hear him, and I don't think I would have understood if I could, and so I joined the dots on my placemat.

My mother saying you don't understand I'm not going.

Leaving so quickly that I didn't get a lolly even though I'd cleaned my plate, and not arriving back home until it was dark again.

I think about what it was that stopped her going, that made her feel unsafe for all that time.

I wonder how many ways there are for a mother to produce that wreckage in her own daughter, and my muscles tense as I think of them.

Locked doors, a belt, bruises in hidden places.

Sharp words, absent touches, thin blankets, empty plates.

I think about the times I thought of her as a hard woman, an unfair mother, and I realise what mercifully pale reflections those moments were.

He says are you asleep, gently, and I open my eyes and he says are you okay?

I say yes, fine, I'm just a bit tired.

He says do you want to stop for something to eat?

I could do with a rest he says, and he squeezes the back of his neck the same way my father used to.

He was always a weary man, my dad.

He seemed to be permanently in the lounge, watching television, slung low in the armchair with his feet up on the table, dark patches on his white socks like mould on soft fruit.

He never seemed to be watching the programmes, unless they were boxing-related, but it was impossible to change the channel without him noticing.

When he did move around the house he moved slowly, easing his workboots off by the door, shuffling through to speak to my mother, settling into his chair as if into a hot bath.

Sometimes when I got back from school he'd already be there, not in his chair but scraping his way through the house, cleaning slowly.

The curtains would always be closed on those days, my mother an absent presence upstairs.

Your mother's not feeling so good today my dad would say, but she never went to the doctor's.

He would cook me tea, burning fishfingers under the grill with tiredness clouding his eyes like bruises.

Once we ate from paper plates, and I didn't think to ask why.

He says there's some services here do you want to stop for a while, and he's already indicating so I say yes and we drive in and park.

We sit in the restaurant in the bridge, picking at overpriced and overheated food, watching the traffic slashing beneath us.

There's a group of women at the table next to us, and I hear one of them saying but I don't understand why he was naked in the first place.

He says so anyway how did you get on then, was it okay?

183

I say well my mum at least admitted she wasn't that
impressed, I think, and my dad didn't say much at all.
I don't tell him what my dad did say.
A woman at the next table says I didn't really think he was
like that, and another woman says well he's not usually is
he.
He says but do you think it was worth going, and I say yes,
yes it was, I think maybe I've started something, I think
maybe they just need a little more time.
One of the women says no it was Phoebe's idea, she said he
needed to show some empathy, to get the apartment,
you know, with the ugly naked guy.

I stand by the entrance and wait for him to come out of the
toilet.
I watch a boy with David Beckham on his t-shirt playing a
football game in the arcades.
I watch a woman with a pushchair waiting for someone to
hold the door open for her.
I look at the pushchair, at the bag dangling from the back of
it, spilling over with nappies and cloths and bottles and
all the other paraphernalia of babydom that I know
nothing about.
I realise that I haven't begun to think about any of these
things, prams, pushchairs, cots, nappies.
I realise that I will soon be a mother, and my stomach
goes sick at the thought of it, greasy and fluid and
unstable.
My face feels red, my legs feel as thin as paper.
He comes out of the toilet, he sees me and says are you
alright you don't look alright, I say yes I just need to sit
down.
As we walk to the car I feel his hand hovering by my elbow,
waiting to grab me.

We drive back onto the motorway and I swallow weakly a
few times, trying to keep the sickness down.

I wipe my face with my fingers and he says is it too hot, do
you want some air?

I say no it's fine, I just, I feel a bit, queasy.

I wonder if this is the nausea I read about in those leaflets,
or if it's just tiredness and stress and travelling in a car.

I want to talk to my mother about it, properly.

I want to say mum I'm so scared I feel like puking, I have no
idea how to deal with this.

To say mum I don't even know how to change a nappy, I
don't know what to feed a baby, I don't know any
lullabies.

Mum, I want to say, I don't even think my breasts are big
enough to produce milk, I don't know how to get it out, I
don't know any of the things you're supposed to know, I
want to say mum will it hurt?

And then I want to ask her if this is how she felt when she
was pregnant with me.

I remember the few times I tried to talk to her about
anything serious while I still lived at home, boys or
schoolwork or friends who didn't feel like friends.

I remember the way her face used to shrink slightly, her
eyes narrowing and looking quickly around the room, her
hands fluttering like birds in a pet shop.

I wouldn't worry about it love she'd say, every time,
things'll be better soon she'd say, and she'd change
the subject, or suddenly remember to do something,
rush out to the shops before they closed.

I remember the disappointment I used to feel, the compar-
isons I used to make with other girls' mums.

I knew girls whose mothers would help them with their
homework, buy them new outfits for new boyfriends,

kiss them on the cheek whenever they came through the front door.

I knew girls, sometimes the same girls, whose mothers would shout at them when they got home late, or ground them if they didn't approve of their boyfriends, or make them help with the housework.

My mother did none of these things.

My mother was polite, and responsible, and didn't always seem to notice I was there.

I think of what my father said, and I think of the grief and rage she must have had stuffed down inside her like a rag in a petrol-filled bottle, and I wonder how she never exploded.

We get closer to home, we come off the motorway and there are lights shining in through the windows, street lights, traffic lights, lights from shop windows and houses and pub doorways, there is music coming from other cars and there are large groups of people talking and shouting and singing.

We go round a mini roundabout, we stop at a green light to let an ambulance through.

He says what's going on, why's it so busy?

I don't know I say, and we drive past the cafe where we had breakfast the other day and I realise we're almost there.

I say well thanks for driving me all that way, I really appreciate it, and he looks at me and says that's okay don't worry.

We stop outside the shop below my flat and he says if there's anything I can do, if you need anything.

I look at him, and I think about all the things I need.

He gets out of the car, takes my bag from the boot, opens my door, hands me my bag.

We say goodbye, and I go up to my flat and sit by the window without turning the lights on, watching the traffic and thinking about how little I said to him on the way back.

There's a hooting, outside, and the twins grab a milk crate each and drag their cricket pitch off the road to let a car drive past.

The car is burgundy red, wide and elegant, ten years old but still the boys are impressed and they run to touch it, pressing sticky handprints against the polished bodywork and trying to climb up onto the bonnet. The car stops outside number nineteen, and the driver gets out and says hey boys now, what you doing uh, you making a mess of my car, and they come and stand in front of him, side by side, hands behind their backs and together they say hello uncle how are you we are pleased to see you, and they giggle and hit each other on the backs of their heads.

The uncle takes a handkerchief from his pocket and says right right, go and tell your mother I'm here okay, and then he turns and polishes the marks of their hands away and they race each other to the front door. The girl with the short blonde hair and the small square glasses, outside number twenty-two, she looks up from a pageful of job adverts and sees the man, he's a young man and he's very well dressed, he turns and sees her looking at him and calls out a greeting, how are you he says and he holds the sun out of his eyes with the back of his hand. She is surprised, she smiles, she says fine and rests her chin on her knuckles and looks at him. He looks back, he hesitates and he almost takes a step towards her.

He turns, and he polishes a hand mark on the bonnet, rubbing at the already gleaming metal as though it were an oil lamp.

The girl goes back to her job adverts, she picks up a red

pen and scribbles out a circle she drew earlier, the moment has passed and she doesn't notice the man glancing over his shoulder at her. Another girl comes out of the house and sits beside her, she puts two mugs of tea down on the stone path and she says was there someone round this morning, I thought I heard voices. She looks at the girl with the glasses and the short blonde hair and she says it wasn't someone who stayed was it? The girl with the glasses laughs and says yeah right, as if, I was talking to the landlord, I was seeing if we could stay a bit longer. The other girl is still wearing her tartan pyjamas, she rubs her eyes and says what did he say? and the girl with the glasses says he said someone's supposed to be moving in tomorrow night. I can't pack she says, I've got too much stuff, I don't know what to do with it all. The girl in the pyjamas picks up one of the mugs of tea, decides it's still too hot, puts it down again. You've got to be ruthless she says, looking at the girl with the glasses, get yourself some binbags and throw it all away, landfill it she says, leave it for the archaeologists. You've got to travel light she says, start in a new place with empty hands. It's good for your karmic energy she says, and the other girl looks at her and laughs. Where did that come from she says, and the girl in the pyjamas shrugs, she says I don't know I read it in a magazine or something and she drinks her tea.

Over the road, the boy with the big hair is squirting more paraffin onto the flaming charcoals, he's grinning and saying fuckin A, that's more like it, and the boy in the yellow sunglasses is turning away and saying that's not how you're meant to do it, it won't burn properly now. The boy with the hair says well at least it is burning Baden-Powell, and the other boy says nothing, he goes into the house and loudly closes the door.

In the hallway of number nineteen, the twins' mother is telling them to please keep out of the way as they run up and down the stairs, into the kitchen, into the front room. Their grandparents are slowly preparing themselves to go out, he is straightening his jacket and placing his small round hat on his head, she is standing behind him and picking small pieces of pale blue fluff from his shoulders, she is pulling her cardigan a little tighter around her. Their daughter-in-law stands and watches, she says is it all okay have you got everything? and she says darling turn that off now your parents are going out. The boys come out of the kitchen with their cheeks squirrel full of pink coconut sweets, they squeeze between the adults and they burst back out of the house.

The young man cleaning his trainers looks up and sees them, sitting in his doorway at number twenty-four, he watches the six of them processing out of number nineteen, the two brothers leading the way, the grandmother and grandfather stepping slowly and carefully, each wincing as they reach the bottom step, and behind them the mother and father, the father still holding a remote control in his hand and he holds it behind his back.

The boy stops scrubbing his trainers, he wipes soap from his hands and he watches the young man by the burgundy car greeting the older couple, shaking the man's hand, kissing the woman's cheek, he sees the mother of the twins looking away down the street as though she is expecting someone to appear. He hears her calling a name and then saying something to her husband, he sees the elderly couple getting into the car and having the doors closed after them by the young man. He sees hands being shaken through open windows, the car driving away, the mother and father on their doorstep going back inside the house and closing the door.

He picks up the brush again, he scrubs at the dark stain

curled across the toe of his left shoe, thinking about last night and swearing quietly.

Next door the girl with the short blonde hair and the glasses stands up and says I'm going to the shop do you want anything?

In the hallway of number nineteen, the mother and the father look at each other, not smiling or searching or waiting for the other to speak, they are just looking.

She says, put that back by the television.

She says, I am going upstairs.

And she walks up the stairs, and although she is much older than she has been, and although her body is quicker to become weary than it ever was, she still feels the movement of herself beneath her clothes as a good and special thing.

She feels the soft slide of cotton against her thighs as she walks, the push of her breasts as she breathes, the pinching of the cloth into the turn of her waist as she straightens her back and pauses on the stairs to glance down at her husband.

He looks up at her, and his face is calm and patient, almost solemn, but inside his head he is throwing buckets of water onto burning coals. He looks at her, and he also is aware of his body beneath his clothes, he is aware of the reassuring miracle of manhood, the flesh-and-blood conjuring trick which stirs the slow energies of his ageing body. He follows her up the stairs, he looks at the way her hair falls down her back, the shift and shine of it, they step into their bedroom and he turns to close the door.

And in a moment the door will be locked, and the stillness and quiet will be left on this side of the door. They will both drop their politeness and reserve to the floor with their clothes, he will close the curtains and she will unveil her body, she will stand against the wall with her arms raised high, waiting for him to drink in his fill of the sight of her, she will lick her fingers, each in turn, as though sharpening them, and then they will be together and the room will fill with movement and laughter and stifled noises.

The rustle and fall of bedclothes.

Murmuring.

A rip of cotton.

A hand clapped over a mouth.

Outside, their twin boys are already playing cricket again, the younger twin hits out and the ball loops high in the air and lands in the garden of number seventeen just as the boy with the white shirt is saying I just wanted to give it a go, I wanted to get in tune with nature and like the cycle of life and stuff, I was reading this thing about reclaiming the masculine hunter and the tall thin girl laughs suddenly and sharply, catching a piece of chocolate doughnut in her throat.

The girl from number twenty-two, short hair and square glasses, she's walking past, she stops and she says do you want anything from the shop what's funny? The boy in the white shirt throws the ball back to the older twin, and the boy with the pierced eyebrow says hucklefuckinberry finn. The girl with the glasses looks at him, confused, and she looks at the boy in the white shirt who says I was just telling them about when I went fishing a while ago, that's all, they think it's funny, I don't know why he says, and the tall thin girl bites her lip. Did you catch anything says the girl with the glasses, and he says I did actually, after a couple of hours, a trout or something, and the short girl with the painted nails pulls a face and says did you kill it?

He says I tried to but I dropped it in the grass, it was flapping around and I couldn't get hold of it, I didn't know what to do, I thought it would just die anyway but it kept flapping for ages he says and the ball bounces off the wall behind him and lands in front of the boy with the pierced eyebrow.

So I picked up this big stick he says, and he rolls up a magazine to demonstrate, a copy of *Hello!*, and he says I stood there watching it drown, trying to hit it.

The older twin runs up and says give us the ball, and the boy with the pierced eyebrow slides it under his legs. Give us the fucking ball he says, and they look up at him with pretend shock and turn away. The ball's over there mate says the boy with the pierced eyebrow, and as the child turns to look he throws the ball, over his head, towards the garden of number twelve. The young boy looks back. Your hair's still wet he says, and he runs away.

So anyway says the boy in the white shirt, I hit it in the end, and he smacks the front step with the rolled-up face of the Duchess of York, twice, to demonstrate, and he says and then it stopped flapping so I took it back up to my mate's house and dealt with it, like washed it and scaled it and took all the guts and shit out, which was fucking obviously grim he says. And then I cooked it he says, and he sits back and looks away down the street and looks proud of himself.

So was it nice? says the girl with the glasses, and he looks at her and says well it looked nice, I fried it up in little steaks with garlic and black pepper and lemon and stuff, it smelt really good and he looks away and she says but what did it taste like? He says I don't know I couldn't eat it.

The boy with the pierced eyebrow takes some money out of his pocket and offers it to the girl with the glasses, he says can you get me some orange juice and she turns and walks down to the shop. The boy in the white shirt adjusts his tie and bites the knuckle of his thumb, he looks at the ground, he stands and goes inside to look for his black shoes.

Upstairs at number twenty, the old couple are busying themselves with the rituals of returning home, the kettle on the stove, the jackets on pegs, unlocking windows and letting a breeze back into the tightness of the rooms.

She hears the toilet flush, she hears his steps in the hallway and his low voice murmuring out a song again, one of his old church songs.

She catches the words thou mine inheritance, and he breaks off as he comes into the room and goes to the window.

He says did I ever tell you I was there when my grandfather died? Says it not looking at her, looking from the window down the length of the street, watching the boys with their cricket, listening to her clinking and clanking with teacups and plates. She says nothing, she takes off her navy-blue shoes and sits in one of the kitchen chairs, picks up her hat and straightens the ribbon.

He says and it might sound strange but it was a beautiful thing. Just to be there with the rest of the family he says. Watching him breathing, and curling his fingers, and sinking into his sheets he says. And he stands there by the window with his hand up to his face, curling his fingers slowly, like the clutch of a newborn baby. Reminding himself of how it was.

It seemed like the right thing to be doing he says, to be there with him. He turns round to look at his wife, do you think so he says.

She pours a cup of tea and says what do you mean? Come and sit down she says.

He pulls out a chair and says I mean does it seem like the right thing to you, having all the family there, well of course she says and she cuts him a slice of cake.

He says the room was full of people, crowded.

I was the last to get there he says, and when I walked in everyone was sat around, looking at him, not speaking. It was dreadful hot in there, and stuffy, and there was a soursweet smell in the room he says.

She looks at him, still standing behind the chair, and she says sit down love.

She brushes crumbs from her floral dress, sweeps them away with her flesh-knotted hand and they fall to the floor. She says why have you never told me this before, and she's thinking all these years and there are still things I don't know, she's wondering if this is a good thing or a bad thing.

He sits down and says I don't know I was just thinking about it, you know, and he pours himself a cup of tea.

They sit, and they sip small mouthfuls of steaming tea, and they look at each other. A breeze catches the curtain and it curls into the room.

He says we were there five, six hours before he died, and every breath sounded like his last. He says I thought he was going to go on forever.

The breeze sucks back out of the room, the curtain falls flat against the window, the bathroom door slams shut.

He says he had his head tipped right back, there was a wetness coming out of his mouth that my mother kept dabbing away with a white handkerchief, and when he breathed in it sounded like there was a bag of ball-bearings in his mouth. All rattling and clacking together he says, and the cup jingles against the saucer as he puts it down.

He says he looked so small, squashed flat into those enormous sheets and pillows.

He says he was wearing red and white striped pyjamas and they didn't fit him properly.

She's looking at him and wondering where all this has come from. She's looking at an unfamiliar expression in his face, a hardness of the skin. It is not something she recognises.

He says his whole face shook with it each time he breathed.

He says he made this wheezing sound, all slow and desperate, like a whale on the beach it made me think of.

She looks at him and she doesn't know what to say.

She says what did he die of, and when he replies oh it doesn't matter his weary anger surprises them both. He says sorry love but and then he doesn't finish the sentence and he looks away from her.

The curtain curls into the room again, and a stack of letters falls to the floor from the sideboard. She moves from the table to pick them up and he says he didn't say a word you know, not a word, he didn't even open his eyes, he just lay there dying.

He says his hair was so thin and light, like a baby's, it looked as though it would blow away if anyone opened the window.

He says you couldn't even see his legs under the bed-clothes he was so faded and gone. It seemed like all he had left was his head and his hands he says, and his chest staggering up and down.

And he says but it was funny you know, it didn't feel like a vigil so much, because of the talking, because after a time we started talking. Little things he says, pleasantries and distractions to ease the tension but by the time he died we were all in full flow.

He says it was strange but it seemed a good thing, that we could do that, just be a family and talk, not spend the whole time staring at him he says, and he stands up and leaves the room.

She watches him go, she listens to the awkwardness of his steps and the squeak of the bathroom door. She looks at his untouched slice of cake and she thinks about his unmentioned visits to the doctor.

He stands by the door and says he looked like a wax sculpture setting into the bed, and when he died he looked beautiful and I was glad to kiss him.

She says come here, come here.

She says what's all this about?

He looks down at her and settles into the hoop of her arms around his waist, he says oh I don't know love I was just thinking. She looks at his chest and she doesn't need to say that she wants him to try again, she looks up at him and she waits.

He says, look, love, it's.

He says, the thing is.

And after a while he unhooks her arms and moves away from her again, back towards the door. He stands there a moment, biting his lip and squeezing his eyes into sparrowfeet, and then he starts to turn back towards her. She looks at him, and he says the thing is love, when he died it was like he was getting better, do you see, and he's looking past her now, towards the window.

Each time his breath softened he sounded more comfortable he says, his face got more relaxed. And then he was almost closing his mouth between breaths at the end he says, and everyone stopped talking and stood up. He talks more quietly now, he says and then he just, went. So slow he says, like a bottle filling with water and sinking he says.

She says, love, and it's a question but she's not sure what she's asking.

He says nothing, he looks at the sky through the window, the light darkening a little. He says it looks like rain but she doesn't turn away from him to look. He says, love, I was just thinking about it, that's all, really, and he turns again and this time he leaves the room and she watches him go and listens to the hacking wetness of his cough.

On the table, an uneaten slice of cake, a half-empty cup of cold tea, crumbs.

There was no one there when I got to work this morning.

My keycard rejected, flicking back like a stuck-out tongue, and there was no one around to let me in.

I was hot and dizzy from the walk, I felt sick again, I needed to sit down.

A security guard came past and said it's a bank holiday love, and I must have looked like I was going to cry because she stopped grinning and offered me a drink and almost touched my arm.

I went and sat in her little office with her, looking at the closed circuit pictures while she made us both a cup of tea and her kettle was so small she had to boil it twice.

She said if you don't mind me saying love you don't look well enough to be at work anyhow.

I smiled and said no I'm okay I'm just pregnant and she said oh congratulations and asked me questions and showed me pictures of her new granddaughter.

She gave me lots of advice, she said drink stout and take folic acid, and mind you take it easy now.

I finished the tea and said thankyou and went home again, and on the way back I was sick by the bins behind the Chinese.

There was a message from Sarah on the answerphone.

It was a long message, so I left it playing while I cleared away the breakfast things.

She said what are you doing are you still in bed where have you been?

She said I've been trying to call you what have you been up to all weekend?

She said and so what about that guy, what's his name, that guy I gave your number to, did he call you, did you see him?

She gasped as though she was suddenly shocked and she giggled and said is that where you've been?

Have you been making babies she said, is he still there now?

There were voices in the background, she said look anyway got to go, she said but anyway I'm in your part of town today so call me and we can meet up.

She told me her mobile number, but she said it too fast and I had to listen to the whole message again before I could write it down.

I took my clothes off and got into the shower while I thought about calling her back.

It would be good to talk to her, maybe, but the idea made me nervous somehow.

I remembered the last time I tried to talk to her about it, and I thought that perhaps I just don't know her well enough anymore.

I filled my hair with shampoo and watched the lather pouring down over me, I looked at my skin and I wondered if anything was different, my breasts heavier, my stomach rounder, my hips wider.

It was hard to tell.

I looked at my body and tried to picture myself as a heavily pregnant woman, I stood with my feet further apart, my hands against the back of my hips, my stomach pushed out.

I felt like a nine-year-old, playing dress-up.

I rinsed off the soap and got out of the shower, and I was just about to brush my teeth when I was sick in the basin.

There was another message on the answerphone, it was Michael, he said just seeing if you're okay and I wondered if you were doing anything this afternoon and he told me his number.

When I open the door I say oh hello, and I look at him and we're both embarrassed.

He's holding a bunch of flowers, thick-stemmed white lilies with bright yellow centres and shiny green leaves.

I look at them, he looks at them, and water drips from the bottom of the wrapping onto his shoe.

Oh, I don't know what to say I tell him, and I don't.

He says oh, I'm sorry, I didn't mean, they're not, I mean it's not anything, I just thought, erm, shall I, and his sentence trails off into a row of faint full stops.

I say, oh, they are nice though.

He says, I just thought, you know, you seemed upset, yesterday, I thought maybe they'd cheer you up, I'm sorry.

I say no, sorry, they're nice, you just surprised me, that's all, I wasn't expecting, I just, look come in anyway, I'll put them in something.

He comes in and stands by the door, and I put the flowers in a vase by the window, the stems curving upwards like the arch of a dancer's back, the petals thick and glossy like morning eyes, the smell of them already beginning to fill the flat.

I make a pot of tea, and I pour it into thin white cups without saucers.

He says are you okay though, yesterday, was it hard?

I can't decide how to answer him, I start to say something deflective, something like well it was okay I think they'll come round, something that will slip from the question like shrugged shoulders from a shawl, but the words stick in my mouth.

I want to tell him something of what happened, the new

201

understanding I was granted, but those words are locked in as well.

I say yes it was, it was hard but not like I expected.

He says what do you mean and I say I don't know how to explain it I don't think it would make any sense.

He says have a go, he smiles and says I'm not as stupid as I look you know and he lifts his palms up.

I say actually can we talk about something else now and he stops smiling and says sorry, sorry.

I say, the flowers, I do like them, thankyou.

He sits at the table, opposite me, and he looks at the flowers and he looks out of the window.

I say I was thinking about your brother this morning, and his head startles round to look at me, I say I was wondering what it's like, being a twin.

He says what do you mean, I say well is it strange, do you feel different to anyone else?

He says I don't know it's hard to say, I've got nothing to compare it to, I don't know what it's like for other people.

It's not like people think he says, we're not telepathic or anything like that, but we've always been very close, we've always known most stuff about each other.

Connected he says, like we're connected.

And then he pulls a face and wipes his forehead with his hand and he says well less disconnected than other people at least.

He says it's hot in here do you mind if I open a window.

He tries to open the window, it sticks and he has to hit the frame with the heel of his hand.

He says you know that thing with his eyes, the blinking, and I nod.

I remember when his brother talked to me that day, blinking so hard that both his cheeks lifted up as if they were trying to meet his eyebrows.

He says that used to be the only way people could tell us apart, especially when we were at school and wearing the same clothes, it was the only difference between us.

He says I used to think he did it on purpose, just to be different, you know, I asked him about it once and he got really upset, he said it showed that even I didn't know him properly, he asked me why he would put it on when it made him look so stupid he says.

It doesn't make him look stupid I say, just a bit shy.

He looks at me, he picks up a pen from the table, a retractable biro, he starts clicking the point in and out, clickclick clickclick.

His hand clenches around the pen suddenly, his knuckles rising hard and white from his hand, he says he is not shy, my brother is not shy, and he weights each word as though he were underlining it with the pen in his hand.

He puts the pen down, he breathes out slowly, and I say I'm sorry I didn't mean, I just, I mean I don't know him really I was just saying.

He says look I'm sorry I think I should go I don't know what I'm doing here.

He stands by the door, and he can't get out because the key's not in the lock.

He waits, and I look at the back of his head and I want him to turn around and I want him to tell me what's wrong.

And suddenly more than anything I don't want him to leave.

He says have you got the key the door's locked, and he still doesn't turn around, he's talking to the door and his voice sounds strange.

I say don't go.

He says my brother isn't shy, but people never give him the chance, people don't make the effort to get to know him, nobody knows him really.

He says I'm not sure that I even know him, and he's still facing the door as he says this and I'm still looking at the back of his head.

I say don't go.

He turns around and he says I don't want to go I don't know where to go.

He sits down and there is a quietness between us for a long time.

He says I'm sorry, I didn't mean to be rude, it's just, I feel like he needs protecting sometimes.

He says he was born a few minutes before me but I've always felt like his big brother I'm not really sure why.

I say you know every time you talk about him I feel worse for not knowing him properly when we lived there, I feel as though I missed out and it was sort of my fault, as though I should apologise.

I hold one hand in the other and say doesn't he ever phone, do you think he could phone here and I could speak to him?

He says no he never phones, just like that, no explanation, and I think maybe I've upset him again, maybe this is too much hard work and I'm out of my depth here.

He says you know I told you he collected stuff, and took photos, I, he gave me them to look after and I think he wouldn't mind if I showed you, I mean I think he'd like it, would you like to see them, and already he's standing up.

I look at his sudden change of mood, I smile and say yes and unlock the door for him and watch him walking out to his car.

I look at my room, at the table with the flowers and the pot of tea, the two cups, I think how nice two cups on a table can look.

A shadow passes across the street, a faint imprint rolling briefly across the pavement and the tarmac, noticed only by the young daughter of the man with the aching hands, she is looking for things like this and she sees it passing as fast as a shiver and she looks up and sees a pair of wings high above her, perfectly white in the huge sky, a thin ribbon of vapour trailing out behind it.

As she looks up, a layer of cloud comes sliding into view, heavy and grey like unwashed net curtains and she watches the wings disappear, she watches the sky darken. She turns around and sees her father standing up, he is picking up his chair, hooking his arm through the seat back and dangling it from his elbow like a bag of shopping. She sees him stepping through their front door and looking over his shoulder at the sky. A cold wind pushes suddenly down the street, her hair lifts away from her neck, the milk crates in the street topple over and the bowler shouts you're out even though he's still holding the ball, the batsman stacking them back up and yelling it doesn't count it doesn't count you never even bowled I'm still in.

She looks up and sees more clouds scuffing in from the south, she sees the clouds swelling and darkening, the whole sky looking like the basin of water after her father has washed his hands. She is excited and she looks around her and she jumps from the pavement into the street. She sees the older girl, the one who told her about angels, she sees her at the end of the street, she comes running round the corner and straight along the pavement, her arm lifted high and the yellow ribbon streaming out behind her like a pennant from a car-radio aerial, she runs straight past and doesn't say a word, her shoes slapping on the pavement like slow applause.

The boy with the paper and pencil, sitting outside his house at number eleven, making a drawing of the street, he hasn't finished but he looks up at the sky and he gathers up his things and backs away into his house.

The man with the ladder, repositioning it against the side of his house at number twenty-five, he feels the drop in temperature and he glances above him and he hurries to put the lids back on his pots of paint, he picks them up and puts them in his hallway, he wraps the brushes in damp rags, he undoes his overalls and he steps back into his house.

The man cleaning his car, on the other side of the road, he curses to himself and he tries to rub the metalwork dry in time, he spreads a large cloth between his two hands and runs it over the roof and the bonnet and the side panels, he looks up and he empties his bucket of soapy water into the drain, he feels a splash of water on the back of his neck.

And there's a smell in the air, swelling and rolling, a smell like metal scraped clean of rust, a hard cleanness, the air tight with it, sprung, an electric tingle winding from the ground to the sky, a smell that unfurls in the back of the mouth, dense, clammy, a smell without a name but easy to recognise and everyone in the street knows it, besides the children, everyone is smelling the air and looking upwards, saying or thinking it smells like rain.

The boy on the front step of number eighteen, running his fingers along the red rims of his eyes, he sees a fat drop of water land on the ground in front of him, it spreads flat, it sucks up dust and it stains the pale concrete. He sees people drifting away into their houses, he sees the quietness that has come across the street, even the twins stopping their argument and looking upwards, expectantly.

He looks at the sheer blackness of the air, and he holds his breath.

He wonders how so much water can resist the pull of so much gravity for the time it takes such pregnant clouds to form, he wonders about the moment the rain begins, the turn from forming to falling, that slight silent pause in the physics of the sky as the critical mass is reached, the hesitation before the first swollen drop hurtles fatly and effortlessly to the ground. He thinks about this, and the rain begins to fall.

One, two, three drops at a time, a slow streak down a bedroom window, a wet thud onto a newspaper page, a hiss onto barbecue coals.

And after these first kissed hints there is the full embrace, the wetness of the sky pouring suddenly down upon this street, these houses, this city, falling with a strange quietness at first, gently gathering momentum until suddenly there is a noise like gravel slung at windows and the rain is falling hard, heavy, bouncing off the tarmac with such force that at ground level it's hard to tell if the rain is coming up or down, pounding the pavement and skidding across the hot dry surfaces of the street, gushing down rooftops into gutters and cracked drains, washing against windows and worn-out windowframes, hammering insistently against anything left open to the sky.

And the people who are still outside are taken by surprise, they gather up their wet newspapers and duck into their doorways, laughing at the sudden change, shaking their heads like bathtime dogs, they turn to each other and say where did that come from, they watch the children getting wet in the middle of it all, the children drenched already, soaked through with excitement, waving their tongues in the air to catch it, the boy with the tricycle, the young girl from number sixteen, the twins, the older twin waving the bat in the air, they are all dancing and shrieking at each other as if these were the first rains for months.

And the twins' sister reappears from further down the street, she is running, her ribbon trailing behind her, a nun-like expressionlessness lighting up her face, she stops beside the young daughter of the man with the burnt hands, she whispers something and they run together, side by side with the ribbon cutting into the rain, like a naked washing line, like a finishing tape, they run to the end of the street and they turn and they run back again, the older girl lost in the hidden delight of her secrets, the younger girl puzzled but exhilarated, she giggles and she tries to skip while they run.

Her father calls to her from his doorway, he calls her name, he says come inside now you are getting wet, and she drops her end of the ribbon and runs to him, the older girl running on, oblivious.

And the rain suddenly doubles, impossibly, a blind blanket of water falling right across the city and now even the twins retreat to shelter and now only the girl remains, the only daughter of the couple lost in each other in their room, she is using her ribbon like a butterfly net, she is trying to catch a baby, a sister, she asked her father where she came from once and he said my darling we plucked you out of thin air and so now she is trying to do the same, she stands in the road and she leans her body up into the rain, closing her eyes against the force of it until a car appears from round the corner, slooshing through the surface water like a snowplough and the girl looks at the car and the music in her head is silenced and the car squawks its horn, and the wheels lock, and there is a slight slide as the car rides over the surface of the water. She looks at the car, and the car knocks into the milk-crate wicket, and the milk crates topple, and she turns and runs into her house, leaving the ribbon lying in the road.

The car sits in the road, its windscreen wipers blipping angrily from side to side, its horn inaudible beneath the thunder of the rain.

And the rain falls hard and heavy, changing the colour and texture of the street, polishing every surface to a dark shine, soaking the dust from the air and drowning all other sound so that people can only watch.

The rain falls against the boy with the sore eyes, leaning out of his upstairs window taking polaroid photographs of it, shot after shot without moving the angle or changing the focus, plucking each newborn image from the camera and laying it wetly aside, the same frame changed each time, the rain falling through his viewfinder like missed opportunities and he watches and presses the shutter release and he doesn't blink and

the rain falls and seeps through the cracks in the felt roof of the attic at number twenty-two, the girl with the short hair and the glasses repositioning an empty icecream tub for the last time, watching the pond-ripples slipping back and forth as each invading drop falls from the stained ceiling, she is packing her possessions into bags and boxes, she is making herself ready to go but she is not sure where she is going or what will happen now, she takes CDs down from shelves and retrieves lost books and clothes from under the bed, she doesn't know where to put it all and she moves with the slowness of a child under orders to tidy her room and

the rain falls sauna-like into the barbecue outside number twenty-three, smoke piles from out of the hissing coals, the boy with the big hair and the grazes rushes suddenly out of the house and hefts a rainbow-striped golf umbrella over it, holding it out at an angle and swapping his scalding hands and

the rain falls against the bedroom window of number nineteen, waking the mother of the twins, she is sleeping with her face pressed against her husband's face, their limbs woven together like the branches of two yew trees, they are sleeping and she is woken by the water pummelling against the window. She doesn't move, she watches the ripples running down the glass through a gap in the curtains, she feels the satisfyingness of things like a physical sensation through her body, as if her breathing was the slow bowing of a cello, a hum and a met yearn playing through her and

the rain falls, catching the trailing edges of net curtains which flow out of open windows like fishing nets lowered over the backs of boats, nets hung neatly between the outside and the in, keeping floundering secrets firmly hidden and

the rain falls, easing, the noise dropping away, light beginning to leak back into the street through thin places in the clouds and the architecture student from number eleven presses his face to the glass and looks at the way the light falls through the water, he thinks about a place where he worked in the spring, an office where they had a stack of empty watercooler bottles against the window, and how he would sit and watch the sun mazing its way through the layers of refraction, the beauty of it, he called it spontaneous maths and he wanted to build architecture like it, he looks at the row of houses opposite and he pictures them built entirely of plastic and glass, he imagines how people's lives might change if their dwellings shook with endless reflections of light, he does not know if it's possible but he thinks it's a nice idea and

the rain falters and she still doesn't move, the mother of the twins, she is deeply happy and she breathes a kiss onto her husband's cheek, she feels a slow wave of it passing through her body like a memory, she closes her mouth and her eyes and holds the soft sound inside herself, letting it circle around the back of her mouth, drinking it quietly back down and

the rain slows further, and the man in the car finally opens his door and moves the milk crates, he flings them to the side and he glares at the twins hiding in their hallway, he drives away and the street is empty, washed and filled by this new and unexpected change and

the rain falls, gently now, past the small window of the attic flat of number twenty-one, the man with the tattoo is in bed again, smoking, and the woman with the henna-red hair is scooping up fallen petals from around a vase of roses, roses she has already kept for longer than they were intended to be kept, she takes the fallen petals and stuffs them into an empty jamjar and the man says what you doing that for? and she puts the jar on the windowsill, she turns to him, shadowed in the rain-darkened room, she says it catches the light that way, the light kind of comes through them and they look alive she says, glowing she says and

as the rain fades away there is stillness and quiet, light flooding rapidly into the street and through windows and open doors, the last few drops falling conspicuously onto an already steaming pavement, there are streams and dribbles and drips from gutters and pipes in various states of dis-repair, there is a quietness like a slow exhalation of tension that lasts only a moment before the children move back into the road, leaping into puddles, their wet clothes and hair drying rapidly under the returning heat of the sun and the boys set their wicket back up and allow play to resume, the storm passing across the rest of the city and out into the hills beyond.

213

When he comes back into the room his face seems lighter, there's an excitement about him, the box looks awkward and heavy but he's holding it as though it were weightless.

He puts it down on the table and immediately starts taking things out, you'll like this he says, you'll like this.

I say won't he mind, isn't it private or something, but already I'm standing close to him and looking down into the box.

No no he says, no, he'll be pleased, he always likes to show people this stuff, and he picks up a wooden case with a glass front and says look I told you about this didn't I?

I look at the row of syringes mounted in the case, the plungers at different heights, one of the needles snapped in half, all of the chambers smeared with a translucent brown coating, like tar from a pipecleaner wiped onto glass, and on the back he's written a date and some numbers that look like a map reference.

I start to ask him about it, but he's already passing me other things, a handwritten letter uncrumpled and pressed in a clipframe like a leaf, a washing-up glove, the bottom half of a broken wine bottle, a bunch of keys.

I look at these things, I say so what's it all for and he says he calls it urban archiving, he told me it was part of his archaeology, he says hold on that broken-glass necklace is in here somewhere.

I go to make some more tea, I stand in the kitchen doorway while the kettle boils, looking at him rummaging through the box, listening to his voice, and I say you're really proud of your brother aren't you, I can tell.

He stops, and he turns and looks at me, and he quietly says of course I am.

I pour another pot of tea, and I take it through to him, I put it down on the table next to the case of syringes and the pressed letter, next to the wine bottle and the keys, next to postcards covered in handwritten notes.

He's sitting down now, he's reading the notes, his excitement seems to have passed.

He picks more things out of the box, a cigarette packet, an unopened can of lager, a white plastic purse with a gold chain looped through its clasps, he holds each object and turns it over in the light, concentrating.

He says do you think there's too much of it?

I say I don't know, I mean some of it, some of it seems a bit, you know, less important.

He says he was talking about that a lot, before he went away, about there being too much, that's what all these things are about, his projects, he was trying to absorb some of it.

I say too much of what, he says too much of everything, too much stuff, too many places, too much information, too many people, too much of things for there to be too much of, there is too much to know and I don't know where to begin but I want to try.

I look up and see that he is reading these words from one of the cards, his voice is slightly different and I wonder if it's his reading voice or if he's trying to sound like his brother.

He picks up another postcard and reads, there are so many people in the world he says, and I want to know them all but I don't even know my next-door neighbour's name, and when he puts the postcard down I see it's actually a photograph, a picture of the old couple next door, taken from an upstairs window, walking down the street.

I pick up the postcards, they're all photographs, stuck onto card, and each one of them is of people living in that street.

There's one of the man with the scarred hands from a few doors further down, he's lifting his daughter up, she is sitting on the chair of his crossed forearms.

On the back of the card, he's written I think his name is Avtar, I wonder how long ago the fire was, his daughter is quite nervous, I don't know her name.

There's another one, of the twins from the house opposite, a picture of them in someone's backyard, pulling bin-bags out of bins, and on the back it says I don't know their names, they're always shouting, their sister is quiet and always seems to be hiding something behind her back.

There's a picture of the boys from number twenty-three, walking down the middle of the road, and on the back they're all named, it says Jamie, Michael knows him, Rob, skateboarder, Jim and Andy I don't know much about them except one of them plays guitar.

None of the people in the pictures look as though they know they're being photographed, they're all looking away slightly, unconcerned, uninvolved.

All the pictures have something in the corner, a window-frame, a curtain, a part of a front door, and all of the pictures look like secrets.

There's a picture of me, I'm walking away down the street, I'm turning my head back to look at something, and on the back he's written my name, he's written something else and then crossed it out with thick repeated lines.

I look at each card, almost everyone on the street photo-graphed and noted, sometimes a name, sometimes a comment, I look at each one in turn and when I have finished I stack them all in a neat pile.

The woman from over the road, the mum of the twins, standing at an open upstairs window, looking into the street, smiling, looking much younger than she must have been.

The man from next door, holding his hat off and pushing his fingers across his head like a comb, on the back it says I think they have an allotment somewhere but I think only his wife goes there.

I remember seeing her, pulling a shopping-bag trolley with a garden spade waving out of the top, trundling past, already wearing her gardening gloves, turning to us and saying hi-ho.

The man who was always washing his car, an empty bucket in his hand, a wet stripe down the front of his shirt as though he'd been running a race.

The young couple from the top flat opposite, I used to hear them arguing all the time but the picture shows them hand in hand and he is laughing.

There are other photos as well, without people, stuck to the cards without any explanation on the back, an armchair in an alleyway, a lamp-post painted red and green, a pigeon flying past with a twig in its beak.

A picture of a pavement by a bus stop, chickenpoxed with grey spots of spat chewing gum.

But mostly the pictures are of people, and mostly people in the street, the boy with the pierced eyebrow, the thin father of the kid with the tricycle, the man in the shop, standing behind his counter and smiling broadly into the camera.

On the back it says he was the only one I could ask, his name is Mr Rozi.

He says did you know all those people, I say I recognise them, I didn't really know any of them, he says no.

He takes more things out of the box, a handful of curtain hooks, a jamjar full of cigarette ends.

He looks at the jar, he looks at me and he laughs, he says some of this stuff, it's a bit, I don't know, and he picks up the curtain hooks and starts passing them from hand to hand, letting them fall from one to the other like dominoes.

I say if he collects this much stuff while he's travelling he'll be driving a lorry by the time he comes back, and he looks up and half-smiles and the phone rings.

I get up and answer it, and Sarah says oh my God I don't believe it.

I say hi, alright, I got your message, what's up, what don't you believe?

She says I just spoke to your mum, I lost your number so I called her to ask for it and she said she was worried about you, she said she thought I knew.

I say knew what, she says what do you think, I close my eyes and swear and turn away from the room, and as I do so I hear Michael picking up the teacups and carrying them through to the kitchen.

I say, oh, so she told you, she says yes I couldn't believe it, I say I'm sorry I was going to tell you, I was just waiting, I was just waiting for, for a little while.

She says how long have you known when is it due who was the why didn't you I mean, and her words come out all tangled and rushed, like a corrupted email.

I say Sarah I'm sorry I didn't tell you about it before, but I really don't want to talk about it now, not right now.

She says oh, sorry, and her voice sounds punctured.

I don't want to upset her, I say shall we meet up, soon, do you want to come round?

Okay she says, okay, maybe at the weekend, that would be

good I say, there's a lot to talk about, we've got a lot of catching up to do, and she laughs a little, nervously.

She says, but, are you okay?

She says, your mum, she was worried, she seemed really worried about you.

I say I'm okay, I'm fine, Michael's here, he just came round, I think we're going somewhere for lunch, I'm okay, thanks for ringing, I do appreciate it, really.

She says, he's still there? it's not him is it? and then she says oh no, of course, and she giggles and she says goodbye and I tell her I'll call her.

He comes in from the kitchen as I put the phone down, he says are you okay and I say I'm fine it's just, it's nothing really.

I look at all the things on the table, beside the box, I look inside the box and lift out a stack of polaroids.

I say, it's my mum, she told Sarah about it, about me being pregnant, and I wasn't going to tell her yet.

I look at the polaroids, they're taken from his bedroom window again, a day when it was raining heavily, there are splashes on the lens and the street is shining wet.

He says didn't you want to tell her at all, I say yes, but not yet, not like this, I wanted to wait until, I don't know.

The twins are in one of the pictures, their heads tipped back into the rain, their clothes soaked, one of them waving a cricket bat in the air.

He says well at least, you can talk to someone about it now, I mean, you know, I'm not being rude but you need someone to talk to about it, properly I mean he says and I look at him a moment.

I look at the other polaroids, the sister of the twins waving her ribbon in the air, a barbecue billowing smoke outside number twenty-three, the dark sky full of rain, the street shining like glass and I look at them all again, closely.

I look at the picture of the twins, and I recognise the clothes one of them is wearing, the one with the cricket bat, and I realise when the pictures were taken and my stomach turns over, like a vase falling from a windowsill.

He takes the last few things out of the box, a thick bundle of spiral-bound notebooks tied together with string, a polaroid camera, pages cut from magazines, photocopied sheets of text.

I think most of this stuff was for his dissertation he says, and he picks up pictures of coffins and funeral pyres, an article about Graceland, he picks at the blu-tac on the backs of the pages.

He did something about funeral rites he says, comparing historical ones with modern ones, he got really into it he says.

I pick out the last pieces from the box, two broken pieces of a small clay figure, I think that was part of it he says, something oriental I think.

I hold the two pieces together, pressing the smooth round head onto the shoulders, holding it up close to look at it.

It looks elegant, peaceful, it's very well made, the eyes closed, the nose a delicate pinch, the shoulders and body almost formless.

I turn it over, I put it down, I put the head by its side.

It's a shame it's broken I say.

He must have dropped it he says.

He starts putting everything back in the box, stacking and arranging it all carefully so that it fits in.

I say do you want to go somewhere for lunch, he looks up and I say I mean, I haven't got any food in, I.

He says no no, that would be good, we, I'd like that.

He says actually I'm not doing anything all day, we could maybe go somewhere for the afternoon, it is a bank holiday he says.

He's looking at me, his hands have stopped moving, I look up and he blinks and I look away, he says I mean that's if you're not doing anything.

No I say, quickly, no I'm not doing anything, no that would be nice, some fresh air I say, a bit of exercise.

He smiles, he says okay, good, he finishes packing the box, he picks it up and he says well shall we go now?

Okay I say, smiling, I'll meet you outside, I need to get a few things, and I open the door for him and watch him walking out to his car, I feel strange and lightheaded.

I pick up my purse, I drink a glass of water and fill a bottle, I look at the flowers again and step outside, into the sunshine, heading for the waiting car.

In the bedroom of number nineteen, the mother of the twins lies awake in bed. Her husband sleeps, undisturbed, and she lies still beside him, locked inside the knowledge of absolute pleasure, thinking about the times when this was not the way of things, the times when there was a shadow over their moments together, the shadow of a thing not happened, the shadow of the family thinking badly of them, of her.

She runs her fingers across the smallness of her stomach, and she remembers when this was a painful thing, a thing to be wept over.

A thing to be prayed over.

She pulls at the slight looseness of the skin around her stomach and hips, runs the side of her thumb along the tiny ridges and turns of the marks left by what was there, by the slow swell and stretch of her body.

She remembers the weight of it, the enormousness, she remembers the miracle of it, her body changing to make room for a new body, for two bodies.

And she thinks about the years of impossibility, the unblessed years, the word her husband's mother used, saying it is a shame that you are unblessed.

And she didn't mean shame the way some people say it, like as a small sadness, like as when they say it is a shame it is raining, this is not how she used the word, she used it in the old way, the word shame meaning humiliation and embarrassment and wrongness. Shame meaning lower your head and do not look at me you are a bringer of shame into my son's household.

She didn't speak quite this clearly, but the things she said meant these things, bitter, spiteful things, and she only said them when neither of the men were in the house.

It was some years ago now, but she still finds it difficult to find excuses for her, the things she said, the way she was.

Her husband makes a noise in his sleep, moves, turns towards her, lays a blind arm across her breast and nuzzles his mouth into her shoulder. She takes his hand and twists her fingers into his, and it looks the same as when their sons were born, when they were laid down toe to toe and they moved together and tangled their legs.

And when she thinks of that moment, of looking at her two newborn sons, her heart blossoms within her, just as it did at the time. She thinks of what it took for them to be born, of all the procedures and rituals, the medicines and the special diets, the calendars and thermometers and endless tests, blood tests and urine tests, and others.

She thinks of the shame of her husband, having to spill his seed into a plastic bottle, she is glad his mother did not know about that. He was quieter for a time after that, after the doctor had talked to him about that test, he said he felt like he was a smaller man, a lesser man. But she kissed him, and she held him, and she told him he was the same to her as he always was, and after a while he believed her and he talked to her about what the doctor had said, the advice he'd been given.

Even now, seven, eight years later, it makes her smile to remember the things they had to do to make the impossible more possible, to call down their blessings. They were things that seemed too ordinary, too mundane, it felt like looking for treasure by guessing six numbers.

She thinks of the things, she kisses her husband's hand and smiles.

Warm baths, a run in the park, less fatty food.

Looser-fitting underwear.

It had seemed so useless, such an insignificant action in the face of barrenness, like a small glass of water in the middle of the desert, like knocking on a huge iron door with the knuckle of one finger. And so their hopes had not been raised, and they had continued with everything else, the charts and the calculations, the temperatures and the weighings, the estimations of the most suitable time. Fertile windows is what the doctor had said, she said you must estimate your fertile windows and make full use of them. It had seemed a funny expression to her, it made her think of a derelict cottage with ivy and moss growing through the cracked panes of glass.

But still, they estimated their fertile windows, and they made full use of them. She smiles, and her body swells with pleasure, with the memory of pleasure, and she turns slightly and presses herself against her husband. She remembers him once, feigning reluctance, saying my love do you think perhaps we are over-estimating these so-called fertile windows? And she had said yes, I think so, and they had made full use of it.

She looks at him now, his eyes closed, his mouth open, every detail of his face lit up by the sunlight flooding back into the room. His cheeks, rough and a little loose around the bones, the day's stubble already itching through the skin, dark points peppered with silver. She thinks of the sound her palm would make as it brushed against those tiny hairs, a rasp like the grating of a nutmeg. She touches his skin, gently, she outlines his eyes and his lips, she follows the furrows of his forehead, pinches the thick hair of his eyebrows between her finger and thumb, tugs it into little tufts. He murmurs something, frowns slightly in his sleep, turns his body away a little, his face wriggling back towards her. She whispers a shush, and trails her middle finger

225

across his forehead, down the length of his nose and onto his lips.

She thinks of his face in that moment, remembers the way it changed so suddenly when she told him, it was like the hugest firework on the darkest night, flashing and sparkling and exploding in front of her, his eyes stretched wide, his mouth lifted open and his teeth flashing white and gold, crackles and hisses of delight bursting out from somewhere deep inside him. Oh is it true? he said, oh really? oh is it true? oh praise be he said, oh I am so happy, oh thankyou thankyou he said, and she'd realised he was saying it to her so she'd laughed and said no thank*you*, thank*you* Mr Baggypants, and he'd laughed, and they'd held each other, and read the letter from the doctor over and over again, talking with joy and excitement long into the night, talking of who they would tell first and when they would tell them, talking of clothes and cots and prams, of decorating the box-room, of good sleep and good food, of extra money, of names. Talking for hours of a good name, for weeks and months as her body swelled and her steps slowed, as the sickness came and went and the excitement grew, as the visits from relatives and friends increased, always thinking of a name. Writing lists, trying out favourites, looking through books for new ideas.

She remembers those last few weeks, isolated in the house, surrounded by people trying to help, surrounded by stories of how it was for them, advice piling up around her like the gifts in the corner of the room.

She remembers how uncomfortable it was, that time, the pain of moving around, the difficulty of sleep, the overwhelming feeling of such bigness, wanting it to be over and yet so fearful of the finishing. She remembers her husband spreading his broad hands across her belly, thumb against thumb and his little fingers not stretching anywhere near her hip bones. How does it feel he'd said, how does it feel to be so strange and new? and she'd said I feel like a mammal and he'd laughed and said but we are, humans are mammals you know. And she'd said no, I don't mean, and been unable to explain what she did mean, that she felt like a damn elephant, a whale, huge and stately and balloon-like but also she meant not like a human at all, like an animal, locked into a process much bigger than herself, more than one human being, she meant that she felt part of a species, part of something that nature was doing and she had no control of.

The night before it happened, he'd spread his hands again, pressed them palm flat to her swollen skin, a skin so stretched that it seemed translucent, held his hands there and said my God this is going to be a hell of a big baby.

She remembers him saying this, she smiles and she shakes her head, she wonders how she could have had no idea, how neither of them could have had the thought even pass through their minds.

She remembers his awestruck idiocy when he found out, when it was over and he was brought into the room and all he could do was look at her and say my God there is two of them.

She touches his lips with one finger again, stroking the knuckle against the chapped edges of his upper and lower lip, he moves his mouth, his eyelids lift a little, like papers rustling in a light breeze. She whispers wake up, she leans her face across to kiss his mouth, she rolls the weight of her body onto him, feeling the warmth of the sun on her back, moving her head so that her shadow bounces in and out of his eyes. He wakes up, he opens his eyes and she spreads her fingers flat across his chest, moving her hips so that his belly rolls a little from side to side.

She says have you slept enough now, are you rested?

227

She says the house is still empty you know.

And he raises his eyebrows, and there is a rolling of bodies, a rustling of tangled bedclothes, a creaking of old bedsprings.

And in a moment's breathless pause, blinking at each other and already wiping sweat from a forehead, she thinks of their further surprise, a few short months after their doubled blessing, the unexpected planting of a third child they had not been ready for, and she knows they were right to seal off further possibility, to let the doctors take scissors and stitches to her husband and close the shutters on their fertile windows. There is not the money she'd said, my body is tired, and he had not been able to deny her that. We have been given more than we asked for she'd said, this is enough now, and he had agreed.

They had kept it a secret, they were not sure his parents would approve, but his mother had made no more comment about extra brothers and sisters for their children. Perhaps she thinks three is enough after all. Perhaps she thinks that they no longer move together in that way, now there is no need.

She draws her fingernails slowly down her husband's back, she listens to the sounds she can draw from out of him, and she thinks well so at least she is wrong about that.

I woke up late this morning, I had to leave for work without having a shower and I felt sticky and straw-headed all day.

Before I left, I noticed that Michael had left the broken clay figure behind, it was still on the table, lying forlornly on its side.

I picked it up and looked at it again, resting the head on the shoulders, looking at the long thin ears, the tiny beads around the neck, the stillness of the expression.

I wondered how it had been broken.

I wondered if I could fix it, if that would be okay, if it was supposed to be like this.

I looked around for some superglue, I looked in the kitchen drawer with the elastic bands and the sellotape and the silver foil, and I found the leaflets from the clinic, the ones I'd stuffed away in there the other week.

I read the sections I'd started to highlight, I read the rest of them, and somehow it seemed a little less alien than it had before, I kept checking the clock and reading a little bit extra, stroking my belly and imagining the quiet bubbling miracle inside.

But in the end I had to put them back and run for the bus with my mouth crammed full of toast.

And I spent all day standing over a photocopier, getting tiny paper-cuts on my hands and thinking about yesterday afternoon.

I thought about how nice it had been to just spend the afternoon walking around, talking, not talking, thinking, telling each other what we were thinking.

We went to the park, and I saw the girl from the shop

downstairs, I think she saw me but I didn't know whether or not to say hello, I wasn't sure that she'd recognise me.

I was sick behind some rhododendron bushes, and it barely interrupted the flow of the conversation.

We had lunch in a cafe by the lake, we sat by the window and looked out over the water, he told me about him and his brother learning to swim on a camping trip in the lake district, how they'd egged each other on to walk further and further out.

It was a hot day he said, but the water was still icy cold.

He told me how they stood there, shivering, calling each other chicken, a step further and a step more, until the water was tapping against their clenched teeth.

He was looking at the lake, at the people in rowing boats, and he said we stopped talking, we were looking at each other, wondering what to do next, and suddenly we grabbed each other and pulled each other forwards, out of our depth, face down into the water.

I said and what happened, he said I don't know, I remember being under the water for a while, throwing my arms and legs around, and then somehow my head was in the air again and we were both swimming.

I told him I couldn't swim and he pointed at my stomach and said so a birthing pool's out then and he smiled and I laughed.

And after we'd talked some more we walked back through the park and across town to an art gallery.

There was a special exhibition on, it was only one piece of work but we were there for an hour, looking and looking and telling each other about it in hushed awestruck voices.

It was in one room, a large room with long skylights, and we stood by the doorway and looked in at it, at them, looking over them, thousands and thousands of six-inch red clay figures, as roughly made as playschool plasticine men, a pair of finger-sized sockets for eyes, heads tilted up from formless bodies.

Each one almost identical, each one unique.

We knelt there, looking at them looking up at us, the thousands of them, saying I wonder how long and I wonder if they all and I wonder what.

A small boy came running up behind us, shouting and then suddenly stilled into quietness, he said it's like being on a stage.

I wanted to steal one, I wanted to put it on my bedside table and wake up to see it smiling kindly at me, but Michael said it wasn't fair, he wouldn't let me, he said it might get lonely.

I wanted to count them, give them all names, make up stories for each of them, but it seemed impossible to even begin.

And so we just knelt there without talking, looking at them looking at us, unblinking, expressionless.

By the time we came out the sun was heavy and low in the sky, we were both hungry but I didn't want to go home.

We went and bought soup from a coffee shop, we sat on high stools at the window-counter and talked without looking at each other, our reflections laid thinly across the glass.

He said you're not too tired are you, we haven't done too much walking have we?

I said no, no, I'm fine, I'm a bit knackered but it's okay I said, I've had a good day I said.

And we both sat there with mouthfuls of hot soup and I wondered again what sort of good I meant, I thought about the last few days, I thought about why he was here, about who he was and why he had come looking for me, what he had been expecting, what he was thinking now.

He said, my brother, he said I only met you a week ago and already I feel like I know you far more than my brother ever did, he said it doesn't seem fair somehow.

I said oh but I feel like I know him, I said you've told me so much about him that I almost feel like I've met him properly, and he said I suppose but it's not the same.

There was a pedestrian crossing further up the road, the signal was red and I looked at all the people waiting to cross, a huge crowd of them, motionless, blankfaced, looking up at the lights.

They looked like the figures in the art gallery.

There was a white van parked outside, two men in fluorescent jackets were loading huge reels of cable into it, shovels, traffic cones.

He said what's the most frightening thing that's ever happened to you?

I started to speak, I was going to say that day, that afternoon, seeing that moment, watching his brother moving to where it was, but he said I mean really happened to you, not something you've seen or read about but happened to you.

I stopped, and I looked at him, and I realised what an important distinction it was.

I said, I don't know, maybe when I was a kid and I got lost at the funfair but, I'm not sure, let me think about it I said, what about you? and I sucked at the thick red soup, I wrapped my hands around the warm paper of the cup.

He said I was in the back of a transit van driving across rough ground, I didn't know where I was and I thought I'd been kidnapped.

I looked at him, I thought he was joking but he didn't smile or say not really.

He said it sounds worse than it was, but at the time I was terrified, I thought I was going to die.

I look at him, he's staring at the van and he says, sorry, it reminded me, that's all, the van, I just remembered.

I said and so what was it, what happened?

He said I was hitching home once, and I'd been there a long time, and this van stopped and these two men said I could get in the back.

He said there were no windows, just a couple of thin slits in the roof, and these shafts of sunlight were scanning around the inside of the van as we turned corners and I was catching glimpses of things in the van, bricks, ropes, a spade.

He said they kept braking really suddenly, and laughing these really high-pitched laughs.

And we'd been driving for too long he said, and they'd stopped laughing, and then we were driving along some kind of dirt track, bumping up and down, and I didn't know where we were.

I said oh my God what did you do what happened, he said nothing, nothing happened, they dropped me off at the end of my street in the end, it was just some kind of joke he said.

He was talking quite slowly, breathlessly, he said and the worst thing was, it was strange, the worst thing, more than the fear of what might happen to me, what they might do or how I might get out of it, the worst thing was thinking that nobody would ever know, that I would just be missing, disappeared, vanished.

He looked at me and he said can you imagine that?

He said can you imagine anything more lonely?

233

When I got back to my flat in the evening, the green message light on my answerphone was flashing.

I stood there looking at it, hypnotised, I left the front door open and the lights off and I looked at the small green light, blinking in the dark.

I wondered if my mother had called, if she'd had time to think and wanted to say now that she wasn't angry or upset, that she was glad I had told her and could she maybe come and visit soon?

I wondered if it was my dad, telling me to be okay, saying that my mother felt these things but found it hard to say them, saying she loves you as much as I do you know.

And I watched the light, on, off, on, off, like a persistent knocking at a closed door, I stood closer but somehow I couldn't press the button marked listen.

I had a sudden idea that my parents had called some people in Scotland, had somehow tracked down the boy who worked at the place where they'd held the wake, had given him my number and told him to call me.

I imagined his rich voice, made thin and brittle by the wires and the machine, bursting suddenly into my flat, saying something like hello well it's been a wee while hasn't it how are you.

I wondered what that sound would do to me, if I would recoil or rise up, if whether inside me, somewhere beneath my heart, something would flutter and jerk in recognition.

I remembered the words I had said to Michael, and I wondered if I could say them again, in response, if I could say I'm sorry but it was just a thing that happened, it wasn't anything, it was just a thing.

And then I looked at the small green light and I thought of Michael's brother, and I imagined his quiet voice hesitating out of the machine.

I imagined Michael having been in touch with him, saying I've met her, telling him that I'd said I'd like to meet him one day.

I imagined him by a public telephone, somewhere on the other side of the world, pacing around it, reaching and withdrawing his hand like an uncertain chess player.

I wondered what he would say, I wondered what I would say if he called again and I spoke to him.

I thought maybe I would ask him about the pictures Michael showed me, the things he'd collected and hoarded, I could ask him why he had them all, if they meant anything.

And I thought I could ask him about the broken figure, what it was, where it had come from, how it had got broken, I thought these would be things we could talk about.

And, of course, I wanted to talk to him about that afternoon, that moment, I wanted to share the remembering of it, I thought somehow he wouldn't be someone who would say actually can we talk about something else now.

I pressed the button, and the machine said you have one messages, first message, and I listened.

There was a pause, the tiny half-kiss sound of someone opening their mouth to speak, the hard jolt of a phone being put down.

I listened to it a few times, listening for clues, guessing, rationalising.

It was a wrong number, a mistake.

Or it was Sarah, wondering whether to come round, she was just passing, it didn't seem worth leaving a message.

That pause, short and huge, not even the sound of breathing, no background noise, no movement in the room.

235

And that half-kiss, the lips parting, no sound passing through them, no air passing through them, just the opening of the mouth and the clatter of the closed phone.

It was nothing, it wasn't anyone, it was just kids, bored, phoning numbers at random, this was how I made it okay, it was just one of those things.

But I had wanted it to be him, this barely known neighbour calling from some other country, saying something like, my brother said, I wondered, I could come back soon, if you like.

It's not that I want him, I don't picture myself lying in bed beside him, I wasn't listening to that sound and hoping to taste it, I just, I wanted to talk to him, I wanted to know, I wanted to say thankyou and sorry.

But it was not him, it was no one, and I went to bed and thought about the people I know and the people I don't know and all the people in between, and it took me a long time to sleep.

The man with the scarred hands eases out of his doorway, he sits down on the step and leans back against the damp doorframe, he is looking at the dark shine of the tarmac and he is thinking about the shine of his wife's hair.

He is trying not to, it is difficult.

He remembers a time, in the early months soon after they were married and they had very little money, and his wife allowed him to cut her hair.

He remembers how easily he held the scissors, how delicate and precise his movements could be, then, his thumb and finger as flexible as when a stalking cat bends its body to the ground.

He remembers the soft weight of her hair across the palm of his undamaged hand, the slish of each careful cut he made, the broken handfuls of hair tumbling down her back and onto the floor like branches blown down a hillside.

The way she closed her eyes and quietly trusted him to not spoil her remarkable good looks. The two of them, in their empty kitchen, the noise of the world drifting in through shuttered windows, no conversation between them, his deep concentration, and when he had finished the bare floor around her chair was like a lake at midnight, still and dark and shining.

He does not speak of these things to people, there is nobody to speak them to here, nobody who knows. If he was asked he would say okay mostly, mostly I am okay, it is okay. But there are times when he feels too much, when if he could tell someone he would say I cannot possibly bear it anymore I want to tear the paper from the walls and fall to my knees and hammer upon the floor with my useless ruined fists.

He listens to the sound of the television from the front room, his daughter is watching, there are young people talking about music and football, he hears his daughter's voice behind him and she says daddy have you ever seen any angels?

He pauses, his face squeezing into a slight frown, he wonders what his daughter is thinking of. He turns and he says I see you every day, and he squeezes her face with his wrists and blows a parpytongue onto her forehead. She wriggles away and says yuk and says no I mean real angels, and she skips onto the garden path and stands on one leg, looking at him, waiting for answers.

He shrugs slowly, he says anything is possible and smiles. Her eyes widen and she says have you have you? He looks at her and remembers the moment she was born, the nurse holding her up into the air like treasure lifted dripping from the sea, he remembers the long silent pause before that first scream of arrival, her tiny face screwed up into wet wrinkles like the stone of a peach.

He says angels? He says I do not know, I do not think so but I will keep looking. He says have you been looking? and she turns away and she nods shyly.

He says hey hey now don't be ashame, it is okay to be looking for these things, it is good okay? and she looks at him.

He says what have you seen? and she doesn't say anything, she stands a little closer and she says I saw wings in the sky at the top of the sky.

He says well that is a special thing, you have seen more than I have ever seen, well done you, and she smiles and her face is like the ribbon pulled from the wrapping of a gift.

He says do you want to see another special thing, and he

points to the rooftops opposite, he says can you clap your hands for your daddy, and when she does so the whole ridgepole of pigeons springs up into the air, ballooning off down the street as a group, circling, landing on another rooftop in a matching single line.

He says, do you see them now, do you see they do not bump into one another, do you think this is special? and she looks at him and she thinks she should nod so she does.

He says you know in the place where you were born in, and he doesn't say back home because he doesn't want her to think like that but that is what he means, back home where they were a family and they belonged, he says in the place where you were born in there would be flocks of thousands of birds, gathering at dusk, and when they turned in mid-air the whole sky would go dark as though Allah was flipping the shutters closed for a second. And not any of those thousands collided he says, do you think this is special?

He says my daughter, and all the love he has is wrapped up in the tone of his voice when he says those two words, he says my daughter you must always look with both of your eyes and listen with both of your ears. He says this is a very big world and there are many many things you could miss if you are not careful. He says there are remarkable things all the time, right in front of us, but our eyes have like the clouds over the sun and our lives are paler and poorer if we do not see them for what they are.

He says, if nobody speaks of remarkable things, how can they be called remarkable?

He looks at her and he knows she doesn't understand, he doesn't think she'll even remember it to understand when she is older. But he tells her these things all the same, it is good to say them aloud, they are things people do not think and he wants to place them into the air.

Angels, he says, and she leans forward as if she is expecting him to pass on a secret. I do not know about angels he says, perhaps there are many, perhaps they are here now he says, and she looks around and stands closer to him and he smiles. But there are people too he says, everywhere there are people and I think it is easier to hold hands with people than it is with angels, yes?

He stops to get his breath back, he knows he is confusing her and maybe boring her, he knows that really he is saying these things to himself.

He says I'm sorry I am talking too much, he says come and give your daddy a hug, and she presses into him and he clamps his arms around her.

Now go and play again he says, the rain has gone, go and find your friend and keep looking for angels he says.

She stands away from him, she turns away, she turns back and kisses him on the mouth and she runs away down the street.

She runs past a rain-jewelled spider's web laid out like lace across a pile of coat-hangers in a front garden.

She runs past a pigeon in a puddle, beating water across its wings.

She runs past number eighteen and she sees the boy who lives there talking to the girl from two doors down, she has short hair and glasses and she is smiling politely and he is blinking a lot and not quite looking at her as he says so you're moving out then, and the armful of air between them is heavy and thick and impenetrable.

She runs past the old man from the next house along, he is standing in his front garden and the sound of his breathing is as though someone were forcing air through a cracked harmonica.

She runs past the young man scrubbing his trainers, he still can't get them clean and he slams his hand into the

240

water in frustration, the bubbles lifting up into the air and drifting down like diamond confetti.

She runs across the road, towards a woman leaning out of an attic window, hanging out a red blanket, shaking it like an air-traffic signal, she runs past the man at number twenty-five, he is back up his ladder, retouching the paint where the rain has streaked through it, a twirl of movement catches his eye and he turns to look through the open window of next-door's bedroom, he sees a boy and a girl, the boy is sleeping, they are both naked and tangled up in each other, the light in the room is clean and golden and happiness is seeping out through the window, the girl looks at him and smiles and whispers good afternoon.

And the young girl runs to the end of the street and she still can't see her friend with the ribbon anywhere, she looks up and she sees a crane arching over the rooftops.

Nearby, a few streets away and a hundred feet up in the air, the man with the carefully trimmed moustache stands motionless and blind. When he opens his eyes he can see the city spread out beneath his feet, the rooftops of the terraces stretched out across the side of the valley, attic windows flashing in the afternoon sun, traffic circling the roundabout, people stretched out in the park, pinned to the ground like collected butterflies. He can see all of this, and the whole city is shimmering and shining so much that it feels as though he's standing on a diving board over a swimming pool, waiting to somersault and twist into clear blue water. But when he looks below him he doesn't see the refracted image of swimming-pool tiles, he sees only the cracked tarmac of the club carpark, stony ground surrounded by a small crowd of people with their faces all turned towards him.

The young man behind him says okay sir, when you're

ready, just relax and let yourself fall forward. He likes this young man, very polite, very trustworthy. He says to him, and you're certain everything is ready, everything is okay, yes? and the young man doesn't hesitate, he says absolutely sir it's all been checked and doublechecked.

Okay then he says, the man with the carefully trimmed moustache and the perfectly straight bow-tie, okay then I will trust you. He swallows, thickly. I will just enjoy the view first okay? he says and the young man says that's fine sir you just take your time. It's a nice view isn't it says the man, it's a beautiful day for this, and the young man agrees quietly, it's a lovely day he says.

He looks at his street, the man, he can see a young girl at this end, he can see the boys playing cricket, he can see a man up a ladder and people sitting on doorsteps. He can see a car just around the corner, and he can't quite tell if it's moving or not.

Okay then he says, and he shuffles a little closer to the edge, okay. The young man behind him says alright then sir, just relax and let yourself fall forward. And keep your eyes open he says, you don't want to miss anything.

And the man with the carefully trimmed moustache and the thinning hair nods, looking straight ahead, leaning forward, dropping away from the platform, soundlessly falling like an empty bottle, like the first weighted raindrop of a storm, turning and accelerating towards the ground.

He should be here by now.

I look out of the window, I look at the clock, I look out of the window again and he is none of the people in the street.

My mother says I was in town today I went into a clothes shop, I bought one of those babygro whatsits, a white one, ever so small it was she says.

It took me a while to choose she says, there's an awful lot of variety these days, there were three or four I couldn't decide between she says.

I press the phone against my ear, I want to hear her better.

She says it's a kind of fleece-type material, it looks ever so snug, it's got a hood with a pair of teddybear ears on it, I thought you might like it.

I say I don't know mum, it sounds like it might be a bit small for me, and she doesn't laugh, she pauses and she says yes well I just thought you might appreciate it.

I say no sorry oh I do appreciate it mum, sorry, I say it sounds lovely mum, thank you.

Her voice lightens, she says I got it in white because you don't know yet, do you?

He should be here by now.

He said seven o'clock, about, and it's nearly eight and he's not here, it's raining and he's not got his car and it's getting dark.

She says so when will you find out, is it soon, it should be, they can do all sorts of things now can't they?

She says not like when I had you.

I tell her I've got an appointment soon, I hear a noise in the carpark at the back and I say hold on a minute, excuse me.

I open the door and look, but it's not him, he's not there.

I pick up the phone again and she says what sort of appointment, a scan I say, they're going to check everything's okay, they're going to find out if it's a boy or a girl.

As I say the words, I picture a boy or a girl inside of me, half the size of my thumb, I picture each of its limbs, its fingers, the faint imprint of freshly forming fingernails, each nail smaller than a pinprick, I picture myself a year, two years, three years from now, a child on my lap, saying hold still, carefully trimming those same fingernails.

She says oh a boy would be nice I've always wanted a boy.

He should be here by now.

He doesn't seem like someone who'd be late, not normally, not unless there was a problem.

Maybe he's got lost, in the dark, in the rain.

Maybe he's trying to phone and he can't get through.

I say mum, look, sorry, I should go, I'm expecting someone, they might be trying to call.

She says oh, okay, oh, who are you expecting?

It's no one I say, it's a friend, and I say it's someone I know from work because I don't want to try and explain.

She says, oh, okay, I'd better let you go then, and she sounds disappointed but somehow she also sounds relieved.

I say thanks for phoning mum, I appreciate it, I really, and she's already putting the phone down.

I look out of the window, I open the door, I check the time.

I think of all the things that can happen to a person when they're trying to reach you.

Cars skidding in wet conditions.

Men falling out of pub doorways with tempers raised.

Boys with needle-thin arms asking for money, a flash of silver in their hands.

I think of him being lost in this weather, the rain heaving down out of the dark sky, I think of him soaked through and shivering, blinking anxiously, looking for street-names, road-signs, familiar buildings.

I put a towel on the radiator to warm up, I put the kettle on to boil, I look out into the thick veil of rain and I wait for him.

And I wonder how this has happened, already, why I can be so worried for someone I've so recently met.

And I know why it is, and I don't want it to be like that.

The kettle boils, clicks off, quietens.

I hear a siren from a few streets away and my heart clenches inside me, I rush to look outside but there's nothing to see.

I feel like flinging open the window and calling his name.

I realise that if something were to happen to him now, if that siren was chasing to the place where he is lying in the rain, that no one would tell me.

That they would find his parents, and let them know, and ask them to come quickly, find his brother, wherever he is, and tell him, and ask him to get on the next available flight.

But that they wouldn't find me and tell me, there is no reason why they would, and I would never know and this all seems wrong.

I put the kettle on again, I turn the towel over so that both sides are warm, I open the door and look into the night.

I see him running across the carpark, his hand held over his head like a tiny umbrella, his face looking up at me.

He runs up the steps, he says sorry I'm late, sorry, I got lost, and he stands in the doorway.

I say are you alright you're soaked, I say come in come in, come here, and I take hold of the sleeve of his coat and pull him towards me and I close the door.

His arms, his whole body is shaking, water quivering and falling from his clothes like rain from a shaken washing line.

His teeth, when he talks, his teeth rattle like polished bones in a box, he says I got lost I tried I couldn't it was I got lost and I say shush don't worry it's okay it's okay.

I say you're soaked, you should, I'll get you something to wear, I'll get you a towel, and I fetch a V-necked jumper from my room, the towel from the radiator.

I hand him the towel and I stand in front of him, holding out the jumper like a shop assistant.

He starts to dry his hair, I say no take your top off first, get something dry on first, and he says oh right, okay, and he hands me the towel and I stand and look at him.

We are both breathing as though we've been running in a rainstorm.

He takes his coat off, he pulls his top off, it gets stuck around his head and he wriggles for a moment, blinded, arms held up, and I look at his smooth wet chest, his nipples, his bare shoulders, the thin drift of hair below his belly-button.

He gets the top over his head, he drops it to the floor, I drop the jumper and I push the towel towards him.

I push the towel up against his chest, and I feel a sudden warmth, I say you need to get dry.

I spread my hands out, holding the towel up against him, holding one hand still, moving the other in a slow arc, my little finger tracing a line around the curve of his shoulder, down the side of his chest.

My thumb, like a compass point, pressed onto his nipple.

But I am not touching him, not really, I am not touching his skin.

It's as though the towel is a pair of gloves that makes what I'm doing okay, innocent.
I look at him, his eyes are closed, tightly closed, his bottom lip is taut and colourless.
I carry on, I sweep the towel down across his stomach, around his waist, up each side of his chest.
I bring the towel up, slowly, softly, draping it from shoulder to shoulder, my hands holding it in place, my fingers curling across the ridges of his collarbones.
And even through the damp cloth of the towel I can feel his heart, beating quickly against the heel of my right hand.

I look up at him, at his closed face.
I say is that better, I say it quietly and I move closer to him as I say it.
He opens his eyes, he opens his mouth to speak, and as he opens his mouth there is a half-kiss of sound, a sound I recognise.
He says yes, thankyou, and I move closer still, as if to hear the words.
I look at him, I lift my face and he lowers his.
He looks at me, he moves a breath closer, I feel his hands hovering around the sides of my face.
Our mouths are as close as the closed wings of a butterfly.
We each move closer, and the distance between us thins further, a veil of silk, a breath.
Everything has stopped.

I close my eyes, I breathe in the sweetness of the hesitation.
He moves away, a sudden release of breath gasping out of him, he pulls back and the towel falls to the floor, he turns away and he lowers his head and he puts his hands into his hair.
He says, I'm sorry, I can't.

He says, my brother.

He picks my jumper off the floor and puts it on, it's too small for him and when he picks the towel up to dry his hair the sleeves only just come past his elbows.

The neckline of the jumper leaves a pale triangle of skin, it flushes pink as I look at it.

He says, I'm sorry, my brother.

I don't say anything, I look at him, he looks at me, he looks away, he looks at me, he says I have to go I'm sorry, he picks up his coat and then he is gone.

On the floor, a puddle of water and a crumpled t-shirt, wet footprints, a towel.

The boy with the pierced eyebrow sees the man with the carefully trimmed moustache making his momentous fall over at the club. He doesn't realise who it is, or what he is seeing, all he sees is a figure falling from the crane, falling through the air and disappearing behind a row of houses.

For a very short moment there is a lump of shock in his mouth, his concentration sucked into the panel of sky the man is falling through; and in that moment, in the time it takes for the orange juice from the carton at his mouth to gush down and fall from his chin, to turn in the air and catch the light and splash into his lap, in that moment his bloodstream is infused with a damburst of adrenalin and his eyes widen and his fingers twitch with the energy of it.

But then he sees the trail of cord hanging loose in the sky, an umbilical from the falling man to the crane above, and he smiles as he sees the cord tighten and recoil, pulling the figure back up, slackening like a question mark against the brightness of the sky.

He puts down the juice carton and watches the man falling again as the adrenalin fades away, breaking down and dispelling itself like a sigh. He wonders what it might feel like, that moment before the cord tightens and recoils, how strong the doubt in your mind would be, if there would be time to imagine the possibilities. He wonders if the relief would be stronger than the fear. And he remembers a man he heard about on the news, a man whose parachute didn't open when he did a jump for charity, he wonders what that might be like, those two or three minutes, that freefall, the roar of the wind and the delirious bellow of death calling in

249

your ears. And the landscape laid out beneath you like a vision, fields and trees and rivers like a picturebook, cars moving slowly along threadlike roads and you wondering if they can see you rushing to meet them. He wonders what he would do, if he would panic, fight it, tread air like a canyon-bound cartoon character. If he would spreadeagle, lie flat to the air to slow his descent, or draw himself in, point arrowlike to the ground, hands pressed together, eyes closed, mumbling come on come on and wanting to get it over with.

He thinks about it, wondering what he would do, wondering if he would be ready, wondering if he would be as lucky as the man on the news who fell into trees and broke branches and bones but didn't die.

He sits on his step, he drinks more juice with the sun on his face, and he wonders how that would feel, how it would be, to know that your own existence is a miracle.

A young man in a car sees the figure falling from the sky, a man in a car coming around the corner at the far end of the street.

Coming around the corner a little too quickly they will say, we noticed.

He comes round the corner and he sees a figure falling through the air, he doesn't see the elastic trailing out behind, he sees four limbs flung out, he is astounded and he stares up and follows the fall.

He is not looking at the road, not at this particular instant, and he is not looking at the child in front of him.

He wasn't looking where he was going they will say, you could tell, it was obvious.

The child looks up. He has been concentrating on the tennis ball, arranging his fingers along the seam in a hopeful parody of his cricketing heroes, and he is just about to turn into his run-up when he lifts his head and sees the car. It's a white car, a small white Fiat, and it's facing towards him. It's moving towards him, but in the time it takes to reach him his perception of distance and movement will falter, become unable to register this fact. The car is facing him is all he can see.

The headlight on the left is cracked, and dirt has squeezed into the crack so that it stands out against the clear plastic casing like a fork of black lightning. The numberplate is printed in glossy italicised lettering, not the usual bold black capitals, he has time to notice this but not to read the letters. The car is clean, very clean, waxed and polished and shining in the sun. He can see the driver's face, he is wearing sunglasses and his face is half hidden by the shimmer of sun across the windscreen but he can still see his face and it's a face he knows, the boy from number twelve who played with them this morning, before he went out with his friends to spend carefully earned money on a car.

The child looks up, and he sees the car, and he sees the driver.

He doesn't move.

Later, when people talk about this moment, they will disagree about why this was. He had time to move, some will say, he could have jumped out of the way, run out of the way, moved just a few feet to the right or the left. Others will say he had no time, that he barely had a chance to see the car before it reached him, that perhaps he didn't see the car at all. Some, perhaps the ones who find themselves unable even to open their mouths when it happens, they will say that the boy had time to move but was unable to, that he was held static for that all-important moment between the seeing and the happening.

He looks up, he sees the car, and he doesn't move.

He can see the road stretching out behind the car, the still-wet surface gleaming darkly, he can see the houses on either side, magnified and distorted in his panic-struck vision so that they loom up like monsters, window-eyes leering, door-mouths snarling. He can see people in the street looking at him, the girl whose daddy has funny hands standing on one leg, and behind her in his garden her daddy with his hands held out, beginning to stand now but so far away, he can see the funny man at number eighteen, the one who can't catch the ball, he is jumping towards him and his whole body seems to be in the air, and he can see the people sitting outside the house next to his, the noisy people, they have all turned suddenly and are reaching their hands out towards him, he can see the small boy on his tricycle, further up the street, heading towards him, feet pumping away as furiously as ever, and he can see somebody on the flat roof of the shop, there are two people, one of them has their hands pressed to the sides of their head, their arms stretched out against the sky like a big O and he can see the sky, the blue sky, it is split from left to right by a tight white vapour trail but the aeroplane is too small to see, there are clouds, only a few, only thin ones, the sun is bright and splayed across a whole corner of the sky, there is a bird stretching out its wings to steady itself on a high branch of the tree outside the old couple's house, there's a cat rolling in the dust outside his own house, a white cat, there are wildflowers growing in the mulch of a blocked gutter on the roof of number fifteen, overflowing and hanging down across the brickwork, tiny white flowers in a spray, larger yellow ones, poppies.

He can see all of this, the boy in the middle of the road.

He can see the street, and the people, and the sky.

But he sees nothing. It is all there, all within his field of

252

vision, the colours and the brightnesses all striking the rods and cones of his young retinae, but there is too little time and he sees nothing.

He looks up, the child looks up, he sees the car, and he doesn't move.

And the young man in the car sees the child, and he slams on the brakes.

He is in the driving seat, he wants to stop the car, he wants to stop it quickly, so this is what he does, he slams on the brakes, with a movement as sudden as the noise of a slamming stable door.

He slams on the brakes.

And in the time it takes to speak those words, everything happens.

Electrical impulses fluster across the cells of his brain, back and forth like runners in a network news headquarters until they converge into a single impulse, a burst of intent which goes laundry-chuting headfirst down the spinal column, leaping and twitching through the shortest route like a cycle courier down a wrong-way street until it arrives at the ankle muscle and yanks the foot to the floor, ignoring the usual feedback control, jamming the foot down onto the pedal so hard that the skin will swell purple and yellow for days after this one day and then the job of the brain is done.

This is what the highway code calls thinking time, but if this was live on CNN the correspondent would be saying no the brakes are not active yet no not by a long way now back to you in the studio.

He slams on the brakes.

Which means that he reacts with panic and presses his foot down onto the pedal as hard and as fast as he possibly can.

And the pedal pulls against its spring mechanism, sinking a plunger into the small reservoir of brake oil, compressing it and sending that compression in a single wave of movement along a thick-walled flexible brake hose, the urgent energy sliding round the rubber curves like opiates through a bloodstream and arriving at the calipers which yield instantly to the pressure, squeezing the brake shoes onto the drilled steel disc, gripping tighter and tighter, gripping like a free climber's last hold on a rockface. But no matter how desperately the brakes embrace the disc the car will not be stopping yet, there is no car in the world that can come to an instant halt under these conditions.

And so this is the beginning of what the highway code refers to as stopping time, and on CNN the correspondent is saying no Christina, the car has not come to a stop yet, I can confirm the vehicle is still moving and I will keep you posted now over to you.

He slams on the brakes is what he does. The child looking at him and everyone looking at him and everyone panic-frozen in the endlessness of Stopping Time.

He slams on the brakes; he stamps on the pedal, the fluid compresses, and the brake shoes clamp against the brake disc. The brake hose shows signs of kinking, the brake shoes are not brand new, the disc is not spotlessly clean or dry, and these things stretch the moment by vital fractions of a second and these things will not be remarked upon in weighty investigative reports.

So he slams on the brakes, the wheels lock, and the car keeps moving on, dragging across the greasy wet surface of the road, the tyres beginning to spill their dark and poisonous residue across the road, and that noise, that noise, now the people in the street hear that noise.

The noise which people sometimes refer to as a screech of brakes but the word doesn't even come close.

It's the noise which will open half the narratives people will tell of this day. I heard this noise they will say, the lucky ones who avoided seeing the whole thing, I heard this noise and turned to look out of the window, or looked up from my newspaper or stopped walking and turned around. This is what they will say, to friends, in letters, in diaries, to people in pubs if the conversation drifts that way. I heard this noise and it cut right through me, like a chainsaw through my head, screaming through from ear to ear, and it was so sudden, and it seemed to go on forever. That's what they'll say, when they run out of ways to express the sound, when they've tried talking about nails on blackboards and screaming fireworks and they've not even come close, they'll say it was so sudden and it seemed to go on forever.

They will mean different things when they say forever. Some of them will mean that as the noise began time seemed to stretch out, that as they turned and saw the source of it an awful inevitability flooded into the street like a shadow across the sun and all they could do was wait for the noise to end. It was like that first descent on a roller-coaster they'll say, and waiting for your stomach to catch up and it seems to last a lifetime, and then they'll look away because that's not really what it was like at all

And others, when they say forever, they will mean that long after it was over the noise seemed to carry on, ringing in their ears, echoing through their heads, replaying through their dreams. I couldn't get rid of it they'll say. I kept hearing that sound, that awful juddering shriek, whenever the room was quiet it would come back, end-lessly sliding down the road, I had to have music on the whole time to drown it out they will say.

That noise. The car, sliding down the road, the wheels locked and the tyres dragging darkly across the steaming surface. The child, looking up, unmoving. And all the people watching, their heads turning like magnets, like compass needles, their hearts jumping like seismographs, caught uselessly in the time it takes for the eye to see and the mind to understand. The sun shines down, music plays, flowers grow, traffic passes at the end of the street, and everything is tipped into the centre of this moment.

The child in the road, the figure in the sky, the car, the noise.

And the young man from number eighteen, moving into the centre, covering the distance without touching the ground, unthinking, an unwitting part in the way of things.

And sitting here now, waiting, trying to be calm, all these
things are rattling around inside my head, like coins set
loose in a tumbledryer.

Michael, rushing back out into the rain wearing my
jumper.

Michael, that night I first met him, saying and you didn't
even know his name?

My mother and father, gathered in a red-faced bundle by
the telephone, my mother saying I'm safe now and my
father unable to speak.

My mother managing to say it's got a hood with a pair of
teddybear ears on it I thought you might like it.

Sarah, wide-eyed, saying tell me about it tell me about it,
listening to my story about Michael, his brother, what
happened after the funeral.

The boy in Aberdeen, naked and beautiful and asleep as I
left his house, him now, working in a bar, unaware of
what he has planted in me.

Michael's brother, his notes and photographs and objects,
his observations, his silences.

Michael's brother, moving to the centre of that awful
afternoon, his hands stretched out

When he left, when I'd watched him hurry across the
carpark and disappear around the corner without looking
back, when I'd decided not to go after him, I picked his
wet top off the floor and spread it across the radiator to
dry.

I picked up the towel and held it to my face, I hid my face in
its warm dampness and I wondered if what I could smell
was him, I was expecting to cry but I didn't.

I phoned him, I wanted to apologise without speaking to him, I listened to his answerphone message and I said hello it's me.

I said I'm sorry, I didn't mean to, I said I don't know whether you're angry or embarrassed but I don't want you to be either, I'm sorry.

I said it was a mistake, I didn't, I said do you think we could just forget about it?

I said I was enjoying becoming friends, I don't want to lose that and, and then I trailed off and said goodbye and hung up.

He phoned back later, when I was almost in bed, the answerphone kicked in and when he spoke he said if you're there don't pick up please I just wanted to say something.

He said I don't want you to be sorry, it was me, don't be embarrassed, it was nice but I can't, he stopped and he said, we can't.

He said, I've got your jumper, I'll bring it round, sometime.

I spoke to my mother again, the day after Michael had been and gone.

She was talking about money.

She said I've been looking in some shops, things are ever so expensive now you know, I was adding it all up and I don't think we can afford it.

I told her my job paid well, I could save, I could buy second-hand, and she said yes in the slow way she does when she means no.

She said of course you know there is someone else who could help out and I said mum no.

She said I've made a few calls, I've got the number of the place where the wake was held, they told me they've got all the same staff they had then, I said mum, no, please.

258

She said that's assuming you know his name? and I told her of course I knew his name and I told her I wasn't going to tell her what it was.

She said it's not right, imagine if I'd done that to your father and we both slammed the phone down at the same time, and I realised that healing would not come so easily, that I must concentrate now on not piling it up inside and not passing it on.

The woman behind the desk calls a name, I look up but it's not mine.

And when Sarah came round at the weekend, finally, she wanted to know everything.

It was awkward at first, I thought it would be easier than talking on the phone but it took a while to get used to being in the room with her, she looked different, older, sharper.

But then she laughed, and her eyes screwed up and she looked the same as always, and we were talking the way we used to, finishing sentences for each other, waving our hands for emphasis, choking on funny stories.

I told her what I'd done to make Michael run away, and she pretended to be appalled but she kept asking for details.

She asked if I'd seen him since then and I told her no but I wanted to, I said he's still got my jumper and she laughed.

I didn't tell her about my mother, about how she reacted, what my dad had told me about her.

She asked how it happened, who it was, and I told her, and I told her a lot, who he was, what we did, the look and the shape of him, his voice.

She was shocked and she was delighted and she said oh but what are you going to do now and I told her I didn't know.

He turns to me and he says are you okay are you worried, and I say no I'm fine I'm just thinking.

And also I didn't tell Sarah about Michael's brother, what Michael had told me about him, the things I'd found out and the things I wanted to find out.

I didn't tell her about those photos, of people in the street, of me, of the twins jumping around in the rain that day.

I didn't tell her about the broken clay figure I've still got, in my room, the two pieces of it on the bedside table, waiting to be put back together again.

I wasn't sure that she'd understand.

The woman behind the desk calls a name, I look at her, she calls it again, it's my name and I stand and I walk towards her.

She gives me a bundle of forms, she points which way to go, and when I turn round I see Michael is still sitting down, looking at me.

I say come on, please, I say I want you to be there with me, and he stands and he walks with me to the room.

The doctor looks at some notes, she asks how I'm feeling and smiles when I say I've been sick a lot, she takes my blood pressure, my pulse, she takes a stethoscope from a case and listens to my breathing.

Michael sits off to one side, looking away slightly, as if he's embarrassed, as if he's not sure he should be here.

She says okay then shall we see how the little one's getting on?

I lie down on the bed, she undoes my shirt and all three of us look at the slight swell of my belly, the smooth tight stretch of the skin, the first hint of fullness.

I look at it, I look up at her, I look at Michael and I feel a

260

sudden pride in what is happening to my body, the miracle of it, the strange neatness of it.

She rubs a thin layer of pale green gel onto my stomach, she says there's nothing to be worried about, I just need you to relax and lie nice and still.

I look over at Michael, I say don't you want to see, he looks back and I say please, come and sit next to me, I want you to.

He looks awkward, he picks up his chair and he puts it next to the bed, he sits down and he says sorry, I wasn't being rude I just.

The doctor pulls a trolley closer to the bed, there's a monitor on it, wires and gadgets, she turns the trolley so I can see the screen.

She says is that okay for you, and I nod.

She holds up the scanner, it's small and white and fits into the cup of her hand, she says this might be cold and she presses it against my belly.

I look at the screen, I see black and white lines, patterns, movement.

It looks like a museum exhibit of the world's first television pictures, I look and I'm scared and I don't want to look.

I feel a warmth, and I realise that I am holding Michael's hand, and that this makes me feel safer, more able to open my eyes and look at the blur on the screen.

I'm surprised, but I'm glad, I realise that this is what I wanted that night last week, to simply make a connection and keep hold of it.

He doesn't say anything.

He doesn't look at me, or the screen, he looks up towards the ceiling somewhere, blinking.

He blinks quickly, tightly, as if he's nervous, like his brother.

I'm sorry he says, quietly, I can't look.
I squeeze his hand, tightly.

The doctor points to a shadow of light, curled like a new
    moon across the bottom left of the picture.
There she says, can you see, these are the hands, there she
    says, this is the head.
I look, and I don't speak, and I recognise what she is
    pointing to, I see the tiny foetal clutch of new life.
I look and I don't speak, and all I can think of is names,
    names hurtling through my head like asteroids.
The doctor points to a shadow of light, curled like a second
    new moon across the bottom right of the picture.
There she says, can you see, this is the sibling's head, these
    are the sibling's hands.
I don't hear her for a moment, I don't understand what she
    is saying.
I feel Michael's other hand reaching for mine, his two hands
    wrapping tightly around mine, I hear him whisper oh my
    God.
The doctor says now let's make sure they're both okay.

Outside, standing by the side of the road and wondering
    what to do now, I realise we are still holding hands.
I feel as though I've discovered I'm pregnant all over
    again.
I feel shocked and excited and confused and close to tears.
I blink, closing my eyes tightly and opening them again to
    the brightness and the colour of the world.
I remember the boy from Aberdeen, his soft warm voice
    saying it's like being called to your place in the way of
    things, I remember my dad saying not anything other
    than a blessing and a gift.
I remember my mum saying have you thought of a name

262

yet, I remember the names hurtling through my head while I lay there looking at the screen.

I smile and I hold up the printout, the two new-moon shapes like echoes of each other, I smile and I say maybe I'll name them after you and your brother, what do you think?

There's a sudden screeching sound, a skid, and we turn and see a car at the traffic lights with smoke drifting away from its tyres.

He says, there's something I have to tell you.

And before the young man from number eighteen gets there, the car hits the child.

There's a thudding sound, like a car-boot being slammed down on somebody's hand.

The boy's legs flip up from under him and he is lifted into the air like the bails of a cricket stump, turning a half-circle across the bonnet and slamming sideways into the car windscreen. There is barely any sound at all, a wineglass breaking on a carpeted floor, a snail snapped under a slippered foot.

The tennis ball pops out of the boy's hand and arcs high over the car, bouncing on the pavement three times and rolling back onto the road.

The windscreen crackles, a spiral spiderweb splintering across its surface without breaking.

The car stops, and the boy rewinds across the bonnet and falls face first onto the road.

And in the moment his body presses against the tarmac, the young man from number eighteen is there, he is a footstep away and he feels the boy brush past his out-stretched hands, he feels the damp stretch of his t-shirt and the smooth stroke of his cheek.

He was not quick enough. He almost caught him but he was not quick enough.

He looks down at the boy, he kneels down beside him and he looks, he is breathing hard and his hands are shaking over the boy's body. He is afraid to touch him. He has no idea what to do. He says hello can you hear me.

He says oh shit oh fuck oh my God.

There is a thunder of footsteps around him, somebody says is he alright and he says I don't know I don't know, people are crouching and kneeling around the boy, somebody says help me turn him over and two pairs of hands slide under his body and roll him over onto his back.

He almost looks undamaged, his eyes closed, his head turned gently against his shoulder. But there is blood, seeping from a long graze down the left side of his face, the skin torn from the top of his forehead down to the sallow of his cheek. And there is blood gathering cloudily between his eyebrow and his ear, swelling beneath the skin like a clenched fist. And there is a little too much stillness about him, lying in the road, watched over by people who don't know what they can do.

Nearby, a few streets away and a few dozen feet in the air, the man with the carefully trimmed moustache from number twenty can see what has happened, he is falling to earth again and there is nothing he can do about what he can see. He rises and falls, rises and falls a little less, and the assistants take hold of him, undoing the ties and lowering his stiffened body to the ground, he looks at them and he opens his mouth but he cannot speak.

A young woman from number twenty-four runs to the middle of the street, she has coloured ink on her hands from drawing diagrams all afternoon, she says let me see, I'm a medical, I mean, let me see, and she kneels beside the boy and pulls her long hair aside to lay her ear against his chest.

They look at her, the people around the boy, they wait.

The young man from number eighteen looks at her, blinking, he was not quick enough and he did not know what to do.

She brings her head up and sinks two fingers into the boy's mouth, she takes her fingers out and squeezes his nose and presses her mouth to his.

There are more footsteps and somebody says there's an ambulance on the way.

The younger twin is standing behind the crowd of people, looking through the gaps, twining his fingers into one another. His mouth is moving, but he is absolutely silent. Tears are spilling from the rims of his eyes.

The young man in the car has not moved, he cannot move, his foot is still stiff against the brake pedal, his face is turned to one side as if from a sudden impact and his eyes are closed. He is barely breathing, small gasps are rushing in and out of his mouth, struggling to reach his lungs. His hands are still wrapped around the steering wheel, his arms locked out straight, pushing away. He cannot move, he cannot look at what has happened.

The young woman from number twenty-four kneels over the boy, her mouth pressed to his mouth.

And the young man from number eighteen, the first to arrive, he is the first to leave, he is backing away with his hand knotted into his hair, he is looking but he doesn't want to look. He stands in his doorway and he feels a kind of breathless pain right across his body, a revulsion, a tight numbness spread across his chest and his arms and he turns away.

She lifts her head from the boy's mouth, she clamps her hands together and pistons them into his chest. The people around them are quiet, awkward, shocked.

The man doing the painting is walking towards the closed front door of number nineteen, he still has a paintbrush in one hand, there is a trail of pale blue drips on the pavement behind him, he is looking at the crowd of people and he is looking at the closed front door.

She says, God, how long is that ambulance going to be, and people look down to the main road and don't say anything.

The man with the paintbrush knocks on the only closed door in the street, he waits, he pulls at his long beard, he knocks again and when the door opens he very quietly says I think you should come and see.

And this is the point at which faces turn away, in embarrassment or pain, as a mother runs wailing across a street, as an ambulance is heard in the distance, as a father stands beating himself around the head, a mutely screaming son clinging to his knee.

The old woman in number twenty turns away, she has been standing by her window with her husband, watching, he is standing tall with one arm around her and the other gripping the windowsill. She is hunched over, turned into his chest, looking up at him, mouthing something like oh lord oh lord oh that poor poor boy oh lord over and over. He turns and guides her away from the window, he lays both hands on her shoulders, protectively.

The young man in number eighteen turns away, he can hardly breathe, he stumbles onto his sofa and tips his face to the ceiling. There is a feeling like a rope circled around his chest, I was not quick enough is all he is thinking, I was not quick enough and the thought clamps down upon him like a vice.

The man with the burnt hands turns away, he turns to the boy's father and takes hold of his wrists, pulls them away from his head. It hurts him to do so, violently, the strain of gripping is pulling and cracking his scarred skin, but he does this, he pulls the man's hands to his side and looks him in the eye and says, enough, now, this is no good, your boy. And the man straightens his distorted face, looks down to his son, picks him up and whispers hushush it is okay.

His daughter stands at her window, not watching. She has taken another ribbon and wound it around her face, across her eyes, there is smooth silk where her eyes might be, she is perfectly still.

And the ambulance arrives, and the paramedic crouches over the boy, his fluorescent jacket rustles and squeaks, he puts down a plastic case like a box of tools, he presses two fingers against the boy's neck. What's his name love he says to the boy's mother. His name is Shahid she says, and the paramedic starts repeating it, shining a light into the dying boy's eyes, hello Shahid, Shahid can you hear me, hello Shahid?

And behind him, watching, his mother is murmuring his name as well. Shahid, his name is Shahid. His name is Shahid Mohammed Nawaz. His name is Shahid.

There are faces at windows up and down the street, faces in frames like portraits in a gallery. The man with the tattoo, the boyfriend of the woman with the henna-red hair, stretching his head from the high window, a jarful of petals in one hand. The architect boy at number eleven, a pen behind his ear and another clamped between his teeth, his fists stacked on top of each other and holding up his chin like a greek column. The girl and the boy at number twenty-seven, naked, a duvet held up across their chests like a beach-towel, squashed together in the small square of

269

the window, their skin creased from being so long in bed and their hands covering their mouths.

And so they pick him up, Shahid, they lay him on a stretcher and they roll the stretcher into the ambulance. And his mother gets into the ambulance with him, and as the ambulance driver closes the doors he meets the eyes of the paramedic and an understanding passes between them. The ambulance leaves the street, the siren is sounding but the vehicle is not moving as fast as it could be.

The man with the sponge, dabbing at his forehead with an unfolded white handkerchief, he offers to drive the father and the children, the father calls to his daughter, she comes running from the house and they all squeeze into his shining car and disappear around the corner.

And that's all there is. That's it. There is no pause or rewind, there is no image enhancement, no recording of the moment beyond a thick streak of black rubber smeared across the road, a stain which itself will soon fade. Later, the police may come and take measurements, make estimates regarding speed of impact, suggest possible causes. They might ask people living in the street what they saw this afternoon, what exactly did they see please. Later, possibly, a court will sit silently considering the facts and opinions, and maybe they will pass judgement upon the young man still sitting in his new car. But the moment will never be again, the moment is gone.

The two girls on the front step of number twenty-two, sitting and watching and not speaking, they look at the girl with the long straight hair, the girl whose lips still taste of the young boy's mouth, they look to her as she walks towards them. She stops, and she crouches by them, she says no, no chance, he was already, he had no chance, and she stands and walks into her house, and the boy with the soapy trainers stands and follows her and closes the door.

The young man at number eighteen, sitting low in his sofa and holding his chest, he can think of nothing else, he will never think of anything else. I could have saved him is what he is thinking, I could have, there was something, maybe, and then underneath this thinking, shamefully, there is the thought that she was watching and she would have seen.

The thin bearded man, from number thirteen, he picks up his son from the floor, he kisses him gently on the cheek and whispers something to him, he holds him to his chest and picks up his tricycle with the other hand, he carries his son back to his house. As they pass number seventeen, the father catches the eye of the boy with the shirt and tie, standing in his doorway, but nothing is said and they both look away. And the son pokes his head above the father's shoulder, like a soldier from a trench, he stares at the end of the street, he blinks once and he stares.

At the end of the street, the man with the ruined hands stands with his arms wrapped around his daughter, he watches the traffic on the main road, re-forming after the ambulance's passing, like the surface of a pond stilling from a stone's entry.

He thinks of the boy's mother, saying his name, he echoes her, he mouths the words, Shahid Mohammed, Shahid Nawaz, he wants to call it out loud, he lifts his face and lets his lips shape the words, miming a bellow, Shahid Mohammed, Shahid Nawaz, he thinks oh Allah have mercy let the whole world hear. He imagines what would happen if the whole street called his name, joining with the mother's small voice, the whole street lifting the words and the words spreading through this city, taking flight like a flock of birds at dusk, clouding the sky, the voices all-present, across fields and forests and oceans, sent out, transmitted, broadcast, on BBC and CNN, satellite and terrestrial and international optic fibres, on billboards and buses and videoscreens, on flyers and posters and news-journals and magazines, the information, the name, pouring down from the sky like electronic rain, out from this one street and sucked down into the lightning-rod antennas that bristle from mansions and shantyhouses across all our misconnected world, a chorus of name-saying, a brief redemptive span of attention.

He imagines this, he whispers the name alone, Shahid Mohammed, and his voice does not rise even above the sound of a passing car.

But he whispers it all the same, like a prayer, he has no faith but the words keep coming, he thinks oh inshaallah let the whole world hear, let the whole world listen for a moment, his name is Shahid, Shahid Mohammed Nawaz, and he is dying.

Halfway across the city, in the back of the ambulance, Mrs Nawaz is holding her son's hand. She is talking to him, she is telling him how special he is and how special he will always be, she is talking in her parents' language and in her son's language, she squeezes his hand and she shakes it a little as she speaks.

At number eighteen, the young man with the dry eyes is realising something is wrong, something is very wrong, there is a scorching pain through his left arm and into his chest, there is a crushing around his ribcage that feels like it will snap his bones. He is trying to breathe, but his mouth feels stuffed full of rags and paper.

In the ambulance, the paramedic glances up at the boy's mother, and he takes hold of the boy's hand himself. He squeezes it, and he says his name, Shahid. Mrs Nawaz squeezes her son's hand tighter, as tightly as she held her husband's hand the day she gave birth.

In his room, the young man with the dry eyes hammers at his chest with a weak fist. Suddenly, almost silently, he is dying, and he stands and thrashes around the room to escape it, pulling down curtains, spilling his box of packed possessions, knocking a small clay figure to the floor.

And there is an interruption in the way of things, a pause, something faint like the quivering flutter of a moth's rain-sodden wings, something unexpected. Something remarkable.

In the ambulance, Shahid breathes suddenly and violently through his nose, spraying blood and phlegm over the hands of his mother and the paramedic, a splutter that sets off sensors and alarms, the siren suddenly louder, the paramedic moving the mother to one side and calling through to the driver.

In his room, the young man lies on the floor, utterly still. Scattered around him there are broken plates and mugs, a torn poster, curtain hooks. He will stay here for three more days, and it will only be once his brother has telephoned, and banged on the door, and fetched the landlord, that he will be found and taken away.

And the ambulance passes on through the city, the traffic parting around it like the red sea, the city bearing it up, fast through the afternoon, along steaming pockmarked streets lined with parades of pubs and shops, past old factories with fading nameplates and retail outlets with neon signs, past the cinema and the bowling alley and the twenty-four-hour garage.

A row of taxis with their doors hung open.

A park full of children and parents and dogs, topless gardeners tugging out weeds.

The ambulance passes on through the city, through a red light, past a dead queue of traffic, up onto the dual carriageway, lifted high on concrete stilts over houses and shops, passing between two tall block buildings, dropping back down and left past a pub with a siege of shirt-sleeved drinkers, right past the supermarket and the carpark crammed with cars.

A man running with a weighted rucksack on his back.

An alleyway with three boys playing basketball, a spokeless wheel for a hoop.

A shop window with a hole the size of a small marble.

A boy in a skip swinging a skinned umbrella around his head.

The ambulance passes on through this city, on through it all, a flash of attention trailing behind it, a fading scorch through a hot afternoon, on past the river, on past the arches, on past the factories and workshops and retail estates, on past the endless rows of anonymous terraced houses, on, finally on, to the last of the roads, past the carparks and signposts and entrance gates, straight through to the emergency doors of the waiting hospital.

And as these streets are travelled, in the time it takes for a hand to be clasped and unclasped, Shahid Mohammed

Nawaz wakes gently, lifted through a gap in the way of things.

And at the entrance to the hospital grounds, four queues of traffic sit facing each other, trapped by traffic lights which have synchronised red for the ambulance to pass, dozens of feet resting on accelerators, dozens of pairs of eyes hanging on the lights.

All waiting for the amber.

All waiting for the green.

ACKNOWLEDGEMENTS

Thanks, for various reasons, to the following;
Tom Davies, Maggie and David Jones, Chris Boland,
Cormac and Jane, Bek, Jitan, Mark and Kim, Alice,
everyone at Squeek, Rose Gaete, Marian McCarthy,
Rosemary Davidson, and my family. But most
of all, thanks to the seven.

Read more from Jon McGregor

RESERVOIR 13

Jon McGregor

The new novel from the award-winning author of
If Nobody Speaks of Remarkable Things *and*
Even the Dogs. Reservoir 13 *tells the story of*
many lives haunted by one family's loss.

Midwinter in the early years of this century. A teenage girl on holiday has gone missing in the hills at the heart of England. The villagers are called up to join the search, fanning out across the moors as the police set up roadblocks and a crowd of news reporters descends on their usually quiet home.

Meanwhile, there is work that must still be done: cows milked, fences repaired, stone cut, pints poured, beds made, sermons written, a pantomime rehearsed. The search for the missing girl goes on, but so does everyday life. As it must.

As the seasons unfold there are those who leave the village and those who are pulled back; those who come together or break apart. There are births and deaths; secrets kept and exposed; livelihoods made and lost; small kindnesses and unanticipated betrayals.

Bats hang in the eaves of the church and herons stand sentry in the river; fieldfares flock in the hawthorn trees and badgers and foxes prowl deep in the woods – mating and fighting, hunting and dying.

An extraordinary novel of cumulative power and grace, *Reservoir 13* explores the rhythms of the natural world and the repeated human gift for violence, unfolding over thirteen years as the aftershocks of a stranger's tragedy refuse to subside.

'Absolutely magnificent; one of the most beautiful, affecting novels I've read in years. The prose is alive and ringing. There is so much space and life in every sentence. I don't know how he's done it. It's beautiful' EIMEAR MCBRIDE

SO MANY WAYS TO BEGIN

Jon McGregor

Longlisted for the Man Booker Prize

David Carter cannot help but wish for more: that his wife Eleanor would be the sparkling girl he once found so irresistible; that his job as a museum curator could live up to the promise it once held; that his daughter's arrival could have brought him closer to Eleanor. But a few careless words spoken by his mother's friend have left David restless with the knowledge that his whole life has been constructed around a lie.

'Extraordinary'   *Daily Mail*

'Subtle, clever and affecting'   *Independent on Sunday*

'An homage to ordinary people and ordinary things, to the parts of our lives that often go unspoken ... moving and honest'
The Times

'A book about the search for greater meaning in the strange dance of chance'   *Independent*

EVEN THE DOGS

Jon McGregor

Winner of the 2012 IMPAC Dublin Award

On a cold, quiet day between Christmas and the New Year, a man's body is found in an abandoned apartment. His friends look on, but they're dead, too. Their bodies found in squats and sheds and alleyways across the city. Victims of a bad batch of heroin, they're in the shadows, a chorus keeping vigil as the hours pass, paying their own particular homage as their friend's body is taken away, examined, investigated and cremated.

All of their stories are laid out piece by broken piece through a series of fractured narratives. We meet Robert, the deceased, the only alcoholic in a sprawling group of junkies; Danny, just back from uncomfortable holidays with family, who discovers the body and futilely searches for his other friends to share the news of Robert's death; Laura, Robert's daughter, who stumbles into the junky's life when she moves in with her father after years apart; Heather, who has her own place for the first time since she was a teenager; Mike, the Falklands War vet; and all the others.

Theirs are stories of lives fallen through the cracks, hopes flaring and dying, love overwhelmed by a stronger need, and the havoc wrought by drugs, distress, and the disregard of the wider world. These invisible people live in a parallel reality, out of reach of basic creature comforts, like food and shelter. In their sudden deaths, it becomes clear, they are treated with more respect than they ever were in their short lives.

Intense, exhilarating and shot through with hope and fury, *Even the Dogs* is an intimate exploration of life at the edges of society – littered with love, loss, despair and a half-glimpse of redemption.

'A rare combination of profound empathy and wonderful writing'
MARK HADDON

'A breathtakingly good writer' *The Times*

'Absolutely outstanding … an incredible book' COLUM MCCANN

THIS ISN'T THE SORT OF THING THAT HAPPENS TO SOMEONE LIKE YOU

Jon McGregor

Tender, sad, funny and riveting, this is an astonishing collection of work by one of Britain's finest contemporary writers

A man builds a tree house by a river, in anticipation of the coming flood. A sugar-beet crashes through a young woman's windscreen. A boy sets fire to a barn. These aren't the sort of things you imagine happening to someone like you. But sometimes they do.

Set in the flat and threatened fenland landscape, where the sky is dominant and the sea lurks just beyond the horizon, these delicate, dangerous and sometimes deeply funny stories tell of things buried and unearthed, of familiar places made strange, and of lives where much is hidden, much is at risk, and tender moments are hard-won.

'Jon McGregor's stories are strange and lovely masterpieces'

SARAH HALL

'McGregor is the nearest thing you will ever come across to a literary Beethoven. Words go beyond being tools of his trade and become an orchestrated, inspired and precisely designed tone poem for each creative idea … One of the most perfect pieces of written English I have ever come across'   *Sunday Express*

'Jon McGregor writes with frightening intelligence and impeccable technique. Every page is a revelation'   TEJU COLE

'Sharp, dark and hugely entertaining, this collection establishes McGregor as one of the most exciting voices in short fiction'

Observer